DONNY
GOES FOR
GOAL!

ACE Fiction

Also by Joe Buckley

Run Donny, Run!
Donny in London

Other titles in the ACE fiction series

Judith and the Traveller Mike Scott
Judith and Spider Mike Scott
Breaking the Circle Desmond Kelly

Born in Co. Offaly, Joe Buckley developed an early passion for sports of all kinds. Student summers were spent working on the London railways before he moved to Canada where he fished and canoed in the mountains of British Columbia. Returning to Ireland, he taught English and Geography in Birr, Ballyfin, Crumlin and Celbridge, using his free time for rugby, canoeing, tennis, music and gardening. He lives in Maynooth, Co Kildare, with his wife Marion and three sons.

DONNY
GOES FOR
GOAL!

Joe Buckley

ACE FICTION

WOLFHOUND

First published 1993 by
WOLFHOUND PRESS
68 Mountjoy Square
Dublin 1

Wolfhound Press receives financial assistance from the Arts Council /
An Chomhairle Ealaíon, Dublin, Ireland.

This book is fiction. All characters, incidents and names have no
connection with any persons, living or dead. Any apparent
resemblance is purely coincidental.

British Library Cataloguing in Publication Data
Buckley, Joe
   Going for Goal!. - (ACE Paperbacks Series)
   I. Title II. Series
   823.914 [J]

   ISBN 0-86327-415-3

Cover illustration: Fiona Lynch
Cover typography: Aileen Caffrey
Typesetting: Wolfhound Press
Printed by the Guernsey Press Co. Ltd, Guernsey, Channel Isles

1

'Sketch!' hissed Murphy out of the corner of his mouth.

Flanagan, who had just taken a deep drag out of Butler's fag, ducked his head and looked across the point of his right shoulder towards the corner of the school. He looked past the scattered groups of boys who leaned against the school wall, or sat on the low classroom window-sills in the early March sunshine. Bill Moloney, the English teacher, currently on 'yard duty' during the midday lunch break, was sauntering towards them, his erect figure framed between the high three-storied wall of the school building and the laurel hedge which separated the senior recreation area from the monastery garden. Flanagan immediately pulled up the collar of his jacket with his right hand, exhaled a swirling cloud of smoke into his right armpit, and carefully eased what remained of Butler's butt into his trousers pocket. He held it gingerly between his index and middle fingers, the lighted end enclosed by, but not touching, his protecting palm, and waited for Bill Moloney to pass.

'Didje see that bit in the paper about the game tomorrow, Don?' Butler's question was an attempt to keep a normal conversation alive while Bill was passing. He knew that guilty silences were like red lights flashing in front of most teachers. The question was aimed at Donny O'Sullivan, a tall slim youth who was sitting on the window-sill beside him, his feet spread on the pavement.

'No,' replied Donny, turning his deepset brown eyes onto Butler's face. 'What'd it say?'

'That youse were goin' to lose!' Butler leered. 'Said it'd be a cakewalk for Bellview, an' all about Sheppard an' how he was over for a trial with Arsenal ...'

'Gerroff!' snorted Flagon, an untidy, blond-haired boy on Donny's left. 'Sheppard'll be no bother. Sure the last time ...'

Flagon stopped in mid-sentence when the teacher's shadow fell across their feet.

'Hello, gentlemen.' Bill Moloney's voice was friendly and interested. When he came to a halt beside him, Flanagan glared from under alarmed eye-lids in Flagon's direction. 'I suppose you fellows are talking football.'

Flanagan started to sidle away but Bill Moloney caught his left fore-arm. 'Aah, Tommy, don't go away just because I'm here.' There was a faint twinkle in his grey eyes. 'I mean, we don't often get a chance to enjoy nature in her most pleasant moods — her sights and sounds ...' He raised his head and sniffed gently. '... and smells.'

Flanagan was suddenly aware that everybody was looking at him with amused sympathy.

'I mean,' went on Bill Moloney, casting his free hand expansively towards the weak midday sun. 'Such warmth as this comes all too seldom, doesn't it, Tommy?'

'Umm, yes, sir. It does. It certainly does.' Flanagan suddenly felt a burning desire to take his left hand out of his trousers pocket, but Bill Moloney's grip on his arm tightened.

'Can you feel the heat, Tommy?' he asked, and his eyes were smiling now. Flanagan's fingers were beginning to blister. He squirmed slightly.

'Yes, sir. It's lovely ...' he began. 'Aaagh!' The heat became infernal. Tommy Flanagan jumped away suddenly, whipping his hand out of his pocket as he did so. He dropped the remains of Butler's butt onto the pavement and began to slap the pocket of his trousers furiously with both hands. His friends were falling around the place as he gingerly opened the pocket with delicate fingertips and peered in.

'Need a fire brigade, Tommo?' asked a short, tubby youth, with gold-rimmed glasses perched on a freckled face. This was Paul Marsh, known affectionately to his friends as Swamp.

Flanagan knew he was snookered. He blushed with embarrassment as he faced Bill Moloney.

'Tommy,' said Bill. 'How many times have I told you that cigarettes are not only bad for the lungs, but very hard on the pocket as well!'

The group groaned in unison. 'Oh, my God!' exclaimed Flagon in mock agony. 'Please, sir. Please don't make me laugh like that again!'

Bill Moloney ignored the good-natured jeering. His face took on a serious frown.

'You're a lucky man, Tommo,' he said, 'that I didn't catch you *in flagrante delicto*, or else I should have had to report you to your Year Head. And,' he raised his eyebrows significantly, 'you know what that would entail.'

There was another collective groan. Everyone knew that the senior year head was Brother Sharkey, familiarly, but not affectionately, known to his students as 'Jaws'.

'I know, sir. Thank you, sir!' Gratitude oozed from Flanagan's every pore.

'Just give them up, Tommy,' Bill advised patiently. 'You'll be more useful to the team then, won't you?'

'Yes, sir.' Flanagan, his bacon saved, would almost have agreed never to copy his homework again. 'You're right, sir.'

Bill Moloney now turned his attention on Donny O'Sullivan, his eyes resuming their kindly expression. 'Have they told you, Donny, that there was a little write-up in the paper about the game tomorrow? Your name was mentioned.'

Donny's eyes widened with interest. 'Kev here said there was something about the game, but he never said anything about me. Was it good or bad?'

Bill inclined his head to one side. 'It's not ... uncomplimentary, but don't let it go to your head. It's not going to be easy tomorrow.'

'Yeh, I know,' replied Donny. The others all nodded seriously, even Butler. Somewhere inside the building a distant bell began to jangle.

'Anyway, I put a photocopy on the senior notice board,' the grey-haired teacher went on. 'So you can study it at your leisure. Which, I believe, is after this next exam.' His arms widened to include the group, now rousing themselves from their rest. 'Let's put our backs into it then, shall we?'

'Bleedin' Mocks!' someone muttered as the group turned reluctantly towards the corner that led to the rear door of the school.

'What've we got now?' demanded Murphy, a pained look on his face.

'Maths, of course,' said Cullen, a lanky youth wearing a leather jacket with an immaculate white shirt underneath.

'What's with the fancy shirt, Stretch?' asked Swamp. 'Didya get a new job?'

Cullen glanced behind to ensure that Bill Moloney was out of hearing. Then he unzipped the jacket and began to unbutton the shirt.

'Got it for a fiver down in the Arcade.' He opened the shirt wide, exposing the inside. It was completely covered with maths formulae written in Biro. 'Takes a Biro perfectly, doesn't it?'

'Well, just be careful,' warned Flagon. 'I think Jaws is supervisin' this one!'

'No sweat!' retorted Cullen, as they jostled their way in through the narrow doorway of the examination hall.

Donny O'Sullivan worked steadily at the Maths paper for over two hours. The hall was silent except for an occasional cough and the stolid creak of Jaws' clerical boots as he paced up and down between the rows of desks. Once, when the Brother's shadow fell across his answer paper and stopped, Donny found himself becoming tense, but he didn't look up or stop writing. He knew Jaws didn't like him and he wasn't going to give him any excuse for comment.

There were fifteen minutes left in the exam, when Donny finally laid down his pen. He had done enough, he told himself. After all, it was only the Mocks, the dry run done in most schools in March as a preparation for the Leaving Certificate Exam later in June. Jaws had by this time grown tired of walking and was now enthroned behind the high desk at the top of the hall, head bent, fingers of both hands cupped round his black eyebrows. Satisfied that the coast was clear, Donny took a letter from the back pocket of his jeans and quietly opened it under the desk. He had read it several times before, but he wanted to read it again, to savour its contents once more.

'Dear Donny,' it began. 'It seems such a long time since I've seen you. Christmas with Gran was OK. We went down to London to see a couple of shows, but all the time I was remembering last summer, and what happened. We weren't back till the day before school started, so I couldn't get to see you ...'

'You!' Jaws' harsh call shattered the silence of the exam hall. 'You with the book under the desk ... Stand up!'

There was a frozen silence. Everyone lifted their heads to see who Jaws was looking at, but his eyes were still shielded by his pudgy fingers. Donny peered from under his brows at the black-robed figure before him, but he could not see his eyes. He folded the letter carefully and prepared to get it into his pocket.

'I said, you with the book under the desk, stand up!' There was an irritating throaty rattle in the Brother's voice. 'I'll give you three. One! Two! Three!'

Donny remained seated, but suddenly a muffled ripple of laughter swept through the hall. Milligan on the right flank, McCallum in the centre, and Dwyer at the back had all stood up. The laughter was snuffed out by the sudden lift of Jaws' head. His pitch-black eyes, matching the flat hair pasted from left to right across his forehead, flickered momentarily over the faces of the three 'coggers' and came to rest on Donny. Their black intensity bored into him. Jaws waited for ten seconds.

'Mr. O'Sullivan. Why are you not on your feet?' his toneless voice grated. Donny was aware of all the heads turned in his direction, of the sudden, still tension.

'I haven't got a book under my desk, Brother,' he called evenly.

Jaws rose slowly from his seat, never taking his eyes off

Donny. He was nodding slowly to himself, an ironic smile playing at the corners of his hard mouth. His eyebrows lifted cynically. 'Nothing under the desk, O'Sullivan?' he intoned as he stepped carefully down onto the floor.

'No, Brother. I didn't say that ...'

'Aha! Changing your story now!' Jaws' pace quickened slightly and Donny noticed the fat fingers of his right hand opening and closing spasmodically. 'I saw you! Are you going to tell me I didn't see what I saw?'

Donny steeled himself and forced down the rising anger. 'No, Brother,' he said. 'All I'm saying is I wasn't looking at a book under the desk.'

Jaws changed his tack. 'But you were reading something, O'Sullivan.'

'Yes, Brother ...'

The brother stopped six feet from Donny's desk. His left hand swept across to indicate the three boys standing sheepishly by their desks.

'At least these three had enough *guts* to admit it ...' He paused for breath. Someone at the bottom of the hall clearly said, 'Wallies!', but Jaws glared into silence the stifled sniggers. 'But you, O'Sullivan! You just didn't have that kind of ... of ... of courage, did you?' He took the last three paces to the side of Donny's desk. 'OK. Let's have it.' He held out his hand.

'I'm sorry, Brother,' Donny said. 'It's a letter ... and it's private.'

Jaws appeared not to have heard him. His eyes grimly surveyed the rows of boys who were now staring at him with barely concealed dislike. At the same time he clicked his fingers and wiggled them impatiently.

'Hand it over!' he ordered. Behind him, Cullen was doing contortions as he tried to decipher a Maths formula under his left armpit.

'No!' Donny's answer electrified the hall. There was not a sound.

'You hand it over, O'Sullivan. Or your paper's cancelled!'

Donny returned the Brother's stare for a moment. Then he

lifted his Maths paper slowly and draped it over the other's outstretched hand. He saw the flush of anger in the Brother's face. Jaws bent suddenly and grabbed at the letter in Donny's hand. But Donny was quicker. His hand closed on the letter and he held it away from the Brother. Somebody at the back of the hall chuckled and Jaws knew he had lost.

'Who's your form tutor?' he rasped.

'Mr. Moloney, Brother.'

Jaws thought about that for a moment. Then he turned away abruptly. 'Report to the principal at 12:30!' he ordered. 'And you three ...' he snapped, his gaze surveying the 'coggers'. 'You go too!'

Donny made no response to this command. Something told him it would be useless. But in his heart he said, 'Like hell I'll go!'

When the bell went to signal the end of the examination, Flagon was the first to come to Donny's side.

'The miserable git!' he exploded. 'He really tried to get you this time. When's he ever going to lay off?'

Donny shrugged his shoulders and began to pocket his pens. 'That's his problem, Flag. Not mine.'

Paul Marsh, the third of the trio of friends, joined them. 'Go easy on that poor man, Don,' he said drily. 'We don't want him to get a nervous breakdown!'

'Yeh, well, if he thinks I'm going up to the boss, he's got another think coming!'

The others said nothing, but he saw them exchanging glances.

'What did you have under the desk anyway?' Swamp wanted to know.

'Just a letter. I was just readin' it.'

'Who was the letter from — if that's not too personal a question?'

'It is, actually,' Donny retorted. 'But I'll tell you, 'cos you'll go mad with curiosity if I don't. It's from Jacky.'

His friends exchanged a knowing glance. 'Aha!' exclaimed Flagon. 'So that was it. *That* would've been nice bedtime reading for a poor brother. Anyway, what did she say?' Flagon sidled closer to Donny, as if expecting a juicy bit of gossip.

'That's goin' to cost you,' said Donny, hoisting his bag on his shoulder and heading for the door.

'Here, hold on, Don,' Swamp called, his face serious and sensible. 'Maybe you should go. Old Boc's not that bad. At least he'll listen to you. But if you don't go at all ...'

Flagon was nodding in agreement. 'He's right, you know, Don. You have to think about the game. If you don't go, you know Jaws'll kick up stink, an' the next thing it'll be a suspension. An' if you're suspended, Clint won't play you on the team.'

'Yeh, Don,' urged Swamp. 'G'wan an' talk to him. He'll listen to *you*.'

Donny knew they were right, but his anger didn't want to let him admit it. 'I dunno,' he said, pretending to be undecided. Suddenly they grabbed him. 'You're bleedin' goin'!' Flagon muttered, pinning him in a neck-lock. Donny knew it was time to give in. 'OK! OK! I'll go!'

'An' what's more,' said Swamp. 'You'd better get up to the boss's office before the others get there, or he'll think there's a bleedin' epidemic of coggers in the place.'

'Here, take this then,' Donny growled, handing over his schoolbag. He headed back along the corridor.

'We'll wait for you,' Flagon called after him.

When Donny reached the principal's office, the door was shut. 'Is someone with him?' he asked Joan, the secretary.

'Brother Sharkey,' she replied, glancing up from her typing. Donny nodded grimly and sat down to wait.

It was fully five minutes before the door opened and the Brother came out. His face was red and he walked past Donny without even a glance in his direction.

Brother O'Connor appeared at the door of his office. 'Come in, Donny,' he said. His tone, as always, seemed relaxed and kindly. Donny went in, closed the door and took the seat that the principal indicated. A grey-haired man, whose bald patch hadn't yet reached his forehead, he sat behind an untidy desk and began to shift papers from one part of it to another. After a few moments, he cleared his throat.

'So you and Brother Sharkey have had another little ... eh ... disagreement,' he said.

'Yes, Brother. You might call it that.'

'He says you were copying, Donny. Is this true?'

Donny shook his head. 'No, Brother. I was finished the exam. I was reading a letter from a friend of mine.'

The Brother nodded slowly, a smile breaking through the corners of his mouth. 'Ah, yes, a letter.' He sighed softly, as if he had heard this inane excuse fifty times already today. 'And who, pray tell, was this letter from?'

'A friend of mine, Brother. I have it here, if you want to see it.' Donny tugged the letter from his pocket.

The brother eyed the pink notepaper for a moment and then nodded, more to himself than to Donny. 'Ah, a girlfriend, I see.'

'Well, yes. She's a friend ... And she's a girl.'

'A good answer, Donny.' The principal was thoughtful for a moment, tapping the end of his pencil against the desk-top. He took a deep breath. 'Maybe you might be a little more careful in the exam situation in future, Donny. After all, the teacher wasn't to know you were reading a letter.'

Donny resisted the temptation to say, 'He could have asked!' He knew that the elderly man in front of him was doing his best for him. 'And you know,' the other went on, 'how conscientious he can be about his work, don't you?'

Donny nodded. He couldn't think of any suitable response.

'So, next time, don't let him see you doing it. OK?' The smile broke through now. Donny smiled in return.

'OK,' he replied.

'And I'll have a word with Mr. Kelly about your Maths paper.'

'Thanks, Brother.' Donny prepared to go.

'By the way, how's your sister? Maeve, isn't it?'

'Yes,' replied Donny, surprised that the Brother knew so much about him. 'She's fine. She's managing better now.'

'And the little one?'

'Stephen. He's great!' Donny resisted the surge of enthusiasm which he always felt when talking about his baby nephew. To him, the principal was still almost a stranger.

'That's good,' said the Brother, getting up and coming round the desk. 'I believe you've been a great help to your sister.'

Donny stood up too, wondering once again where the principal got his information. He turned towards the door.

'And good luck in the game tomorrow,' the Brother said, as Donny went out.

'Thanks, Brother.' Donny had a warm feeling inside him as he strode free. Milligan, McCallum and Dwyer were sitting on the long bench by the secretary's desk. Their eyes searched Donny's face as he approached. He just looked down at them and shook his head sadly. Before he turned the corner he heard Brother O'Connor's surprised exclamation. 'Gentlemen! To see me? Surely not!'

Flagon and Swamp were waiting at the end of the corridor. They watched as Donny approached.

'Well?' said Flagon, as they fell in step with him. 'What'd he say?'

Donny shrugged his shoulders casually. 'He just wished us the best of luck in the game tomorrow, that's all.'

There was a pause. 'Yeh,' said Swamp. 'An' I suppose he gave you a medal for sortin' out "The Fish"!'

'Not exactly,' replied Donny. 'But doesn't the poor man have to live in the same aquarium with him. He knows what he's like.'

'Then why doesn't he sort him out himself?' demanded Flagon. 'Instead of havin' to pick up the pieces all the time when he has a run-in with the lads.'

'Aw, I dunno,' said Donny seriously. 'I think Jaws is not so bad inside, if only you could understand him.'

They looked at him in amazement. 'Now, don't start on about environment an' hereditary an' all that psychological stuff!' retorted Swamp. 'It's all a load of ...'

'No, no,' Donny insisted. 'Sure if I hadn't read that book, I never would have found out what a pair of weirdos I hang around with!' Then the slagging began in earnest.

'By the way,' remarked Swamp, as the three of them slurped tea and ate hunks of brown bread in the Marsh house fifteen minutes later. 'That letter. You never told us what she said.'

'Yeah!' agreed Flagon. 'What's the story?'

Donny shrugged his shoulders. 'No story. I'm going to a disco.'

'A disco!' exclaimed Flagon. 'You don't hear from her for weeks an' weeks, an' suddenly it's a disco. Where's the disco?'

'It's in a rugby club — Corinthians. Tonight.'

'Yeh, I heard about that place. But if they find out you're from Walkinstown won't you have to have a character reference from the principal, the parish priest an' the bleedin' bishop to get in there?'

'Yeh, that's for ordinary Joe Soaps,' Donny replied. 'But Jacky's dad's on the committee, or something.'

'Oh, excuse me!' said Swamp with exaggerated politeness.

'But what are they doin' holdin' a disco on a Tuesday night? That's a stupid night for a disco.'

Donny shrugged his shoulders. 'I dunno. It's somebody's birthday, I think.'

'So you're going then?' asked Flagon.

'Thinking about it.'

'That means he's going,' stated Swamp. 'Did you *tell* her you were going?'

'Yeh. Phoned last week.'

'She never thought of askin' the rest of her friends to it, did she?' Swamp asked again.

'Naw, she only needs one man,' Donny joked, and they were off again.

Later, when Donny was on his feet ready to go home, Flagon gave him a word of warning. 'Here, Don. Make sure Clint doesn't hear that you were on the town tonight. You know how he is about everybody gettin' into the scratcher early the night before a match.'

'An' no booze either,' added Swamp significantly.

'*Or* women,' went on Flagon.

'Piss off, lads!' was Donny's good-natured reply.

2

Donny left Swamp's house at ten to five. Every Tuesday and
Thursday he had to collect little Stephen from Mrs. McIntyre,
who minded him five days a week while Maeve was at work. On
these two days, however, she liked to leave a bit early to visit her
mother above in Crumlin. Donny had reluctantly agreed to
collect his nephew at five o' clock, take him home or for a walk
and keep him alive till Maeve arrived at around a quarter past
six.

This chore hadn't turned out to be as bad as he had expected,
however. For one thing, Mrs. McIntyre nearly always had
Stephen's nappy changed when Donny arrived, which was a
great weight off Donny's mind; for another, he actually enjoyed
being with the baby most of the time. You could have good crack
with Stephen. He always roared laughing when Donny popped
his face up from behind a towel or when Donny fell in a heap on
the floor with his feet in the air like a dead spider. The only
problem was that Stephen got the hiccups if you made him laugh
too much, and the hiccups made him cross. After that it was
harder work. Donny would put him on the floor and the two of
them would do a wobbly crawl around the place, or he would lie
on the floor, sit the baby on his chest and let him slap Donny's
face with his little fat hands.

This evening, in answer to his knock, the door was opened by
Mrs. McIntyre's daughter, Orla, whom Donny knew to be in

Third Year at St. Mary's, which was just around the corner. She was about fifteen, not tall, a little plump. She wore the maroon skirt and cardigan that all the St Mary's girls wore. Donny knew she was a friend of Swamp's sister, Helen.

'Hi.' Her greeting was casual but friendly.

'Hi,' he responded. 'How's he today?'

'Ah, he's grea',' Orla clipped her 't's' in true west-Dublin fashion. 'Me mammy had to go a bi' early.'

'Yeh. Sure. That's OK,' replied Donny. 'I'll just take him.'

In the pokey sittingroom he found Stephen being propped up on the settee by another girl. Her uniform was identical to Orla's. Her hair was long and straight and mousey-coloured, and she would have looked like any one of hundreds of the St. Mary's girls if it hadn't been for her eyes. They were widely spaced and very brown and there was a kind of curiosity in them when she looked at Donny.

'Hi, Fiona,' said Donny.

'Hi,' she said softly, and looked down at Stephen again. 'Here's your uncle now, Stephen.'

Donny was trying to figure out whether he was being slagged or not, with the 'uncle' bit, when Fiona looked up at him again. 'He's a grand little fella,' she said, starting to get up. Her voice was husky.

When Stephen saw Donny, he let a yelp of delight out of him and promptly keeled over on the settee.

'Yeh. He's not bad,' said Donny as he lunged to grab the baby. 'OK, Mister. Up you come.' He lifted Stephen high towards the ceiling. 'You've been drinkin' again, haven't you?' he joked. Stephen whooped and crowed with delight.

Orla came in pushing the buggy. 'You're in time today. For a change,' she remarked.

'Yeh. I knew *you* were lookin' after him,' Donny retorted good-naturedly. Orla was great crack.

She left the buggy and came over to look into Stephen's eyes.

'You'd prefer to stay with us, wouldn't you, Steve?' she asked him. Stephen slapped at her nose and said, 'Doo-doo!'

'See,' she laughed. 'I told you.'

'Don't mind these women,' Donny advised the infant. He sat him into the buggy and began to strap him in.

'How's Paul Marsh keepin'?' It was Fiona's quiet question.

Donny noticed the look which passed between the two girls.

'He's great — still.' Fiona had asked the same question the previous week. 'I'll tell him you were askin' for him.'

Fiona was indignant. 'Not me!' she protested. 'It's her!'

'OK. I'll tell him *Orla* was askin' for him, then.'

Orla started. She blushed. 'Oh, no. Don't.'

Fiona's laugh was husky and mischievous. 'Ah, go on. Let him tell him,' she said. 'Sure you'd never know.'

'Well, whatever you like,' said Donny laughing. 'I was only messing anyway.' He pushed the buggy towards the hall. 'Seeya. An' thanks.'

The two girls followed the buggy right out to the footpath, talking baby talk to Stephen and kissing him on the pudgy cheek. 'Seeya,' they called, as Donny pushed the buggy away down the street. Then Fiona's voice, 'An' don't forget to tell Swamp ...'

Donny smiled to himself as he trudged home. Old Swampy and Orla, he thought. He shrugged his shoulders. Yes, he agreed. It was high time for Swamp to get a bit of romance in his life.

When Maeve arrived home, she found Donny stretched on the sofa, watching TV. He had Stephen propped on his stomach, and the baby was walloping his way through a bottle of milk.

'God! I'm knackered!' exclaimed Donny, as his sister hung up her coat.

'Hard day at school?' she enquired.

'Naw. School was OK. It's your man here. He'd wear you out.'

'Ah, it's good practice for you,' she retorted.

'Humph!' he retorted. 'You won't catch me getting married.' She was silent for a moment and he wondered had he hit a sore spot. Maeve's marriage was certainly no advertisement for the state of wedlock.

'That's gas, coming from a bloke that's after being invited to a party tonight. And that's going, what's more!'

Donny smiled to himself. This was more like the old Maeve.

Since she had returned from England and gone back to work, she had regained that old sense of humour which he liked so much. It was almost like the times before Liam, her shiftless husband, had appeared on the scene, before everything began to go wrong. But Liam was gone and now there was little Stephen. He was an extra personality in the house, and for the first time since his parents died, Donny had begun to feel that he was part of a real family again.

3

It was nearly eight-thirty when Donny started to get himself ready for going out. After a bath and hairwash, he searched in the wardrobe for his good jeans and sweater. They were the only decent ones he owned and he tried to keep them for special occasions. He dressed and surveyed himself in the mirror of the dressing-table. He wished he had a smart jacket to wear instead of the sweater, and he decided that he would ask Murty in the bar for a couple of nights' work during the week in addition to his three at the weekend so that he could make some extra money.

At nine-fifteen, he took the bus to Terenure and walked through the quiet suburban streets towards Jacky's house.

Daylight was a faint pink glow in the western sky and in the lamplit streets the smell of smoke hung in the air.

When he came to the large red-brick house, Donny turned into the drive, stepping onto the paving slabs set into the lawn to avoid contact with the large Volvo parked behind a red Toyota Starlet. He rang the doorbell and watched the hazy outlines of the lighted hallway through the frosted glass of the front door. Butterflies gyrated in his stomach. Almost immediately, the distortions in the glass took on a blue tint and Jacky's shape materialised.

'Hi, Donny,' she whispered, as she swung the door open. She looked different. Her fair hair was all fluffy round her head and the deep blue dress revealed her shoulders. But there was the same brightness in her eyes that he remembered from before and there was no mistaking the pleasure of her smile. 'Come in,' she said, louder now.

'Hi, Jacky,' he said, stepping into the wide hall, trying to be cool. 'Not too early, am I?'

'No. Just right.' She closed the door and he saw that she had grown taller. For a moment, the thought flashed through his mind that he was in the company of a stranger, but he blotted it out. 'Here, let me take your jacket. Mum and Dad are in the sitting room.'

Donny was glad to remove the old denim jacket. He had only worn it in case of rain. 'Come on,' she said, hanging the jacket on the knob of the stair banister. She grabbed his hand and pulled him towards the open door on his left. Her confidence gave him courage. The room was warm and rich, but he had no time to observe it.

'Ah, Donny.' A tall tanned grey-haired man put down his pipe on the hearth and got up to face him.

'Hi, Mr. Anderson,' Donny said. He was on the point of saying, 'Long time no see,' but he stopped himself. 'How are you?' he asked instead.

'Fine, fine.' The man took Donny's hand and shook it firmly. 'You remember Myrtle, don't you?' he went on, turning to the elegant woman seated on the other side of a blazing fire, who was observing him with slightly arched eyebrows.

'Yeh, I remember,' Donny said, stepping over and offering the woman his hand. She took it, shook it formally and gave it back to him. Her hand felt long and elegant and cold and it was encrusted with rings. 'I hope you are keeping well,' he continued.

'Delighted, I'm sure,' she replied. 'Won't you sit down?' Her accent was unmistakably English. Donny retreated to the large sofa directly behind him and sat on the edge of it.

'I'll be ready in a tick,' Jacky said and disappeared through the doorway. Donny wished she had stayed.

'Jacky has been telling me about the game tomorrow. Am I right in saying that there was something in the papers about it?' Mr. Anderson seemed genuinely interested in the subject.

'Yeh, there was a small write-up,' said Donny modestly. 'In

The Irish Times, I think. It's a replay. Quarter final. We were lucky to draw the last time, though.'

'I take it there is only one Donny O'Sullivan on your team?' Mr. Anderson continued, a slight smile deepening the creases on his weather-beaten face.

'Yeh,' said Donny.

'A "key player"? Am I right?' The man's eyes twinkled good-naturedly.

'I dunno,' replied Donny, smiling. 'It's probably something the reporter put in to fill space.'

Jacky's mother was looking at Donny with increasing interest. 'Oh, so you play rugby, Donny?'

'No,' replied Donny helpfully. 'This is soccer we're playing tomorrow. Leinster Senior Cup.'

'Oh, how nice.' She seemed a little disappointed with his answer. 'Maybe the boys at the club tonight will be able to persuade you to try rugby. It's quite an exciting game.'

Donny was trying to figure out an intelligent answer to this statement, when he heard rapid footsteps in the hall and Jacky came in through the doorway. She wore a cream-coloured jacket with pink flowers on it.

'I hope Mum and Dad haven't been too boring, Donny,' she joked.

'No,' her dad responded. 'We've only been talking about football. You know Donny's got this big game tomorrow.'

'Oh, yes? Where's it being played, Donny? You didn't tell me.'

'It's over on the Bellview ground,' replied Donny. 'We had them at home last time, but ...'

'At what time?' Jacky seemed really interested.

'Three o'clock. You'll still be in school, though,' he joked.

'Oh, I just might go on the hop,' she said mischievously. 'We've only got French and Maths last two periods.'

'I hope you're not being serious, Jacky,' Mrs. Anderson said politely but firmly. 'You know how important the Leaving is for you, if you want to go to college.'

Jacky planted herself on the sofa beside Donny. 'Oh, I think

I'll take a year off next year. Travel and see the world a bit.' She nudged a surprised Donny in the ribs as she said this.

Her mother turned to look at her now and her response was almost icy, Donny thought. 'My dear,' she said, 'we've been through all that already.' Now her gaze shifted to Donny. 'I'm sure Donny will tell you how important it is to get into college and get a good degree. What will you be doing next year, Donny?'

Donny was taken by surprise. The truth was he didn't know. He knew what he wanted to do, but whenever he thought about the financial aspects of going to college, he was dismayed. Maeve was just able to manage for herself and Stephen, while Donny's weekend pub-job hardly provided enough to keep himself going.

'Uh, I'd like to do engineering,' he blurted. 'Electronic. Probably in Kevin Street. But it depends on the results of the Leaving, you know.' For some reason which was not clear to him, he felt under pressure. Jacky's mother was still looking at him steadily, her eyebrows slightly raised. He felt that he should continue talking, but he couldn't think of anything to say.

'Right,' said Jacky's dad, suddenly getting to his feet. 'Are we ready to roll? I'll just get my jacket.'

Several minutes later Donny and Jacky were sitting in the back of the big Volvo as it purred through the darkened streets. Donny wasn't completely relaxed. He felt now, as he had felt before, that Jacky's mother didn't quite approve of him. Moreover, the thought of going into the rugby club where he would know nobody except Jacky was beginning to bother him a bit. While Jacky talked excitedly, Donny nervously fingered the crumpled tenner in his jacket pocket and wondered would it be enough to get him through the night.

When the car cruised to a halt on the tarmac surface of the club car park, Donny noticed that there was a queue of young people at the entrance.

'Right,' said Mr. Anderson, turning to hand two cards to Jacky. 'Take these. They're complimentaries. Just show them to Trevor at the door and you won't have to queue. Give us a ring when you're ready to come home.' His teeth glinted as he smiled. 'And enjoy yourselves.'

'Thanks,' said Donny. He felt better then. Mr. Anderson seemed to like him, and there was something genuine about the man which Donny liked too.

When the car had pulled away towards the dim street lights, Donny followed Jacky past the bubbling line of young people to the crowded entrance. She squeezed past a girl and stepped up into the foyer. Donny was about to do likewise when a male voice behind him said, 'Hey! What's going on? There's a queue, you know!'

Donny turned to look at the speaker. He was a tall youth, with curly blond hair, a handsome face and a green blazer with a fancy crest on the breast pocket.

'It's OK. We've got complimentary tickets,' said Donny.

The youth surveyed Donny from head to toe. A girl in a pink dress, leaning against him, laughed aloud.

'Complimentaries?' the youth said, a sardonic smile hovering round his lips. Then his eyes shifted to look over Donny's shoulder. 'Oh, hi, Jacky,' he said.

Jacky appeared at Donny's side. 'Hi, Bruce,' she said cheerfully. Then to Donny, 'What's the matter, Donny?'

Donny was about to answer, but he was cut short by the other. 'I'm sorry, Jacky,' he said. 'I didn't realise he was with you.' He now looked directly at Donny, an easy smile creasing his face. 'No hard feelings, OK?'

Donny nodded briefly. 'No sweat,' he said. The shrill laugh of the girl in the pink dress cut through the air as he turned towards the foyer.

'What happened?' Jacky asked.

'Ah, nothing really. Your man in the blazer thought we were jumpin' the queue.'

'Who? Bruce?' she seemed surprised.

'Yeh. But don't worry about it. It was nothing.'

Inside the clubhouse, the air was vibrant with the beat of drums and the thrumming of the guitars. The coloured lights flashed with the beat, and Donny, standing alone while Jacky went to the cloakroom, began to relax, his nerves responding to the rhythm.

After several minutes, he felt a hand on his arm. It was Jacky. 'Come on. Let's dance,' she said, pulling him out onto the floor, which was now beginning to fill up.

Donny felt more comfortable on the dance floor, amidst the swaying and gyrating bodies, and he let the music take him away. But he couldn't long remain oblivious of the young woman who danced in front of him, her face serious except when their eyes met and she smiled up at him. His mind went back to the previous summer in London, when he and Flagon were working on the railways and Jacky was staying with her grandmother in Leatherhead. He remembered the golden August weekends when he would take the train south from London, the long hours spent at the cottage by the river, and the fun they had, when it seemed that life could have gone on like that forever. Reality had pushed its unwelcome way in, however, when the holidays came to an end and it was time to come back to school in Dublin.

During that September, Donny had become more aware than ever before of the great gulf that existed between his world and Jacky's. Her world was that of the classy school in Mount Merrion, of rugby and tennis clubs, of holidays spent cruising on the Shannon on her father's boat, or doing the shows in London. His was so different. Ever since his brother-in-law, Liam, landed himself in jail in England for dealing in stolen merchandise, Liam's estranged wife, Maeve, and her brother, Donny, had a hard struggle to make ends meet. True, the small three-bedroomed house in the working-class housing-estate was hers, thanks to the wisdom of their dead father, but the social welfare money had not been nearly enough to keep Maeve and Stephen. That was why Donny had taken the job in the local pub at weekends, working first as a lounge-boy and being recently promoted to a serving role behind the bar. With this work and babysitting Stephen, Donny had little time for socialising or for meeting Jacky, despite the several letters which she had written.

He had promised Jacky that at Christmas they would get together but, inexplicably, she went off to England with her mother for the two weeks, so they had never met. He had phoned her house twice during the first week back at school, but there was no reply the first time, and Jacky was out at some kind of a Careers evening the second time. As well as that, Christmas had left Donny stony broke, so he kept putting off making another call until he had saved some money. And then the football training had begun in earnest. So Donny began to feel more and more that he wasn't going to see Jacky again. That was until her letter came.

Now as he watched her elegant figure beside him, Donny began to chide himself for his lack of courage. They had shared bad times and good. There was a bond, and he knew he should struggle to keep it from being broken.

Now she moved closer to him. 'Well, what do you think, Donny?' she called into his ear. Her closeness smelt of fragrance. He caught her arms to keep her close.

'Cool,' he said. She laughed and swayed away from him. 'Who's your man, anyway?' he asked. 'The guy at the door?'

Her eyebrows arched. 'You mean Bruce?' He nodded. 'Oh, he's just a fellow I knew ... I know.' Donny sensed embarrassment, but waited for her to finish. 'He lives near me. We've known him for years.'

'Oh, yeah. Just a friend, eh?' he chided her gently.

'Yes,' she smiled. 'Just a friend.'

When the number ended, the crowd began to drift away.

'C'mon. Let's have a drink,' Donny suggested. 'And you can tell me what's been happening.'

They headed for the bar. Just inside the doorway, Jacky stopped. 'Hi, Bruce,' she said. Donny recognised the blond head immediately. The girl in the pink dress seemed to be attached to Bruce by an invisible belt.

'Hello, Jacky.' Bruce's voice was suave and relaxed. 'Haven't seen you around in a while. You must be studying hard.'

'Not really. By the way, this is Donny O'Sullivan, a friend of mine. Donny, this is Bruce.'

Bruce's face broke into a half smile. 'Yes. I think we've met,' he said. Donny nodded in response. He didn't smile.

'And this is Gloria,' Bruce said. Gloria detached herself momentarily from Bruce's waist and said, 'Hi.' Then she laughed that high-pitched laugh again, although Donny could see nothing particularly funny in what had been said.

Bruce chatted easily for several minutes. Donny noticed that he looked at Jacky nearly all the time. Gloria seemed to be particularly interested in a photograph of a rugby team which was hanging on the wall beside her. Before they left, Bruce turned his attention back to Donny.

'Haven't seen you around here before, Donny. Are you new in the area?'

'Yeh. You could say that.'

'Do you play a bit? We could always do with some new players.' The question seemed innocent enough.

'No ...' Donny began to explain, but Jacky interrupted.

'Donny goes to St. Colman's. They're playing in the ... What is it again, Donny?'

'Leinster Senior Cup,' Donny said. Bruce seemed at a loss. 'Football,' Donny went on. A glimmer of recognition grew in Bruce's eyes.

'Oh, yes. That's the Walkinstown school. You're in the other half of the draw from us, I think. Who're you playing tomorrow?'

'Bellview,' said Donny.

'Right.' Bruce seemed to recognise the name. 'I'd say you're up against it tomorrow, though. Bellview are a strong team. We beat them by only a goal in a friendly a few weeks ago.'

'Do you play soccer too, Bruce?' Jacky seemed surprised and interested.

Bruce was casual in his reply. 'Well, we squeeze it in between the rugby and the cricket seasons. It gives us a bit of a break after the cup campaign. We haven't such a bad team this year, so we've entered for that competition. I often think we should take the game more seriously, though. You know what they say, "A game for gentlemen ..."'

Gloria was by this time tugging impatiently at Bruce's blazer. Bruce's resistance was obvious. 'Well, we must be going, as you can see,' he said and Donny detected a faint hint of irony. He

looked again at Jacky. 'I might see you around.' He nodded to
Donny, looked down peevishly at Gloria, and the two of them
drifted away.

'Bruce is nice,' Jacky said. 'And Dad says that he's terrific at
rugby. They won the cup this year, you know.'

'Yeh. I know.' Donny had read about it in the papers and he
knew also that Bruce's school, St. Edmund's, were reputed to
have a very strong soccer squad this year.

'Didn't you like him?' Jacky seemed to have sensed Donny's
luke-warm response.

'Well, it's hard to know when you're only talking to a bloke
for a few minutes ...'

She rounded on him. 'I know you don't like him, Donny
O'Sullivan. Come on. What is it?'

'Nothing, really. It's just what he said about soccer. You know
the rest of that, don't you?'

'No. What is it?'

'Well, they say that rugby's a game for hooligans played by
gentlemen, an' that soccer's a game for gentlemen played by...'
He paused.

'Hooligans,' she said, her eyes widening as the meaning
dawned on her. 'But that's not true, Donny. Anyway, Bruce
didn't mean it like that, I'm sure.'

Donny shrugged his shoulders. 'It's no big deal anyway,' he
said, smiling. 'Bruce can think what he likes.'

She smiled then. 'Right again, Donny O'Sullivan,' she said.

At the bar Donny stood his full height and ordered two
Budweisers in his deepest voice. He took them to where Jacky
had found two seats by a table.

'What happened at Christmas?' Donny asked after a while.

She put down her drink. 'Mummy decided to stay two weeks
instead of one,' she said. 'Of course I wasn't consulted at all! I
should have sent you a card, but I thought I'd see you when I got
back. I thought you'd phone.'

'I did, but you were out.'

'That was only *one* night, Donny!' she said with spirit.

'Yeh. Well, with the job at the weekend, and the football ...

And anyway, I have the feelin' that your mother isn't too keen on me.'

'Oh, Donny!'

'No, I mean, that stuff about joinin' the club, an' where will I be next year. Why does she have to go an' say stuff like that?'

'Don't mind Mum, Donny. She's a terrible snob. We're always telling her that. She's different when you know her.'

'Yeh, an' I'm not too crazy about your man in the fancy jacket, your friend, Bruce,' he chided.

'Ah, don't mind him. He just carries on like that sometimes, but he's really all right.'

Just then Donny noticed three youths with green blazers standing at the bar, sipping Budweiser from bottles. The stocky, dark-haired one in the middle was looking in Donny's direction. He said something to the others. They turned to look, smiled, and turned back to the bar. Donny put his drink down. He saw that Jacky's eyes had followed his to the three at the bar.

'Three more fancy jackets,' he remarked. 'What're they lookin' at?' He was beginning to feel a little uncomfortable.

'Ah, don't mind them either,' she said impulsively. 'Let's go and dance.'

Back in the dance area, the lights were soft and the number was slow. Donny put his arms round Jacky's waist. She leaned against him, her arms on his shoulders, her hair brushing his cheek. He became aware of the slimness of her waist where his hands were, and of the rhythmic movement of her hips. He felt the pressure of her breasts against him, and smelled the sweet fragrance of her perfume. He felt good.

Suddenly he was jolted by a rough push from behind. He released Jacky and turned. The stocky dark-haired youth that he had seen at the bar was glaring at him over the shoulder of a girl in a white dress.

'Watch where you're driving!' said the other. His voice was slightly slurred. Donny felt the pressure of Jacky's hand on his arm. 'Don't mind him, Donny,' she hissed. 'He's been drinking.'

But Donny was annoyed. 'At least I'm fit to be in the driver's seat,' he said. The girl tried to push her companion away, but he caught her arms and pulled her to one side. 'You've got an awful lot to say for a knacker!' he called above the noise of the music. Donny felt himself tensing up. 'No, Donny. Please!' Jacky pleaded. He brushed away her restraining hand.

'D'you want to say that outside?' he demanded, taking a step closer to the other. He steeled himself, expecting the head-butt. He had his arm ready to block. There was an ugly look on the other's face.

'I'll say it any god-damn place I want,' he said hoarsely. He lunged forward, but Donny pushed him away with open hands. He didn't want to fight. Then, from the watching crowd, two blazer-clad youths appeared and grabbed the stocky one.

'Come on, Rocky,' said one of them. 'Take it easy.' It was Bruce. Donny watched as Bruce and his companion hauled the stocky one protesting away.

Donny was shaken. 'That's it!' he exclaimed. 'I'm getting out of here!' He headed for the door.

'Wait, Donny. Wait!' Jacky pleaded.

He turned on her, indignation flaring within him. 'You can see what's happening here! These guys are lookin' for aggro.'

'No, Donny. Everyone knows ...'

He didn't let her say any more. 'Would you mind just ringing your dad?' he demanded.

'No, Donny. Will you just *listen* to me?' Her eyes flashed. 'I'm telling you Rocky's always like that. Everybody knows ...'

'Everybody except me!' he retorted ironically. 'I suppose he dunts all the other blokes in the back here, an' they just turn an' say "Thanks"!'

'No, Donny. But he's a trouble-maker. He goes drinking before the disco and he tries to make trouble when he comes in here. They all know that.'

'Yeh, well, wouldn't you think they "all" would do something about it!' he demanded. 'I mean, there's no way that was an accident. He did that deliberately. You could see it in his face!'

'But he's always carrying on like that. All you have to do is ignore him.'

'Oh, yeh? An' what do you think would have happened if your

fancy friends hadn't come an' dragged him away?'

He saw the hurt in her face immediately. 'That's not fair, Donny. Bruce was trying to help.'

'Yeh, OK,' he admitted. 'But if he hadn't done it ...'

'Donny, all you had to do is turn your back and walk away.'

Donny shook his head in exasperation. 'That's not the way it works, Jacky. If I'd done that he'd have thought I was chicken, an' done it again. And then ... Well, I just don't want to be mixed up in aggro the first night I come here. That's all.'

'But, Donny, maybe it *was* an accident.'

'No way, Jacky. That was no accident. He was lookin' for trouble. You just said yourself that he does this all the time.'

'But what about the disco? It's not even half over,' she pleaded. Donny's resolve began to weaken. Maybe he was over-reacting, he told himself. Or worse, maybe he was afraid to stay. Maybe he was letting a muscle-bound posh run him out of the place.

'OK,' he said. 'But if that bloke ...'

He never finished the sentence, because over Jacky's shoulder he saw a commotion under the balcony. He saw Rocky struggling to break free from the grasp of three other youths. Rocky was glaring in Donny's direction and he was shouting something which Donny couldn't hear because of the music.

Donny made up his mind then. 'I'm going,' he stated. 'If you want to stay, I can find my own way home ...' He didn't mean it to sound narky, but that's the way it came out.

'You needn't bother,' she said shortly. 'I'll ring Dad.'

He followed her out to the foyer. A glance behind told him that the commotion had moved deeper under the balcony. He could see a group of youths huddled together in the shadows and then they passed out of view. He stood beside Jacky as she dialled the number. He heard her say, 'Dad, will you come and get us?'

Then a pause. 'No. Nothing's wrong. We're just tired, that's all.' She put the phone down and turned towards him, but her eyes avoided his. 'He'll be here in a few minutes,' she said. 'I'll go and get my jacket.'

'OK. I'll wait for you outside.' he said, heading for the door.

The night air was cool. Breathing deeply he let the tension out of his shoulders. Maybe he shouldn't have come. Maybe the difference between his world and Jacky's was too great.

The door of the clubhouse opened and Jacky came out, buttoning her jacket. Looking at her, he felt a pang. Was this how it was going to end? She came and stood beside him but was silent. And the silence became unbearable.

'Lookit, Jacky,' he said. 'I'm sorry it happened like this. I know you're disappointed.'

She was silent for so long that he thought she was sulking. 'Donny,' she said quietly. 'I thought you'd enjoy ... I thought *we'd* enjoy it. That's why I asked you to come. But I still think you shouldn't have said anything to him. If you'd just ignored him ...'

Donny sighed and tried another tack. 'Look, Jacky, I know Bruce is a friend of yours. But I find it really hard to believe that this Rocky guy just waltzed over and dunted me in the back without the others knowing about it.'

'But they don't like him, Donny. He's just a trouble-maker. Even on the rugby team he gets into fights. They all say that.' She stopped as if she knew there was no point in going on.

They were still silent when, a few minutes later, the powerful headlights of the Volvo swung in through the tall stone pillars of the entrance and the big car crunched to a halt beside them. They answered Mr. Anderson's questions as casually as they could. He must know something is wrong, thought Donny. Would Jacky tell her mother? he wondered. No doubt *she'd* be delighted to hear that the evening had been a flop, he thought grimly.

Back at the house, Donny made the excuse that he had to be in bed early because of the game on the following day. He didn't stay for supper. At the door he tried again to retrieve the situation. 'G'night, Jacky. Thanks for asking me. I'm sorry it didn't work out better.'

'Me too,' she replied. He saw the confusion in her face.

'I'll give you a shout in a few days,' he said, and turned to go.

'Donny? Good luck in the game tomorrow.'

'Thanks,' he said, and walked away.

4

Donny met Flagon in the school corridor next morning before class.

'Well?' queried his friend. 'How was last night?'

'It was OK' said Donny. Flagon's eyebrows lifted in response to this lukewarm reply. Donny decided to tell the truth. 'Well, no, actually. It was crummy.' He told Flagon about the disco and the incident with Rocky.

'Sounds like a real shit-stirrer,' was Flagon's comment when he had finished. And then another thought struck him. 'Maybe you were moving in on a pad that he thought was his.'

Donny shook his head. 'You mean, him and Jacky? Naw. I don't think so. She says he's a wally. No, I think he was just shapin', because I was new in the place an' I didn't have a fancy green jacket to wear.'

'Well, don't worry about that ponce,' said Flagon. 'Maybe he was lucky that the others hopped on him,' he added.

'I'm not so sure about that,' retorted Donny. 'He had plenty of meat on him. I think he plays in the scrum. An' anyway, if I had started with him, the others would probably have hopped on me. Jeez! Can you just imagine it? Here I am with the daughter of the club treasurer an' the first time I set foot in the club the aggro starts an' I get duffed around the place an' thrown out by Roy of the Rovers and his mates.'

'Yeh,' chortled Flagon. 'That'd make you flavour of the

month up in Andersons, all right.'

Donny thumped the door of the empty classroom with the heel of his fist. 'Shit!' he exclaimed. 'Why'd I have to go to that bleedin' kip in the first place!'

Flagon was silent. Frustration was nothing new to him and he was humble enough to respect it in his friends. As well as that, he knew the answer to the question and he was tactful enough not to blurt it out, because he knew that Donny knew the answer too.

The squad left their classes at twelve-thirty and had a light lunch in the assembly hall. Because it was on their minds, they talked about anything except the match. Butler entertained the group at his table with a yarn about his brother who was on his way to a fancy dress ball wearing a gold dress and a wig belonging to his girl-friend. He dropped into a pub beforehand with a few friends and was playing the part so well that a visiting Polish sailor made a pass at him. When he couldn't shake off the attentions of the love-sick sailor, he told him to go away — in his normal bass voice. He was lucky to get out of the pub in time because the offended sailor started rounding up his mates. 'The brother reckons they weren't plannin' a singalong either,' remarked Butler significantly.

The bus came at one o'clock and the group filed into it. By this time, Clint, the team trainer, had materialised and was directing operations in his usual laid-back fashion. Of medium height, with straight mouse-coloured hair and glasses, his real name was Peter Eastwood, but since he had overheard two First Years in the corridor outside his room calling him 'Clint', he had cultivated the dead-pan expression which was the trade mark of the film star in question. The general opinion among the squad was that far from being offended, he was actually flattered by his nickname. Now he was making sure that the bag of gear, the spare footballs, the First Aid kit and the water bottle were safely stowed on board the coach.

'Give her sally!' was his comment to the bus driver, when they were ready to go.

On the bus, talk gradually came round to the game, but none

of the squad could bring themselves to be ⌐
would almost be a sign of weakness.

'Hey, Anto!' yelled Butler, leering over the heads
who was at the back. 'Who's takin' the pennos today?'

'Your Granny!' yelled back Curtis, the sandy-haired captain,
who had missed a penalty in the drawn first game.

'Well, she'd do as good a job as you anyway!' retorted Butler.
'With one leg tied behind her back.' General merriment all
round.

As the bus drew near to Bellview school, Donny found
himself thinking about Jacky. What if she skipped out on classes
and came to the game? The idea was crazy, he told himself. Not
after what happened last night. And as he thought about those
events, he began to have doubts. Maybe it was he who had been
at fault. Maybe he just had been out of his depth. But then he
remembered Rocky and the incident on the dance floor and
another voice in his head cut across these thoughts. No, it said.
You would have been crazy to become involved in a mosh in that
place. You were *right* to get out. But what about Jacky? the first
voice insisted. You went and upset her after all the trouble she
went to, asking you to the party. It wasn't her fault, and you went
and ruined her night for her, you thankless bastard. While Donny
was struggling with these conflicting thoughts, the bus drove in
through the imposing gateway of Bellview School.

The dressing-room buried in the bowels of the Bellview
gymnasium was long and narrow, with a low ceiling and high
windows. Scraps of mud with circular stud holes in them lay
under the wooden seats. The team shuffled in. Several players
stood while others sat on the long wooden forms that lined three
of the walls. Flanagan had now become the entertainer and the
others responded with loud guffaws to his pithy jokes. Nobody
seemed interested in getting changed for the game.

'OK, you guys!' barked Clint, who had just come back from
inspecting the pitch. 'Put a sock in it now. We have a game to
play here.' The banter faded out. 'You'd swear you guys were
going to the Point on a Friday night, to listen to you. Just get
togged and I'll go over the team.'

again quickly, naming the player
ld play four at the back with Murray
d for the moment, and two up front. In
nd began to put on the pale blue jerseys
t had his homework done. Sheldon, the
, was good in the air, but suspect with the
keep the ball low. Munroe, the right winger
w... ...tler would pick him up, push him out to the
wing a... ...mmit himself unless he was sure. If Butler ran
out of steam, he would switch with Miler, the right full-back.
The centre-forward, 'What's-his-name', was useful but one-
footed, and remember, that was his left, so keep on his left side,
and don't let him fire one off inside the penalty area. And
Sheppard, he was Donny O'Sullivan's man. Donny was to stay
'glued to Sheppard's ass' all day. And remember the quick break
out of defence, because we had speed on the wings too.

'Right. Get stretched off,' he told them, when they all had their
boots on. They did their warm-up exercises while the referee
came in, inspected their studs and said his mandatory few words.
Then it was time to go. Clint said, 'Good luck.' Then he stood
by the door and slapped each of them on the back as they passed
out.

One side of the pitch, snuggling at the base of a hill behind
the low, grey school, was lined with a scattering of Bellview boys
when the St. Colman's team emerged. There were no St. Colman's supporters — the game hadn't been considered important
enough to warrant any of the pupils missing class to go and
support a team which, as Murphy had wrily remarked, 'wasn't
going to win anyway'. There was a half-hearted murmur from
the Bellview supporters when they saw the opposition, a scattering of boos, a half-serious broadcast of insults. Sprinting past
them, Donny heard the words, but didn't listen to them. He had
more important matters on his mind. Near the far goalposts, he
saw the Bellview team already limbering up, their maroon-and-
yellow strip bright against the drab leafless hedge behind. He
picked out the stocky figure of Sheppard with the number eight
on his back. The pitch looked smooth and level.

St. Colman's lost the toss. Sheppard elected to play against the fitful breeze that swung down from the western flank of the mountains. The black-clad referee's whistle blasted and the game was on.

Donny nudged the ball forward off the centre spot to Flanagan, who casually turned and stroked it back towards Curtis, the St. Colman's centre-half. But there was no pace on the ball. Leaden-footed, Donny saw a Bellview forward rush after it. Curtis, sensing the danger, galvanised himself into a sudden sprint. The two players clashed on the ball. It squirted up into the air between them. Curtis, recovering, leaped at it but his head stabbed empty air. The Bellview number eight pounced. He took the ball on his left foot, switched suddenly to his right and smacked it hard and long. It sliced between Miler and Murray towards the St. Colman's goal. O'Reilly, between the posts, had just landed after touching the crossbar three times, as he always did at the beginning of matches, when he saw the bullet coming. His feet suddenly did a little dance. He steadied himself. The ball began to curve to his left. He launched himself sideways. To Donny, now running back from the centre circle, everything seemed to happen in slow motion. The ball seemed to be destined for the top right-hand corner of the net, when O'Reilly's clawing hand touched it. He pushed it upwards a fraction. It thumped off the crossbar and came whizzing back into the field of play. Flagon, rushing goalwards from his mid-field berth, steadied himself and walloped it out of play near the corner flag. The rising Bellview roar dipped to a groan of disappointment. Corner!

Curtis went berserk. 'Whaddya mean givin' me a pass like that?' he screamed at Flanagan. 'For Chrissakes!'

Clint, on the line, was having a fit too. 'Flanno!' he roared. 'Get the bleedin' finger out!' Flanagan held up his hand sheepishly, acknowledging the blunder. 'Donny!' came the roar from the line again. 'That's your man! You can't let him take potshots like that!'

'Shit!' thought Donny. Number eight was Sheppard. He was the one that had nearly scored. But Clint was screaming now.

'C'mon. Get your donkey into the area! There's a bleedin' corner! Curtis, back post! Murray, near post! Butler, pick up eleven! Donny! *Donny!* Onto eight!'

St. Colman's were rattled. The din on the sideline grew louder. The corner swung across. 'Tommo's ball!' roared O'Reilly, rushing out. His fist caught the ball a glancing blow. It soared skywards as O'Reilly fell in a heap. He started to scramble to his feet. Above him, Curtis steadied himself, head back, watching the flight of the ball. The big Bellview centre-forward bumped shoulders with him. The ball began to fall. Curtis leaned into his opponent and poised himself for take-off, but just at that crucial moment, O'Reilly erupted from the ground beneath him. The ball hit Curtis on the shoulder and bounced high, back towards the empty goal. O'Reilly sprinted like a madman but he knew he wouldn't make it. He was about to launch himself in a spectacular but despairing dive when Miler, the St. Colman's right full, rushed in from his left, stretched a long foot out and snaked the ball off the line and away towards the right touchline.

'Things can only get better,' thought Donny grimly when the roaring died down. Then he remembered something and scanned the touchlines anxiously to see if Jacky were there. Part of him wanted to see her alone there, watching him. Another part was thankful when there was no sign of her. He was playing badly enough, he told himself grimly. If Jacky came now, he'd be up shit creek completely.

It was ten minutes before St. Colman's had their first shot on the Bellview goal. They had been buffeted by wave after wave of Bellview attacks, had scrambled the ball off the line again, and conceded two more corners, when Flagon, playing at midfield on Donny's left, nutmegged the Bellview centre-half ten yards outside the Bellview penalty area. He hastily lined up to let fly with his favourite right foot. Unfortunately he hit the ball slightly off centre and it screamed over the end line fifteen yards wide.

'Hard luck, Flag,' Donny encouraged, but from the touchline came another Clint bellow. 'Hold it up, Dave! Hold the Goddamn thing up! Wait for the support!'

Five minutes later, Bellview scored. Monroe, their winger, latched onto a ball near the right touchline. He pushed it on with McCarthy shadowing him, towards the corner flag. McCarthy's outstretched boot was fractionally too late as Munroe sent over the cross. Curtis and Murray, the St. Colman's defenders, both leaped to intercept the ball, but Donny, covering near the penalty spot, knew it was too high. He gauged its flight, poised himself to head it away, but at the last second someone smacked into him from the side. As he fell he heard the solid thump of a header, and the roar of the Bellview supporters told him the ball was in the net even before he looked.

'Shit!' said Donny. He saw O'Reilly dejectedly picking the ball out of the back of the net. Away to his right a Bellview player was being mobbed by his teammates. It was Sheppard. The supporters were dancing jigs on the touchline. On the opposite line, Clint was holding his head, looking at the ground.

'Shit!' said Donny again.

The score was still one-nil at halftime. The goal seemed to have taken the fire out of the Bellview attack. In the dressing-room, the St. Colman's team sat around the walls, heads down, saying nothing, waiting for Clint to begin. For five minutes he tore strips off them, pacing in front of them like an angry father. 'Right,' he said, when the tirade came to an end, 'I've said it before and I'm only going to say it once more, because it's what I believe. This team can beat Bellview. But you blokes have to believe it too. Now you can do either of two things. You can go back out there, let them walk all over you, and spend the rest of your last season in the Cup sitting on your arses watching someone else win it. Or you can go out there and play football, and play like a bleedin' team and not like a bunch of oul' wans, so that when you come back in here, win, lose or draw, you'll be able to say you played your best. And I believe your best is good enough to win this game.' He turned on his heel, walked out through the door and slammed it behind him.

Nobody said anything for a long moment. The only sound was their breathing, now nearly back to normal. Then Donny said, 'He's right, you know. We're playing total bleedin' rubbish.

Anyone can see that.'

'Yeh,' agreed Curtis, the team captain. 'He's right. C'mon, lads. Let's have a bleedin' lash at it. Come on!' He got up from the seat and glared at them fiercely. Donny jumped up too, then Flagon, then the whole team. 'Yeah!' they said. 'Come on!' Then Curtis opened the door and charged out. His foot caught in the metal doorstep, however, and he tripped. Flanagan, on a charge behind him, couldn't stop himself. He got a dunt in the back from Murray and then the whole team fell on top of the first three, a tangled mass of bodies in the narrow corridor outside the door of the Bellview dressing-room. There was mayhem for a few moments, and the corridor echoed with a string of muffled curses, but nobody laughed. The fall and the contact seemed to generate more fire in them. The door of the Bellview dressing-groom remained closed and St. Colman's were out on the pitch a full five minutes before the opposition appeared.

Bellview kicked off to start the second half. Confidently they stroked the ball in neat triangles around the St. Colman's forwards. Sheppard, in midfield, took it from the centre-half but passed it back lazily when Donny closed on him. Kavanagh and Donoghue, the St. Colman's front pair, ran like redshanks around in circles, but couldn't get near the ball. Sheppard went looking for the ball again but Donny went with him this time, shadowing his every move. Mullen, the Bellview right fullback, decided to kick it long. Munroe, their right winger, raced forward under it, but the ball never reached him. Butler timed his intercepting jump perfectly and knocked it down to Murphy, on the left side of the St. Colman's midfield. Murphy threaded it through to Flagon, who pushed forward into the space that opened in front of him. Two Bellview players closed on him and he stabbed it across to Donny, moving through from midfield. Donny spotted Kavanagh wide on the right and played a long ball towards the corner, right into his path. Kavanagh tapped it on and then crossed. Donny, racing for the six yard box, heard Curtis behind him before he saw him. 'Anto's ball!' roared Curtis. In the last second before contact, Donny ducked away from the ball, his years of training telling him to leave it to the caller. Curtis soared skywards. His forehead met the ball with a solid thud and it sped downwards towards the Bellview keeper's feet. The keeper, stooping low, stopped the ball with his left hand but couldn't hold it. Donny saw it loose. He lengthened his stride and then launched his right foot at it. The keeper scrambled forward, arms outstretched, fingertips zeroing down on the spinning ball, but Donny's foot reached it first. The ball slid under the keeper's body and over the line. Goal!

Donny was still on the ground on the goal-line when the others landed on him. The breath was squeezed out of his lungs. 'Ya budgie ya, Don!' Curtis shouted in his ear. The others were hugging him and slapping him and shouting. Then Flagon dragged him upright and pushed him outfield, aware of the presence of the disgruntled Bellview defence. From the touch-line came Clint's call, 'Nice one, Don. Nice one, Anto!'

It was one goal each and St. Colman's were back in business.

The next thirty minutes saw the contest see-saw first one way, then the other, as both teams strove for the winner. The goal had injected self-belief into the St. Colman's players and gradually their style of play changed. They became more comfortable on the ball, and began to play one-touch football in tight corners so that instead of rushing their passes, the team was able to hold on to possession. When they lost the ball, they began to harry the opponents so that they had less time to settle. Yet Bellview didn't collapse. Sheppard, their captain, worked ceaselessly to try to settle them, but every time he got the ball, there was Donny shadowing him, closing off the passing lanes, pushing him out wide so that he couldn't run at the St. Colman's defence. He began to knock long high balls in towards the tall Bellview centre-forward, but Curtis gave him a torrid time, and anything that passed him was snapped up by Murray, the sweeper. Some-how, the massed supporters on the touchline sensed the game slipping away from them. They were less of a confident crowd now, and more a bunch of individuals, getting more anxious by the second. Then, with just four minutes left, they were com-pletely silenced.

Flagon, who was now playing a more forward role, latched

onto a pass from Murphy just on the eighteen yard line. He had his back to the Bellview goal but a little shimmy to the right shook off the defender for a second. Flagon turned left, saw Donoghue ahead and to the right. Donoghue called for the ball. Flagon shaped as if to pass it, and the defender drifted out. Suddenly there was a space in front of him and Flagon took the ball on, but the tall centre-half began to close on him. The goalmouth opened before him. Flagon wound up for a shot, but it never came, for the Bellview defender caught him from behind and tumbled him down onto the penalty spot. The referee's whistle shrilled. Penalty!

'You OK, Dave?' came Clint's call. Flagon dusted himself down. There was no doubt about who was going to take the kick. Flagon picked up the ball and placed it on the spot. There was not a sound from the Bellview touchline. Flagon stepped well back, looked at the goals and sprinted forward. Just a metre from the ball he stalled. The keeper started to go right. Flagon casually stroked the ball into the net on the other side. Goal!

Donny thought the final whistle would never come. It was desperation stakes as he and the others defended furiously, while Bellview threw everything at the St. Colman's goal. Then the long blast came and the game was over. Jubilation. Wild leaps in the air. Hugs. Back slaps. Shouts of exultation. St. Colman's had won.

Behind Donny a voice said, 'Well done, Donny.' He turned, grinning. It was Sheppard. 'Well played,' he said. Donny took the outstretched hand and shook it. The firm grip told him that Sheppard meant what he had said.

'Hard luck, Paul,' Donny said, sensing the disappointment in the other. 'It was just a kick of the ball.'

In the dressing-room, joy gave way to disbelief. They couldn't believe it. St. Colman's were in the last four in Leinster for the first time in the history of the school.

'Jeez! Wait till the lads hear this!' chortled Murphy. Then Clint came in and there was a chorus of 'Shhhhh!' Everyone wanted to hear what he would say. His speech was short. 'Well done, lads. You played your best. This is the day that the team has come of age.' He didn't get any further because of the eruption of boisterous cheers and shouts from the squad.

'Sir,' said Butler, when the noise subsided, 'you shoulda seen the way we came out of the dressing-room after half time.' A ripple of laughter swept through them as they remembered. Clint's curiosity spurred Butler to continue. 'Anto here gave us all the blood-an'-guts crap, an' got us all fired up ...' Butler started to laugh as the scene came back to him. 'Then he pulled open the door an' made this great charge out ...' They were all laughing now, but quietly. They wanted to hear Butler tell the rest. 'An' we all charged out after him.' The tears were streaming down Butler's face and his voice was seizing up. 'But didn't Anto trip over the doorstep, an' the whole bleedin' lot of us fell out on top of him ...' Butler had to stop as the fit seized him again. Clint was laughing now, looking round at the others for confirmation. 'We nearly bleedin' killed one another!' roared Butler. 'Right outside the Bellview dressing room!'

'Yeh,' remarked Flanagan, when there was a lull in the merriment. 'We'll have to do the same thing at half time in the semi-final. It works wonders on the pitch!'

5

Next morning, the school was abuzz with the news that the senior team had beaten Bellview and were through to the semi-final of the cup. At assembly, Brother O'Connor, the principal, made a special point of congratulating the players and their coach on their excellent play and he wished them luck in the semi-final which had been fixed for the following Wednesday. As the applause rang out throughout the school body, Flanagan leaned over to Donny and said, 'He wasn't even *at* the bleedin' game!' The team were well pleased with the boss's comment all the same.

At the mid-morning break in the senior area, Curtis was the centre of attention. He had the morning paper. The others crowded around him as he read aloud the short report of the game. 'St Colman's surprise Bellview,' he announced. A chorus of approval. 'Dark horses, St. Colman's, came from behind to score twice in the second half — through O'Sullivan and Byrne — to oust fancied team, Bellview, in this quarter-final replay of the Leinster Senior Cup.' General back-slapping of Donny and Flagon. 'Bellview captain, Paul Sheppard, had put the Churchtown team ahead after forty minutes when he headed home a Munroe cross, with the St. Colman's defence flat-footed.' General slagging of the defence, Curtis in particular. 'Yeh, but wait, lads,' the latter went on. 'Who was it that made the goal, eh?'

'G'wan. Read on, Anto,' ordered Miler.

Curtis cleared his throat dramatically. 'A breakaway goal in the first minute of the second half, however, restored St. Colman's confidence — O'Sullivan finishing after good work by Curtis. D'ye hear that, lads? They improved steadily until Byrne was taken down in the area after eighty-six minutes. He converted the spot kick to put St. Colman's through to a semi-final joust with St. Brendan's, winners of this competition two years ago.'

They were impressed and pleased. Curtis folded the paper. 'If ye think that's good, just wait till we win the bleedin' cup,' he told them.

'Hold on, Anto,' called Murphy. 'Giz a look at who's in the other semi?' Curtis opened the paper again and searched.

'Yeh. There it is,' said Murphy, pointing. 'St. Edmund's and Greenfields.'

'Ah, Greenfields'll win tha', no bother,' announced Miler. 'Them other lads are all a bunch of rugby players.'

Butler chipped in. 'They're supposed to be shit hot this year — St. Edmund's. I know a bloke that goes there, an' they've got this Italian bloke, Borgee or Bargee or somethin', an' they're sayin' he's the best that ever played in the competition.'

'Gerroff outta that!' scoffed Murray. 'That's just 'cos he's an Italian. Sure didn't we nearly *beat* them in the World Cup. He'll be no bother ...'

'Yeh, *nearly*,' said Flanagan drily.

As the argument warmed up, Donny listened. He didn't particularly want to hear about St. Edmund's, but it occurred to him that if St. Colman's won the next match, there was a possibility that they'd meet St. Edmund's in the final. And Donny had mixed feelings about that eventuality. The argument, however, was not resolved, because the bell sounded for class again.

It was during the Maths class, the last one of the afternoon, that Donny found himself thinking once again about Jacky. For the last few days, he had imagined her coming to the game. He had dreamed about her standing on the touchline while he blinded her with skill on the pitch. But she hadn't come, and he knew the reason why. It wasn't that she couldn't get off from school, or that, standing on the touchline, she wouldn't have known anyone except himself and Flagon, and they were both playing. No, he told himself, she didn't come because she had finally realised the difference that lay between them. She was disappointed in him. He just didn't have the class. He had lost face in front of all those posh friends of hers. He was an embarrassment to her now. But what else could he have done? he argued. Sure, he could have taken Rocky on, but anyone except a fool could have seen that that would have been stupid. He would have gotten himself thrown out of the club and maybe a split head, or a broken nose to boot. And that, he thought ironically, would have made him number one in the popularity stakes in the Anderson household, for sure.

Donny was jolted out of his reverie by his sudden awareness that several of the lads who sat near him were staring at him. He looked at Spud, the Maths teacher. *He* was staring at him too.

'I'm sorry, sir. I didn't catch that,' said Donny, feeling certain that Spud must have asked him a question. Spud gave him his characteristic disappointed look and moved on.

'You, Miler,' he said patiently. Miler gave him the answer.

After school, Donny and Flagon waited for Swamp at the school gate.

'How's it goin', Don?' Flagon asked.

Donny glanced at him. It was more than a casual question. 'Ah, it's OK, Flag,' he answered.

'You didn't phone you-know-who, I suppose?'

Donny kicked at a spent ice-cream stick on the tarmac. 'Nah,' he said. 'I'm not sure if I'll bother, after Tuesday night.' Flagon nodded his head, as if he understood everything. 'Yeh,' he said. 'I know.'

Donny knew that Flagon, too, had been having problems with keeping in touch with *his* girlfriend. He had met her in London last summer, and while he had managed to write several times and even to phone once, he was frustrated by the great distance between himself and Leandra. He was currently saving furiously for the air fare over, having sworn that he was never going to travel by boat again.

Swamp arrived, his rucksack hanging by its one good strap from his hunched-up right shoulder.

'Cheer up. It might never happen,' he exhorted, through a mouthful of half-chewed apple. He nibbled studiously at the butt and then flung it in the general direction of a lone evergreen tree to his right. His two friends studied him for a moment.

'Nice apple, eh, Swampy?' Flagon enquired sarcastically.

Swamp licked his fingers and smacked his lips. 'Lovely, actually.'

'Any more in the bag?' asked Donny hopefully.

'Nah. The kid only had the one.'

'Robbin' the First Years again, eh?' It was Donny's turn to slag.

Swamp sniffed disdainfully. 'They can't expect their maths homework to be done for nothin', can they? Especially when it keeps them out of detention.'

Flagon nodded wisely. 'I should have known,' he said.

'By the way,' Donny remarked, changing the subject, 'who's that girl I see hanging around with your sister?'

Swamp shot him a quick glance from under the rims of his glasses. 'Can't say,' he said stonily. 'My sister's very popular. She's got lots of ...'

'Orla,' Donny interrupted. 'Her name's Orla. Her mother looks after Stephen.'

'Oh, yeh. I know the one.' Swamp casually picked a tooth with a fingernail. It didn't seem to have occurred to him that Donny had answered his own question. 'Orla McIntyre. What about her?'

Donny winked at Flagon. 'She was askin' for you the other day.'

Swamp's guard slipped. There was a momentary flash of interest. 'Oh, yeah? Askin' for me, is it?' Then the guard went up again. 'Wouldn't pay any attention to that. Lots of girls askin' for me.' He examined his fingernails studiously.

Flagon shook his head sadly. 'They're wastin'their time, o' course. A man of destiny wouldn't let himself be bothered by a bunch of silly girls.'

Swamp's eyes were smiling when he looked at them. 'Well, I wasn't really going to say it. But when you put it like that ...'

'Anyway,' Donny cut in, 'I'm off to collect Stephen. See ya, lads.' He turned towards the school gates.

'See ya, Don,' replied Flagon. Swamp, who had been watching Donny's back, his eyes huge behind the glasses, suddenly stirred himself. 'Ah sure, hang on, Don. I'll stroll over that way with you. You could use a bit of company.' Donny stopped. He and Flagon exchanged meaningful glances. Old Swamp was still his own man.

On the way to McIntyres, Donny couldn't get a word in edgeways, because Swamp was pontificating on a report he'd read in the papers about a caveman whose body had been found deep-frozen in the Alps.

'Three thousand years old!' Swamp enthused. 'An' he was still wearin' the gear he had on when the frost got him.'

'Oh, yeh?'

'An' he had a mushroom on a bit of a string in his pouch, an' all. Jus' goes to show you that they knew all about antibiotics in those days.'

Donny didn't know if Swamp was having him on. 'Yeh,' he retorted. 'An' I suppose he had a hypodermic needle stuck up his ...!'

'Oh, you can laugh all right. The trouble with you, Donny, is that you're one of them cynical sceptics that's always prepared to knock a bit of culture ...' Swamp was in full flow.

Mrs McIntyre, that stout, kindly lady, opened the door in answer to their ring. Donny did the introductions. He wanted to say, 'Ol' Swampy here wants to check out Orla.' But of course he didn't. Instead he said, 'This is my mate, Paul.'

'Come in, Paul. You're very welcome,' she said warmly. Swamp pushed the glasses up along his nose and stepped up into the hallway. Donny led the way into the small sitting room. The two girls were sprawled on the floor. Between them, flat on his tummy, lay Stephen, his face flushed with excitement. When he saw Donny, he shrieked with happiness.

'Hi,' said Donny.

'Hi,' replied Orla. Donny noticed the surprise in her face when she saw Swamp behind him.

'This is Paul,' Donny went on. Orla stood up, her cheeks already reddening. 'Hi,' she said.

'An' this is Fiona.'

Fiona, on her knees now, glanced briefly in Swamp's direction, then looked back at Stephen.

'How was he today?' Donny asked.

'Great!' exclaimed Orla. 'Fiona has him dancin'. C'mon, Fee, show us.'

Fiona hauled Stephen upright by the hands, then lifted him around the waist till his tiny toes just touched the floor. Then she began to lilt a tune, bobbing him up and down in time to the rhythm. Donny watched her face. It was calm and serious. Stephen chortled with pleasure.

It was nearly half an hour before the boys left the house. During that time, Swamp, enthroned on the settee, had delivered a lecture on spiders. (He had recently been reading the *Guinness Book of Animal Marvels*, he told them.) The two girls watched him with a kind of fascinated horror as he expounded on the habits of the American Black Widow, who always kills her mate after mating, and whose bite can kill a human being.

'One spider actually caused an earthquake,' he went on dramatically.

'How?' demanded the two girls, both of whom were sitting on the floor, near the great guru's feet.

'Got into a seismometer, an' registered 9.1 on the Richter scale — the worst earthquake in human history!' Swamp chuckled at the idea.

'Ugh! I hate spiders,' was Orla's response.

Out on the street, Donny had gone only twenty yards down the road, when Swamp halted.

'Here, Don. How about askin' the two girls to meet us later at the shoppin' centre? We can have a few cokes or coffee an' a bit of a chin-wag.'

Donny's first impulse was to slag his friend. What was more, he had lots of homework. But at the same time he felt a certain responsibility to Swamp to help him out in his first romantic venture. As well as that, he was curious.

'Yeh. OK. Good idea,' he said.

'I'll just nip back an' ask them so,' said his plump friend.

Several minutes later, when Swamp emerged from the house there was an exaggerated swagger in his gait.

'All systems go!' he called from a distance. 'Eight o'clock.'

By this time, Stephen was expressing his impatience with the hold-up by banging his head against the padded back of his seat.

'OK. OK. You little twerp!' said Donny affectionately. 'We're going.'

'Nice girl, that Orla,' Swamp mused, as they turned into the village. 'School uniform does nothin' for her, though.'

Donny arrived at the shopping centre a little early. He knew Swamp would like that. The two girls were already there, sipping Coke in the open-plan restaurant. They were now in casual sweaters and jeans, and Donny found himself agreeing with what Swamp had said about the school uniform.

Swamp arrived a little later in his Reebok tee-shirt and hooded sweater. 'Sorry I'm late,' he said. 'The oul' wan went a bit mad when I said I was goin' out, so I had to humour her. Now, what's everyone havin'?'

'Wow!' thought Donny to himself. 'The last of the big spenders!'

The drinks and crisps were ordered and the four young people sat around the table. The talk ranged from parents to homework to pocket money and discos and rock concerts and then back to parents again.

'I think,' announced Swamp, 'that parents should have to go back to school like the rest of us. Only they'd have to learn how to treat kids properly, an' psychology an' all that stuff.'

'That's right,' agreed Orla. 'Instead of always goin' on about when *they* were kids. My mum never stops!'

'Ah, don't mind her,' Swamp advised. 'I think some of them were never kids. Sure there was no such thing as a teenager back in them days. They switched from being kids to being grown-ups all in one go. An' another thing ...'

As Swamp became more eloquent on the subject of parents, Donny couldn't help thinking that it was easy to go on like that when you *had* parents to complain about. He glanced at Fiona's face. She seemed serious, almost sad, and she was twisting her glass round and round on the table surface. His reverie was interrupted by a question from Swamp. 'What do you think, Don?'

There must have been something in Donny's face that gave him an answer, because suddenly Swamp exclaimed, 'Aw, Jeez, Donny. I'm sorry. I wasn't thinkin'...'

Donny waved away his apology. 'It's OK, Swampy. No sweat.'

He looked up to find Fiona watching him through deep brown eyes and he grabbed at the first subject that came to his mind. 'I suppose you'll all be at the game next week?'

The girls' puzzled looks betrayed their ignorance. Swamp was indignant. 'You mean to say that neither of you knows what game is on next Wednesday? Where have you been *livin'* for the past few weeks? Do you realise that this is a *historic occasion* ....!'

And Swamp was in full flow again.

At nine o'clock, when the centre closed, the four friends drifted out into the forecourt. There was daylight only in the low western sky and the street lights were flickering on. They were more relaxed with one another now.

'Oh, my God!' Orla suddenly announced, looking at her watch. 'I have to go. I told Mam I'd be home before half past.'

'I'll go that far with you,' Swamp offered.

'I have to go, too,' Fiona said. 'See you.' She started to back away.

Donny found Swamp and Orla looking at him meaningfully. 'Hang on,' he said. 'I'll go with you. Where do you live?'

She seemed flustered. 'It's OK. I'll be all right ...'

'No,' he insisted. 'I'll go.'

'It's not far,' Orla cut in. 'Blake Road.' Donny didn't really feel he was being pressured into something. The truth was that he wouldn't have been happy with Fiona's going home on her own.

Now that he was alone with the girl, Donny searched for something normal to say. He realised that, although he had spent over an hour in her company, he didn't really know anything about her.

'How do you like it around here?' he started, conscious of the smooth rhythm of her stride beside him and of her tallness.

'It's OK.'

He tried again. 'Better than where you were before?'

'Yeh, a bit. It was a kip.' They turned the corner by the old Methodist church. Donny reckoned he wasn't going to get much mileage out of this subject so he searched for another.

'Swamp is nice,' remarked Fiona, suddenly.

'Yeh. He's a panic at times,' he replied, relieved.

'Is he goin' with anyone?'

'With a girl, you mean?' She looked at him, startled. Then the implications of what he had just said struck him. His laugh drew a smile from her. 'No, I didn't mean anything like that. It's just that ol' Swampy ...' He didn't want to say that Swamp never had any interest in girls, so he said something which struck him as being equally true. 'Well, he's always stuck in a book. Eats 'em, actually. So, he kinda neglects his social life.' She didn't reply, and suddenly Donny found himself thinking of Jacky. It was kind of ironic, he thought. Here he was getting Swamp fixed up with a girlfriend while, for all he knew, his own relationship with Jacky could be on the rocks. He found himself comparing Fiona and Jacky. Apart from the difference in accents —Fiona's was true north city — and in the colour of hair and eyes, there was a striking difference in personality. Jacky was confident and bubbly, full of energy and fire; Fiona was quiet, almost moody and he sensed a certain unhappiness deep within, as if something painful had happened that she wanted to forget.

He tried to steal a glance at her face in the dim street light, but her eyes caught his momentarily and she looked away quickly.

'Have you got a girlfriend?'

The question took him by surprise. 'Well, yeh. Sort of.'

She frowned. 'Sort of?'

'Well, it depends on what you mean by girlfriend. You know the way kids go on. They get one of their mates to ask a girl will she go with them, but even if she says yes, they don't see much of each other. So a fellow might have a girl but she's not really his friend, if you know what I mean.'

She laughed now, a clear musical peal in the gloom. 'Yeh, I think I do, now.' A pause. 'So what about your ... friend?'

He thought for a moment. 'I suppose I haven't seen much of her lately. But she is — at least, she *was* — a friend, a real friend. She doesn't live around here though.' And suddenly he didn't want to talk about Jacky any more. Not until he was sure. And then he resolved that he would have to get in touch with her and talk to her.

'This is my road, now,' Fiona said. 'I'll be OK here. Thanks.' She didn't seem to want him to go any farther.

'No, I'll go the rest of the way. I can turn right at the end.'

The house, when they came to it, was in darkness. Even the dim light from the lamps couldn't conceal the unkempt garden and the paint peeling from the door.

'Thanks for the Coke an' stuff,' she said.

'No sweat,' he replied. 'See you.' He watched as she hurried along the side of the house, until the shadows at the back swallowed her up. After a few moments, a light showed in a side window. He stood there absorbed in thought for several minutes. What a strange girl. And what a strange deserted house she lived in. He was thoughtful as he walked home.

That evening, after Stephen had been put up for the night and Maeve had settled in front of the TV, Donny slipped out of the house and around the corner to the telephone kiosk. He felt a little nervous as he put in the coins and dialled. The moment before the phone was answered was always the worst. Finally, there was a click at the far end and he cringed as he heard the aristocratic tones of Jacky's mum.

'Hi, Mrs Anderson,' he said, trying to sound relaxed. 'Can I speak to Jacky, please?'

There was a slight pause. Then, 'Who is speaking, please?'

The voice was polite and slightly distant.

'It's Donny,' he said.

'Oh, Donny. I didn't recognise your voice.'

'Like hell!' thought Donny. 'Is she there?' he said aloud.

There was another pause. 'No, I'm afraid she's out, Donny.' He hated the way she said his name. So condescending. 'Can I take a message?'

'Nah. It's OK. What time will she be back?'

'I think it will be late, Donny.' The woman's voice seemed strangely hushed, he thought.

'It's OK. I'll call tomorrow, maybe,' he said hurriedly.

'Very well,' she said.

Donny put the phone down, then stared at it for a long moment. 'Shit!' he said softly. There was nothing to do but go on home.

Donny rang Jacky again on Friday night. He went down to the pub a little before eight o'clock so that he could call before starting work. There was another tight knot in his stomach as he dialled the number. Please, he thought, let Jacky answer it. To his dismay, however, he heard the mother's voice again. 'No,' she said, in reply to his query. 'I'm afraid she's gone out again.'

Doggedly Donny asked what time she would be home. There was no reply, just some muffled sounds at the far end, like a distant argument. Then the mother's voice again. 'It's going to be late again, I'm afraid, Donny.' Donny waited for the woman to say more, but she didn't.

'OK. Thanks, anyway,' he said abruptly, and put the phone down again. This time he was in no doubt. Jacky's mother didn't want him calling and as long as she kept answering the phone, it was never going to be any different. Whether she was in the house or not, Jacky was always going to be 'out'.

'The bitch!' he said.

It was on Sunday afternoon, while he was pushing Stephen in his buggy through the park, that Donny decided what he was going to do. All weekend the problem had been nagging at him, swinging him now one way, now the other. Several times he decided to forget about Jacky and her stuck-up mother and her rugby club full of prigs. But each time the memories kept flooding back to him. He had known her for over two years now. He recalled her big eyes under the woollen cap in the dim light of the cabin cruiser, on the night he had first met her. That was on the Shannon in Athlone. During that first year they met often, going to the pictures or the occasional disco. And then there was that hectic and magic time in London last year. He remembered the gaiety of her laugh when she was happy and the fire in her eyes when she was annoyed and he resolved that he owed it to Jacky to go and see her, in person, and talk to her face to face. There was no other way.

The football squad trained for a full hour and a half on Monday after school. It was gruelling stuff. Clint ran them until their legs and lungs screamed for rest. Then there was the ball work, the work on the off-side trap, the set piece plays, the penalties.

'Right,' he told them when the session was over. 'No work tomorrow. And to bed early tomorrow night.' They trooped wearily into the dressing room at the back of the small gym.

'Is he expectin' us to go out an' play a bleedin' game the day after tomorrow?' Miler demanded, stretching his long legs across the floor from the bench where he had collapsed. Their silence eloquently voiced their agreement. Yet, as Donny looked around the dressing room, he sensed a hidden satisfaction that the session had been hard. They might complain, but deep down they knew they needed the workout.

'Will you do me a favour, Sis?' Donny asked, as he and Maeve had their tea that evening. 'I need a note for tomorrow afternoon.'

She looked at him, eyebrows raised. 'Pray tell, what for?' she asked. He decided to tell her the truth. He needed to take the three classes off so that he would be able to get across the city to Jacky's school before she left it.

'Hmmmm,' replied Maeve thoughtfully, when he'd finished. 'You'll have to think about the future, Donny. Jacky's a lovely girl, but don't you think that it's all a bit too intense? You're very young, you know ...'

'Yeh. I know all that stuff, Sis. It's not as if we want to go off an' get married or live together. It's just that ... well, I like her — a lot. We've been through a lot together. I just don't want to let that go just because her mother isn't crazy about me. Not unless ...'

'Unless what, Donny?'

'Well, unless Jacky wants to finish it.' He hated saying it. 'That's why I want to see her, to talk to her.'

'OK,' Maeve said after a short pause. 'I'll give you the note. What do you want me to say? That you're going to see your girlfriend?' She laughed.

'Nah. Just say I've a dental appointment at half-two.'

Donny didn't go back to school after lunch on the following day. He waited till two-thirty and then went round to the Number 18 bus stop. He had presented Maeve's note to Bill Moloney, his form tutor, earlier in the morning. All Bill had said was, 'Hope you're not in pain, Donny,' and handed it back to him.

He had been waiting at the bus stop for about seven minutes, when a dark approaching figure caught his eye. It was Brother Sharkey — Jaws. He walked with a jerky stiff motion, and even at a distance of over fifty metres, Donny knew that Jaws had already spotted him. He was glad he'd got the note from Maeve.

'Hi, Brother,' said Donny, trying to sound friendly.

Jaws didn't return the greeting. 'Why aren't you in school?' he snapped instead.

'I gave a note to Mr Moloney,' Donny replied evenly. The black eyes bored into him. Donny was aware of another person arriving behind him to stand at the bus stop.

'Why aren't you in school?' The voice was harsher now; the face expressionless.

'I'm going to the dentist,' Donny lied.

'Where's the dentist?'

Donny thought quickly. 'In Ranelagh,' he said.

'What time is your appointment?'

A sudden surge of resentment rose in Donny. What right had this man to interrogate him in the public street? He was tempted to say, 'Half-two', just to get the Brother off his back, but something in him rebelled against giving in like this. 'I gave the note to Mr Moloney,' he repeated calmly. 'He has all the information.' In the distance behind him he heard the rumble of the bus. He saw the flush begin high on the Brother's cheeks.

'So you're refusing to give me this information?'

Donny stood his ground. 'No, Brother. I'm telling you where it can be found.' The tyres of the bus rasped on the tarmac beside him and the hot diesel fumes swirled around him. Donny turned abruptly and stepped up into the vehicle. He paid his fare and headed for the stairs, aware of the dark figure that still stood motionless at the bus stop. He didn't look back, however, until the bus was well away. Jaws was standing staring after the vehicle. He was still there when the bus turned the corner. With a certain sense of foreboding Donny watched the suburban streets slip by. He should have told the Brother the time of his appointment, he decided. It might have satisfied him. Now, the chances were that he would go to Bill Moloney in a thick humour and make a big deal about Donny's refusal to give him the information. And then he would surely find out that Maeve had written that the appointment was at two-thirty. Donny looked at his watch. It was five to three now. 'Damn!' he said aloud.

It was twenty to four when Donny reached the imposing gates of Mount St. Oliver's. He walked in a short distance along the tarmac avenue and stood looking for a few moments at the impressive two-storied building which stood over fifty metres away, half-hidden by a line of conifers. Already several parents were sitting in their cars in the wide space in front of the building. Donny didn't want to be too conspicuous, so he turned and came out again. He would wait in the shadow of the high wall directly across from the entrance, he decided. From there he would be able to spot Jacky as she came out, without having the whole school gawking at him.

At five to four a stream of cars was entering the gates, driven mostly by women. Donny had been watching them idly for several minutes when he saw a red Toyota approaching. With a shock he realised that it was Jacky's mother's car. He put his hand up to scratch his head and shield his face from the driver.

As the car swept in through the gates, he glimpsed the aristocratic profile and he was certain that the driver was Mrs Anderson.

'Ya bleedin' thick!' Donny exclaimed, furious at himself for not thinking of such an obvious thing. He went over to the gateway, watching the Toyota winding its way through the low shrubbery along the driveway. Now what was he to do? His first thought was that he couldn't let Jacky's mother see him. He'd look a right nerd if he was standing there when she came out and she drove right past him. 'No, thanks!' he said to himself. He stepped to one side of the gateway to allow another car to drive in and it was then that he saw the 'Entrance Only' sign. In the distance, in front of the school, girls were getting into cars and cars were driving away past the front of the school until they were out of sight behind a low red-brick building. Donny started to run, scanning the remaining cars for the red Toyota. When he saw it pull out from a line of parked cars, he broke into a sprint. Another car coming in behind him jammed on the brakes as he raced across the driveway. He leaped across a thorny shrub onto the lawn beyond, hoping to take a short cut. But his runners slipped on the damp grass and he fell sprawling. He scrambled to his feet but his first glance told him that he wasn't going to make it. The Toyota was even now beside the low red-brick building. As he watched, it swung out of sight and was gone. He stumbled to a halt, dusting himself down, slapping at the mud and grass stains on the knees of his jeans. In frustration he swung his right leg at a tall yellow weed that lay across his path.

'Damn it!' he said aloud. Just to his left, there was a movement behind a shrub with dark green leaves. A nun's bonnet had suddenly risen and a stern nun's face was glaring at him indignantly. He held up his hands apologetically. 'I'm sorry, Sister. You weren't meant to hear that.' Then he turned on his heel and headed back towards the entrance. When he looked back, just before reaching the gates, the little nun was still glaring after him.

It was nearly a quarter to six when Donny arrived back to Walkinstown. After he got off the bus he tried to phone Jacky's home three times, but each time he got an engaged tone. Finally, he banged down the phone and thumped the kiosk door open in annoyance. 'Poxy phone!' he said aloud. A slight woman waiting outside looked at him, startled.

'Is it not workin', young f'lla?' she asked.

'It's bleedin' engaged!' he replied rudely, turning towards McIntyre's house. His watch told him he was already twenty minutes late for collecting Stephen. 'Shit!' he exclaimed.

When Orla ushered him into the sitting room, he found Fiona walking round the room, jogging the baby on her shoulder. As soon as his eyes lit on Donny, the little fellow broke into a wail of annoyance and relief. Reluctantly, Fiona handed him over.

'Here's your late uncle now,' she told the baby.

'Sorry,' Donny mumbled. 'I got held up.'

'Detention?' Orla smirked, picking up the scattered toys.

Donny wasn't in the mood for jokes. 'Naw. A sort of a wild goose chase,' he answered cryptically. 'Anyway, I hope I didn't keep you from anythin'.' He had been surprised to find Fiona in the house and now her hovering by his shoulder making baby talk at Stephen irritated him. He resisted a mean urge to ask her had she moved in. Instead, he focused on the baby who was trying hard to sob on his shoulder. 'What have these two women been doing to you at all?' he asked, a slight edge to his voice.

Orla exploded with indignation. 'Oh, will you listen to your man! And he half an hour *late*!' She stuffed random toys into Stephen's bag.

'We gave him his tea,' Fiona said quietly.

Donny took a deep breath. He was tired and hungry, and he just wanted to get home to his own place. 'That's cool,' he said, hoping it didn't sound ungrateful. 'Thanks.'

Fiona's eyes seemed huge when she looked at him. 'You're welcome,' she replied. He wondered was she being sarcastic.

Donny thought of saying something about Swamp as he left the house, but he didn't. It was up to them to ask, if they wanted. A short distance up the street, Fiona's voice called after him. 'Tell Paul that Orla sends her lo ...!' The last word seemed to have been cut off. Donny glanced behind to see Orla trying to clamp her hand over Fiona's mouth, amid shrieks of laughter.

'I will,' he called. Shrill laughter followed him up the street.

7

It was on his way to the first class on the following morning that Donny was waylaid by his form tutor, Bill Moloney.

'Donny, a quick word,' he said. Donny stepped to one side out of the stream of bodies on the corridor and waited for the genial teacher to go on. 'I've had a complaint about you. I think you know from whom.'

Donny nodded wearily. 'Brother Sharkey, I suppose.'

'He says you cheeked him yesterday evening when he was asking why you weren't in school.' The teacher paused, as if expecting a satisfactory reply.

'I'm sorry, sir. He was hassling me. I told him that I'd given you a note and that you knew the reason why I was absent. I thought that would be OK.'

'Well, I'm afraid it's not.' The teacher's tone was not harsh, and Donny knew why. Bill Moloney was well aware that Br. Sharkey didn't like Donny O'Sullivan. He had had to deal with disagreements between the two of them before. 'He's calling it insubordination, and he wants me to slap a detention on you.' His tone was almost apologetic.

Donny looked steadily into the grey eyes of his English teacher. The look said, 'Well, are you going to do it?'

Bill said, 'I'm not going to do it — just yet. But if this problem keeps cropping up, I may have to.' It was a gentle warning. 'Look, Donny. I know you two don't see eye to eye, but just try not to give him ammunition. OK? It puts me in an awkward position.'

Donny knew that the teacher was on his side. He looked at his shoes. 'OK,' he said then.

The semi-final was to be played in Tolka Park, on the north side of the city. Today, three bus-loads of supporters, all from the senior school, were going to the game, so there was a buzz in the building at the eleven o'clock break. The team and subs gathered into Clint's room for the last-minute check. Donny noticed that the slagging was strangely muted. The group was quiet and serious. When Clint finished talking, Curtis got up and cleared his throat.

'Right, lads,' he began. They could see that he wasn't comfortable in front of them. 'We got this far. No team from this school was ever here before. So ... we're all goin' to give it our best shot ... an' then some more. We'll never have this chance again.' He looked at Clint then and the teacher's face told them that he was impressed. Curtis had never been the best when it came to making speeches.

'OK,' said Clint. 'Lunch at half-twelve. Bus at one. See you then.' There was hardly a word spoken as they filed out.

At one o' clock, after a light lunch, Clint got them onto the coach and told the driver to head for Dollymount Strand.

'We're just going for a walk ... together ... away from everything,' he told them from the front of the bus. 'I know you guys are ready for this game, so just keep it ticking over. Talk about what you're going to do. Keep the concentration.'

They walked for perhaps half a mile on the wide deserted strand, just the group and Clint. They talked quietly, or just listened, enjoying the freshness of the breeze that swung in off the sea.

At ten past two, the coach dropped them outside the high walls of Tolka Park. They filed in through the narrow doorway set in the high, wooden gate and Clint led them towards the dressin-grooms.

'Put the gear in, and we'll have a look at the pitch,' he told them.

Donny walked with Flagon out to the centre circle. The stands and the terraces were empty, the only movement coming from three lonely seagulls that strutted around importantly at one end. Beyond the high walls, Donny could see the drab, red-brick chimneys of the city houses.

'Not great, is it?' remarked his friend. The surface was level, but right through the middle, from goalmouth to goalmouth, lay a wide brown swathe where the grass had lost the battle with the multitude of studded boots that had ravaged it in recent weeks.

'At least it's dry,' replied Donny. 'But we'll want to watch the bounce. It'll hop like hell on this.'

A movement near the centre of the stand caught his eye. A stream of students, many with green-and-white scarves, was entering through the opening that came up from the main turnstiles. The St. Brendan's supporters had arrived. When the first chant began, Clint motioned to the team. 'C'mon,' he said. 'Let's go and get togged.' They trooped in under the stand to the strains of 'Ye're all a load of rubbish' from the growing St. Brendan's crowd.

'Where the hell are our gang?' Miler wanted to know.

'They'll be here,' retorted Murphy.

'Right,' Clint said, as they entered the low-ceilinged dressing room. 'Let's keep the concentration.' He went among them, handing out the numbered strips, checking their socks, the tie-ups, the studs. Clint's quiet words were the only sounds in the room, apart from the clatter of studs on the concrete floor, and the rustle of the gear.

Donny, intent on tying his laces, was aware of the atmosphere. He had never experienced anything like it before. He felt a bond with the lads, and he knew that, like him, they all felt the excitement, the sense of occasion, and above all, the determination.

'Right,' said Clint, after the referee had inspected the boots and gone. 'We got to play for ninety minutes. These guys will be good. Make no mistake about that. If we go behind, we won't panic. We've been there before. Just keep playing football, and help one another. Remember, we encourage one another. There will be mistakes, sure. But no narking. This is a team, and if we play as a team, we'll get the result. OK, go on, and good luck.' He pulled open the door and they streamed out.

Donny heard the din before he saw the pitch. It sounded as if an army of drummers were hammering away at a battery of metal drums. When he cleared the narrow tunnel and crossed the last concrete slab before the turf, he recognised the sound. The St. Colman's supporters had arrived and the lively ones had established themselves on the topmost seats of the stand; they were at that moment busily banging the galvanised steel wall behind them with their hands. The noise rose to a crescendo when the team appeared.

Donny didn't look up at the supporters. Instead, he raced out onto the turf, sprinting to the centre circle and then away towards the empty goalmouth to his left. St. Brendan's, in their green-and-white strip, were already taking potshots at their keeper in the other goal.

St. Colman's won the toss, and Curtis elected to play into the wind, a dry breeze from the east. The din from the stand became deafening as the St. Brendan's number eight kicked off. The game was on.

Donny didn't enjoy the first fifteen minutes. His memory of them later was of a frantic merry-go-round, in which he and Flagon and Flanagan, the other two mid-fielders, chased like terriers after the ball, but never seemed to get hold of it for more than a split second. He remembered, too, Clint's shouts from the dugout, and the exasperation that slowly crept into his tone as the St. Brendan's mid-fielders played rings round his own.

It was when he went to the touchline beside the crowded stand to take a throw, near the end of the first quarter, that Donny first heard the remark, 'Come on, the scrubbers.' Normally, he paid little attention to remarks from spectators, but there was something so clear and deliberate about this one, that he had a quick look. The boundary railing was crowded with supporters, most of them sporting the green and white of St. Brendans. But after a quick glance along it, Donny found himself staring into a pair of brazen eyes. He recognised the sneering features immediately.

It was Rocky Stewart.

Donny started to turn away. As he did, however, he heard another voice. 'Come on, Donny!' it said. He knew immediately that it was Jacky's. He turned to search for her. Behind him, Flagon, in a clear space along the touchline, was screaming for the ball. 'C'mon, Don! Do it!' He heard Jacky call again, and this time he saw her. She was about ten metres to his right, leaning out over the concrete fence. She waved and he grinned at her. Then he had to take the throw and get back into the game.

Donny had to work hard to get his concentration back. Those few seconds had raised conflicting emotions: anger at Rocky's insult, pleasure at seeing Jacky.

At half time, the game was scoreless. During the last ten minutes of the first half, O'Reilly, the St. Colman's keeper, had pulled off two top-drawer saves to keep his team in the hunt. At the other end, Donoghue and Flanagan each sent a shot harmlessly wide. The pressure was on.

As Donny headed for the dressing room, bracing himself for the tirade Clint would deliver, his eyes searched again for Jacky. She was leaning out over the fence. On her right stood Rocky Stewart; on her left was the unmistakable blond head of Bruce. Caught between two minds, Donny kept going, suddenly glad that he didn't have to pass close to her. He heard Jacky's call again, but he didn't look up. He passed through the gap in the railing and the encouraging St. Colman's mob gathered there.

'Donny! Donny!' Girls' voices called from above. Orla and Fiona were leaning over the parapet at the tunnel entrance. Swamp, with his scarf and flushed face, was beside them. 'C'mon, Donny. You can do it!' he called.

Clint made them all sit down. Then he sat down too. In his hand he held a small notepad. When they were all quiet, he started. He was amazing. He had a detailed brief for every player. What they were doing wrong. What they had to do. The tactical changes. They would go back to the four-four-two formation for the first fifteen minutes and then listen for instructions from the dugout. 'Get your God-damn heads up. They're going down!' he almost shouted. 'We have guys losing the ball and standing there, watching it go. We have guys winning it, but getting rushed into making stupid passes. When,' he demanded, 'when did we ever practise wellying the ball from the full-back line up and over the heads of the midfielders?' There was silence. They all knew the answer. Never. 'Every time we get the ball, what are we doing with it? I'll tell you what. Giving it straight back! What kind of bloody football is this? Only for Eamon in the goals we could be packing up the gear and going home now.' They were all silent.

'Right,' he said more calmly. 'So their midfield is good. They can play a bit. But remember this: they can't play if they haven't got the ball! And they won't score if they haven't got the ball. So for the first ten minutes, what are we going to do with the ball?' Another silence. 'Get it, and *keep it*! I don't care if you keep passing it around in your own half for the whole God-damn ten minutes. But you have to get it, and keep it.' He looked at Curtis, a long, hard look. 'Now, talk about it,' he told them. Then he got up, opened the door, and went out.

Curtis looked around at them. His eyes were bright. 'Come on, lads!' he commanded them. And then they began to talk.

Donny tried hard to fire himself up along with the others. But he felt an emptiness in his stomach that he couldn't swallow down. His mind kept coming back to the same question, no matter how hard he tried to force it away. How could Jacky have come to this game with those two blokes? Especially after what had happened at the club the night of the party? He couldn't believe it. OK, St. Edmund's were playing the other semi-final on the following day. If they won, they would be playing either St. Brendan's or St. Colman's in the final. That was why Bruce and that other jerk were here. Spying! But why did Jacky have to be with them? Maybe she *wanted* to be with them. Maybe she didn't care. Maybe ... But no answer would come, and the sick feeling grew.

'C'mon, Don!' he heard Flagon urging, and his friend thumped him on the back. 'Let's show them a bit of the old skill.' All around him the others were standing, restless on their feet, eager for the door to open again.

'Right, Flag.' Donny knew he wasn't playing well. He knew

he had to rouse himself, but he was dreading going back out and having to see Rocky Stewart there beside her. He could imagine the expression on Rocky's face ...

Suddenly the door was open again and Curtis was shouting at them. 'Right, let's go! C'mon, Flanno. C'mon, Murph! C'mon, Don!'

They streamed out, hard studs clacking on the concrete. Clint, standing just outside, caught Donny by the arm as he passed. 'Don,' he said, 'you have to keep tight on that number six. He's the one that's making the play. OK?' Donny nodded and began to pull away. 'We need you, Don!' was Clint's last call.

Donny understood the message. It was Clint's way of telling him that he wasn't playing up to scratch, that he wanted a better effort, or the likelihood would be that Donny would find himself sitting on the subs' bench.

The din from the St. Colman's supporters, as the team reappeared, was deafening. Donny was glad. At least he wouldn't have to respond to any remarks from the sideline. He thought he heard a girl's voice calling from above, but he couldn't pause to look, because the players behind him were pushing him onwards. Probably Orla and Fiona, he thought to himself. Back on the pitch, he did his warm-up exercises meticulously in the way Clint had taught them. When he was finished, he jogged around the centre circle, doing his best not to look towards where he had last seen Jacky at the boundary fence. But the spot became like a magnet to him, its power growing with every passing second. And eventually he had to look. He saw Jacky's face clearly, framed between Bruce's broad shoulder on one side, and Rocky Stewart's lower, more burly one on the other. She was staring at him, her hand half raised as if to attract his attention. Before she could make any sign, however, there was a surge of sound from the St. Brendan's supporters and Donny looked away. The opposition was just coming back onto the pitch.

Flagon touched off the ball to begin the second half. Donny turned it and stroked it back to Curtis. The captain pushed it all the way back to O'Reilly, in goal. The keeper saw the St. Brendan's number nine bearing down on him and he kicked it

wide to Miler on the right. Miler steadied it and sent it across to
Curtis again, who touched it on to Butler. Challenged, Butler did
two complete circles with the ball, shielding it from his marker,
before chipping it forward to Murphy, who had run into space
near the touchline. 'That's more like it!' roared Clint from the
dugout. Seeing that Murphy was in trouble, Donny shook off his
marker and sprinted towards the ball. Murphy stretched his long
left leg and tapped it into Donny's path. Donny hit it first time
with his right and it skidded on the hard surface back to Miler,
now wide on the right flank. 'Now we're sucking diesel!' came
Clint's satisfied call.

St. Brendan's got possession only twice in the first ten minutes. The first time was when Flagon's pass to Butler across the
centre circle was intercepted by a despairing lunge from the
number seven, and the ball sliced back towards their lanky
central defender. But Donoghue arrived just after the ball and
hounded the centre-half so much that he had to kick for touch on
the halfway line. The second time was more dangerous. Curtis
was shaping up to deal with another back pass, this time from
Butler, when he stumbled just at the wrong moment. The ball
bounced over his foot and the Brendan's centre-forward was
onto it like a flash. As he controlled the ball, however, O'Reilly
came racing out from the goalmouth, spread himself low across
the forward's path, and wrapped himself around the ball and the
other's feet as well. 'Great save, Eamon!' Clint called.

St. Colman's gradually edged forward into the opposition
half. Donny, growing more confident after his first few touches,
began to probe the defence, threading passes through the centre
or spraying them to the wings where Flanagan and Murphy, the
wide midfielders, were making forward runs to support
Kavanagh and Donoghue, the front two. He worked hard at
closing down Glennon, the St. Brendan's elusive number six, to
discourage his team-mates from passing the ball to him. But he
wasn't always successful, and his blocky opponent occasionally
made raids on the St. Colman's defence. Once, when the mid-
fielder turned him the wrong way, Donny saw Flagon appearing

suddenly on the other side to force Glennon into a defensive back pass.

'Nice one, Flag,' panted Donny.

Another time, when Glennon was racing forward, the ball at his feet, Donny launched himself, feet first, and stabbed the ball away. Glennon dived dramatically over Donny's outstretched foot, looking for the free kick, but the referee was having none of it. 'Play on!' came his strident command.

Soon afterwards, Donny got hold of the ball on the edge of the centre circle. He looked up, scanning the spaces, pushing it forward in readiness for the pass. The defence, anticipating the move, sagged back to cover the runners. Donny pushed the ball into the space that opened in front of him. He pushed it again. From just outside the area, he saw a gap to the keeper's left and wound up for a strike. Just as his right foot started the downward swing, however, something hard struck it. Next moment, Donny was sprawled on the turf, clutching his ankle, grimacing in agony. Shrilly the referee's whistle blasted and Donny heard the official's throaty command to the St. Brendan's player. 'Here. None of that. Just play the ball the next time, or you'll walk!' Next moment, Clint was hovering over Donny, pulling his sock down, pouring the cold water onto the ankle.

'How is it, Donny?' he asked.

'Sore as hell,' Donny groaned. 'Lemme up.' The limb was painful, but he could walk on it. 'It's OK,' he said then.

'If it's not, let me know,' Clint said as he hurried off.

St Colman's nearly scored from the free kick. Flagon's curling shot whizzed only inches wide of the top left-hand corner of the St. Brendan's net. The rising yell from the stand was suddenly quenched.

Soon afterwards, Donny had to take a throw from a point on the touchline near the stand. He collected the ball, which had rebounded off the fence onto the field, and found himself looking directly at the place where he had last seen Jacky. She wasn't there, but Bruce was, gazing in Donny's direction, a lazy smile on his lips, and Rocky Stewart was on his left. As Donny stared back, Rocky looked up at Bruce and said something into his ear.

They were both laughing as Donny came to the touchline. 'Come on, the scrubbers!' came Rocky's sneering comment, and suddenly Donny's anger exploded. With one swift movement he dropped the ball and, just as it hit the ground, he struck it a stabbing kick with his right foot. His aim was unerring. Rocky saw the ball coming and, in a desperate reflex action, lifted his arm. But the ball smacked off his chest below the arm and knocked him back a pace with the force of the impact. Donny bent coolly to pick up the ball, a smile of satisfaction on his face. But he had no sooner turned back towards the pitch, than he heard the whistle blast shrilly. The grey-haired referee came racing towards him, his hand ominously reaching into his back pocket.

When Donny saw the yellow card, his anger boiled up again. He dropped the ball. 'What's that for, ref?'

The referee waved Flagon brusquely away. 'Ungentlemanly conduct!' he snapped into Donny's face. 'Name, please.'

'An' what about the names that ... that fella was callin' me?'

'Name!' There was an edge to the ref's voice that was a warning. Flagon's face hovered anxiously behind the official.

'Donny O'Sullivan,' he said then. From his left came a sneering laugh.

'Right. Get on with the game,' barked the ref, backing away from him and thrusting the card up in the air in front of Donny.

Another derisive guffaw came from the railing, and Donny stiffened.

'C'mon, Don.' It was Flagon's voice. 'Never mind the poxy bastard!' And Flagon's arm round his shoulders turned him away from the touchline.

From that moment, something changed inside Donny. His resolution grew, till it became a hard thing inside him, and for the next few minutes he played like a demon. He raced around midfield, taking command of the ball when it came his way, or relentlessly harassing Glennon when he managed to get it. Once, he crunched head-on into the number six and the two of them rebounded onto the turf, while the ball spun away towards touch. Before long the fans in the stands had taken up the chant, 'Don-ny! Don-ny!' to the rhythm of a galvanised metal drum.

St. Colman's were firing on all cylinders.

The goal, when it came after thirty-five minutes, was a scrappy affair. Flagon got hold of the ball in midfield, played a neat one-two with Donny and sent a lazy pass wide to Kavanagh on the left. Kavanagh's effort at a first-time cross went all wrong. When he hit the ball with the inside of his foot, it glanced off the shadowing defender's shin and wobbled back towards the eighteen yard line. Donny came onto it with his right but his shot whacked against the centre-half's chest. The ball shot skywards behind the line of defence. Donoghue raced in, but the keeper was quicker. He flung himself on the ball as it bounced the second time. Donoghue slowed and began to turn away but, just as he did, the ball squirted out from under the keeper, right across his path. Donoghue swerved at the last second and caught it with the toe of his left boot. It dribbled goalwards. From the stands came a rising surge of sound. But the stocky St. Brendan's right half was racing towards it. Just before it reached the goal-line, his outstretched foot caught it and shot it upwards. It whacked off the underside of the bar, bounced straight down, caught the defender's arm as he slid into the net, dribbled in after him, and the St. Colman's supporters went mad. Goal!

The last twenty minutes were hectic. It was desperate, heroic stuff from both teams. The din from the stands was continuous and deafening as the ball flowed from end to end. There was the crunch of tackles and the thud of bodies whacking off the hard turf. There were desperate goalmouth scrambles and thumped daisy-toppers from way outside the area. St. Brendan's hit the woodwork once. At the other end, Murphy and Kavanagh pulled brilliant acrobatic saves from the St. Brendan's keeper. In the stands, the supporters alternated between wild hope and black despair. But when the final whistle blew, St. Colman's had won and were through to the final.

Donny just had time to shake hands with his opposite number before the rejoicing horde engulfed him. Swamp, his face flushed and sweaty, grabbed him and hugged him. 'Ya budgie ya, Don!' he roared hoarsely. It was all wild and boisterous: a mill of jubilant faces and slapping hands. All around him, Donny could see that the rest of the team were enjoying the same fate. 'Jays, lads! Go easy. Mind me ribs!' he laughed as he struggled towards the dressing-rooms and saw Orla and Fiona pushing towards him.

'Donny!' they called. He waited.

'Donny! Well done!' exclaimed Orla. 'You played great!'

Fiona stood smiling behind her, a St. Colman's scarf around her neck.

'What're you two doin' off school?' he demanded in mock seriousness.

'We're on the hop,' retorted Orla. 'Blame her. She wanted to come an' see youse playin'.'

Fiona smiled. But now the press behind was becoming more insistent, as the rest of the team zeroed in on the dressing-room.

'Listen, I'll see you later,' Donny said. 'I have to go an' tog in.'

'See ya!' they chorused.

But Donny didn't go down into the dressing-rooms. Something else was on his mind. He scanned the nearby railings and the stand behind but he could catch no glimpse of Jacky or Bruce or Rocky. He worked his way to open ground on one side, vaulted over the railings onto the concrete beyond and searched through the clusters still scattered on the stand, but to no avail. Maybe, he thought. Maybe she went down to the dressingrooms. Surely she was waiting there. He went down and into the gloomy passageway, now jammed with excited well-wishers wanting to see the team. But when he finally reached the door of the dressing-room, there was still no sign of Jacky. Frowning with disappointment, he pushed through the half-blocked doorway and into the room.

Inside, there was mayhem. Curtis was braying like a drunken donkey at anyone who came within a roar of him. Clint, red-faced and delighted, ushered in a beaming Brother O'Connor, whose soft Kerry tones were drowned in the welter of excitement and joy. The jubilant jam in the passageway outside became so bad that Clint had to plant himself in the doorway and roar hoarsely, 'I'm sorry! You'll have to wait. If you give them space, they'll be out in ten minutes!' and he shut the door in their faces. Then he put his back against it and cleared his throat. Curtis held up a commanding hand and stilled the tumult.

'Well done, lads,' said Clint. 'That was a bleedin' great performance. You've proved something out there today — not to me — but to yourselves. This team has character. It'll take a good team to beat it.' There was a raucous roar of approval from the squad and from the few lucky supporters trapped inside the room. 'There's a bit to eat upstairs in Mooney's later on. But remember one thing. There's training this Friday and next Tuesday after school. Just make sure you're there.'

They laughed and hooted. It was just like Clint to be thinking of the next game already.

Donny showered and dressed quickly. He felt a strong need to know for sure if Jacky was really gone. He picked up his kit-bag, and brushed past Clint, who was chatting with Curtis.

Outside, the crowd had thinned considerably, and Mr Hendron, the Maths teacher, was issuing dire warnings to the stragglers to shift their asses, or the buses would leave without them. Donny hurried out onto the lower benches of the stand and scanned the remaining clusters of spectators. But Jacky was not among them. He went down the steps and along a passageway to the main gates, but the pavement outside was almost deserted. 'Well, that's that,' he said softly to himself and headed back to rejoin the team. He didn't know what his next move should be. He would have to think about it.

8

Half an hour later, on the bus back to Mooney's, when he had grown tired of waving his school scarf out of the skylight of the bus, Flagon plopped down on the empty seat beside Donny.

'How's it goin', Don?'

'Great, Flag,' Donny replied, cheerfully.

Flagon was silent for a moment. When he spoke, his tone was quieter. 'I saw her there. With those two blokes,' he said. 'Are they the St. Edmund's crowd?'

'Yeh. The butty bloke was the one that dunted me in the club. He was shoutin' remarks all the way through the game.'

'Well, he'll be quiet enough next week after the final. I wonder if he's playin'.'

Donny smiled in anticipation. 'Yeh. That'd be good all right. That's one bloke I wouldn't mind playin' against.'

Flagon went on. 'I didn't see her after the game.'

Donny tried to be casual. 'Nah. She must've had to go.' He looked through the window at the drab streets outside. ''S funny. I was hopin' all week that she'd be there, an' now ...' He tailed off.

Flagon decided to take the bull by the horns. 'Did she not say an'thin' durin' the game? Or at half time?'

'Nah. Maybe I shoulda gone over to her at half-time, but with those two ponces there with her ... I just didn't.'

Flagon turned to look at him now. 'Don, I think you should

go to her house an' knock at the bleedin' door an' just say your piece.'

Donny thought about that. 'I dunno, Flag. I wouldn't be able to say what I want to say with her parents there, even if they didn't slam the door in my face. 'Cos the way I feel right now, there could be a bit of language flyin' around.'

'Well then, take a few classes off *before* lunch one of the days, an' see her at the lunch break, up at her school. She doesn't go home for lunch.'

'I dunno, Flag. I'm beginnin' to wonder if the whole thing is worth all this messin' around.'

Flagon gave him this studied look now. 'That's funny, comin' from you, Don. 'Cos last year, in London, anyone could see that you two were made for each other.' The bus was coming to a halt outside Mooney's. Flagon stood up and took his kit-bag from the shelf overhead. 'C'mon, anyway, Don. We have a bit of celebratin' to do first.'

The meal in Mooney's was great crack. Everyone, including Donny, was in high spirits. They had arrived with a growing sense of their own importance and after the meal, when Clint rose to speak, he didn't let them forget it.

'This is the first team from this school ever to get to a semi-final of the Leinster Senior Cup, not to mention the final.' He looked around at them with fatherly pride. 'You guys have made history again today. This is a big day for our school, and for me personally. I want to thank you guys for the effort there today, for the teamwork, for the support and encouragement you gave one another. And I'll tell you another thing. It'll stand to you in the final.'

When Clint sat down to cheers and whistles and uninhibited applause, Flanagan roared for Curtis to get up and make a speech. The others took up the call. 'C'mon, Curto!'

'Get stuffed!' replied Curtis. His motto had always been that actions speak louder than words, and he felt distinctly uncomfortable standing in front of a group of people who expected him to talk to them. They knew that, and that was why the clamour became even louder. 'Curto! Curto! Curto!' Finally he conceded.

He stood up to more whistles and catcalls. Pushing back a lock of sandy hair from his forehead, the captain waited for the shouting to stop, a flush already glowing in his cheeks. He cleared his throat and they were silent.

'Yiz all played OK. Now will yiz all go home to bleedin' bed,' he growled, and sat down again.

'Great speech, Curto!' bawled O'Reilly, and the slagging began again.

When the meal was over, the supporters, who had been gathering in the foyer outside, were allowed in, their faces still alight with the flush of victory. It wasn't long before Donny heard the familiar, 'Yo, men!' and turned to see Swamp heading for them through the crowded tables. He had Orla and Fiona in tow.

'Here comes Robert Redford with the two women,' remarked Donny to Flagon. 'Wouldn't you think that one would be enough for him?'

'Yeah,' replied Flagon, giving Donny a funny look.

'Good bit of grub, lads?' enquired Swamp, as he pulled in chairs for the girls.

'Not bad,' said Flagon. 'Not enough chips. But the trifle was OK.'

'Is there a meal after every match?' enquired Orla.

'Yeh,' replied Swamp. 'There's always grub when they win a semi-final. But our school never got beyond the first round before. The lads were a bit hungrier this year, though.'

'Yeh, but wait till we win the final,' joked Donny. 'We'll be sick for a week.'

'You'll be sick for longer if you don't win it,' remarked Swamp. 'Here, is anyone buyin'?' He looked around expectantly.

'Yeh,' said Flagon. 'Clint is. Just go an' order a round, an' tell the barman to put it on the coach's tab.'

Swamp gave him a scathing look. 'Yeh. Pull the other one. It's got bells on it.'

Fiona suddenly spoke. 'Why don't we go somewhere an' have a proper drink?' They all looked at her.

'Yeh. I'd love a gin an' tonic,' said Orla.

'Hey! That's not a bad idea,' said Flagon. He was serious.

'Wouldn't be served,' Swamp decided.

'We could go up to Carey's, couldn't we, Don?' said Flagon. 'The lads'd serve us there. You know them all.'

Donny was lukewarm. He didn't want to blot his copybook in his place of work. On the other hand, he didn't want to put a damper on the spirits of the group. 'Yeh, but what about dosh?'

They all began to search their pockets.

'I've got one sixty-three,' announced Orla, excitedly.

'Plus two quid, an' sixpence,' added Flagon.

'Right, an' here's another quid,' said Swamp.

'I have a tenner,' said Fiona quietly. Everyone looked at her.

'You're OK, then,' said Flagon.

'No,' she said, her dark eyes fixed on Donny. 'There's enough to buy a drink for us all.'

The others began to protest, but Fiona forestalled them. 'No, I want to.' The protests fizzled out.

'Right,' said Flagon. 'What're we waitin' for?'

Carey's pub was almost deserted when the group trooped quietly in and settled themselves in a dimly-lit alcove farthest from the bar. 'Go on, Don. You order,' urged Flagon. Donny collected the various amounts — they had all agreed to buy their own first — and went to the bar. Tommy, the barman, was friendly.

'Ah, how's it goin', Don?'

'Great, Tommy. Can I get a few drinks?'

Tommy looked up along the bar. 'Yeh. Sure, Don. Fire away.'

Several minutes later, Donny returned to the alcove with a laden tray. 'Ya boy, ya!' exclaimed Flagon.

'Gin an' tonic for Fiona an' Orla. Lager for Flag. Kaliber for Swamp, an' a pint for meself.' He put the tray to one side and sat down. There was satisfaction all round.

'Yeah. This is the life!' said Flagon, taking a long swig from the frothy pint.

'Yeh. Good luck in the final,' said Orla, raising her glass.

Donny was feeling good now and, as the beer began to have

its effect, his spirits improved even more. Gallantly, he went to order another gin and tonic for Fiona, when her glass was empty long before the others. 'Go easy on that,' he joked, as he put the drink in front of her.

'Ah, there's plenty more where that came from,' she replied, her voice a little huskier than usual. 'Sure, you can only live once.'

'That's the name of a film, isn't it?' croaked Flagon, wiping a white moustache off his upper lip.

The talk came round to pubs that were known to serve young people and to those that wouldn't. Swamp began to lecture on the advantages of I.D. cards, and was in full flow when Orla told him to put his sock in it.

'Who wants I.D. cards?' she wailed. 'Sure we wouldn't be able to get a drink at all then!'

'Yeh,' retorted Swamp. 'You'd be just as well off. Sure, even the smell of the stuff is enough to get you on your ear!'

'He thinks he's God Almighty, you know,' declared Orla, appealing to the rest of the group. 'Him an' his Kaliber! I don't know how I stick him!' But she was smiling when she said it.

Time moved on, and the pub gradually filled with patrons. Donny began to think about Maeve. He couldn't get in touch with her, and he didn't want her to be worried when he hadn't come home. He was about to excuse himself, when Fiona declared that she wanted to buy everyone a drink. Donny hesitated. Before he could say anything, however, Flagon broke in. 'Yeh, one for the road! Great idea!' he said.

'Don't get one for me,' Orla told Donny. 'I have to go home to me Mammy. But get the others one.'

No-one disagreed, so Donny shrugged his shoulders and went.

It was half past nine when Donny finally got up. 'Have to go,' he announced. 'See you tomorrow.'

Fiona, who had almost finished her third gin and tonic, looked at her watch. 'Oh, God! Is that the time? I'll have to go, too.' And she stood up.

Donny hesitated again. Then suddenly he found that Flagon, Swamp and Orla were all looking at him. He looked at Fiona and he couldn't see any way out. Ignoring the smirk on Flagon's face, he said, 'How're you for gettin' home, Fiona?'

'Oh, I'm OK,' she said, stepping unsteadily through the gap between the stools. 'It's not far.'

'OK. See you,' called Donny to the others and turned towards the door. He wanted them to have to guess whether he left Fiona home or not. He suspected a conspiracy.

Outside, he waited for Fiona. It was dusk and the street lights were on. 'Shit!' he said to himself.

'Oh, Donny,' she said, as if surprised to see him. 'I thought you were gone.'

'Nah. I'll go some of the way with you, anyway.'

'But there's no need, Donny.' Her face looked pale.

'Ah, it'd be safer,' he said.

'Whatever you like.' She thrust her hands deep into the pockets of her jacket and turned towards home. He fell into step with her, but her stride was not smooth.

'Will they be wonderin' about you, at home?' he asked. He realised that he knew nothing about Fiona's family.

'They?' she said. Her tone was charged with irony. 'My mum might...if she's at home.'

'Is she workin'?'

She didn't answer, and when he glanced at her, unsure whether she had heard or not, he saw that her face was white in the dim street light.

'Oh, God! Me head's swimmin'!' she exclaimed, stumbling over to lean against the high wall beside her.

Donny thought she was going to fall, so he took hold of her arm. 'Are you OK?'

She pulled her arm away and, leaning her back against the wall, she held her forehead with both hands. Her breathing came in quick gasps. 'Oh, God! I shouldn't have taken that third one. I'm all dizzy.' She leaned forward. 'Just gimme a minute. I'll be OK in a minute. If there was some place I could sit down.'

Donny remembered the low wall outside the houses round the corner. 'C'mon,' he said, taking her arm again. He could feel the resistance. 'There's a place round the corner.'

Soon afterwards, sitting on the wall, Fiona began to feel worse rather than better. 'I shouldn't't've ...' she moaned, her voice slurred. 'I can't go home like this. Me head's goin' round in circles.'

'Maybe if you could ... throw up,' Donny suggested, realising, when he had it said, that it wasn't the sort of thing you normally said to girls. The suggestion seemed to release something in her, because suddenly Fiona twisted round and emptied the contents of her stomach into the shadows behind the wall. Donny stood there, helpless. He resisted the impulse to say, 'Get it up outta you. It'll do you good' — a phrase he had heard Swamp use once, when Flagon had been plastered after Christmas, because he hadn't got a card from Leandra.

'I'm sorry, Donny,' she mumbled when the fit of retching was over. 'I shouldn't be botherin' you. You just ... You're very good.'

'It's OK,' he answered. 'C'mon. See if you can walk.' He helped her to her feet and she stood unsteadily for a moment, before sinking back onto the wall.

'I can't,' she gasped. 'It's me head.'

Donny looked up and down the street, hoping for some inspiration, but none came. He was kicking himself for getting mixed up in the business in the first place. Then he decided. 'C'mon. My gaff's not far from here. You can have a cuppa coffee there, an' then you'll be all right.'

Her dark eyes searched his face. 'Will there be someone there?' she asked, warily.

'Yeh. But it's only me sister an' little Stevie. An' *she* won't mind.'

'OK,' she agreed. He took her arm and they set out.

Several minutes later, they reached Donny's house. He had supported Fiona for most of the way, with his arm around her waist. But as they neared the house, she insisted that she was feeling better and could manage on her own. Donny was relieved. He didn't particularly want to land on Maeve's doorstep with a girl that was 'paralytic' with drink.

He opened the front door and, seeing the kitchen in darkness, he led the way into it, turned on the light and indicated a chair. 'Have a seat. I'll just tell Maeve I'm home.'

'Where were you?' Maeve asked, when he opened the sitting-room door and stepped in.

'We won the game,' he said.

Her face brightened with pleasure. 'Oh, that's great, Donny! That's brilliant! But where were you till now?'

'Ah, me an' Flag an' Swamp an' a few friends went for a drink after the game — to celebrate, you know.' Her face showed her disapproval. 'It was only one or two. Anyway ...' He closed the door quietly behind him and lowered his voice. 'Don't ask questions now, but I have a girl with me, an' she's not feelin' the best.' He mimed putting a drink to his lips. 'So I'm goin' to make her a cup of coffee before she goes home.' Maeve started to rise from her seat, but he signalled her to stay put. 'It's OK. I think she's a bit embarrassed. I'll see you in a few minutes.'

'What was the score in the game?' she called after him as he shut the door.

'One-nil!' he shouted back.

In the kitchen, he found Fiona sitting by the table with her head resting on her arms. She looked up as he came in. There were dark shadows under her eyes. He answered her unspoken question.

'It's OK,' he said. He put on the kettle to boil and busied himself with the coffee things, aware that she was watching him. 'Like a bit of toast?'

She shook her head. 'Just the coffee, thanks.'

'The phone here's disconnected. Only for that you could ring home ...'

She pushed back a lock of hair that had strayed over her eyes. He noticed her long slim fingers. 'It's OK. They mightn't be there anyway.' He poured the steaming water into two cups and pushed one towards her. 'Thanks,' she said. Her face seemed less severe now. 'I hope your sister doesn't mind ...'

He waved away the idea. 'No sweat. She's used to me bringin' girls home from the pub.'

Her look was startled until she saw his grin. Then she smiled too. 'Yeh, every night, I suppose,' she retorted, her hands holding the cup possessively.

'Ah, no. Only at weekends,' he joked.

Fiona felt better after the coffee and, when Donny and she'd had a few polite words with Maeve, they set off into the lamplit streets again. Donny was a bit concerned about his homework. It would be at least half an hour before he would be able to tackle it. On the other hand, he consoled himself, at least Fiona would be sober when he arrived home with her. Anyway, the teachers would probably be lenient, considering the great victory in the Cup.

Another thought began to bother him now. Where had Swamp and Orla disappeared to? After all, Fiona was Orla's friend. She had come to the game and pub with Swamp and Orla, yet when things had gone a bit off-side, they had left Donny holding the baby. Surely they must have noticed that Fiona wasn't the best when she followed Donny from the pub. There was something a bit fishy about how things had gone, he decided. He would corner Swamp the following day and ask him a few questions.

'I'll be OK now,' Fiona's voice broke in on his reverie. They had just arrived outside her house. 'An' thanks, Donny, for the coffee, an' all. Lots of fellas wouldn't have bothered.'

Donny halted. 'No bother,' he said. A weak light showed through the frosted glass of the front door of the shabby house.

'What about ...?' He inclined his head towards the house.

'Ah, they're not bothered what time I come in at. 'S long as I don't disturb them.'

'They?'

She looked down at her toes. 'Me mum ... An' *him*.'

'Your dad?'

She shook her head. 'Me da's gone. There's this other bloke, that's livin' with her. He's a ...' She seemed to be about to say something more, but she changed her mind.

Donny was uncomfortable. He felt caught again. He wanted to head back home, yet he didn't want to turn and walk away from Fiona after what she'd just said.

'Bad, is he?'

She nodded, now fumbling with the cord of her jacket. She seemed to be teetering, as if she couldn't decide between two courses of action. Suddenly she stepped close to him, kissed him lightly on the cheek and turning, hurried along the path towards the side of the house. At the corner, she stopped and looked back. He saw her hand lift in a brief wave. Then she was out of sight.

On his way home, Donny thought about Fiona. What a strange girl! And what about the house? There was something ominous or threatening about it. He wondered about the 'man'. Why did Fiona seem to hate him so much? Was it because he had replaced her father? Or was there something more? And then there was her reaction whenever he came too close to her. She seemed jumpy, as if she thought that at any second he was going to attack her. He couldn't figure it out. Finally he shrugged his shoulders and let it fade from his mind.

He hadn't gone far, when he found himself thinking about Jacky. The memory of her there at the railings with Bruce and Rocky began to smart again, like a sore inside him. What if she had latched onto Bruce again? She *had* almost admitted that she'd gone out with him before. Grudgingly, he had to admit that Bruce had a lot going for him. Big house, posh school, plenty of money and his father's car whenever he wanted it, probably. The thought discouraged Donny. How could he compete with that? He recalled what Flagon had said about Rocky. Maybe he *was* interested in Jacky. But she had said she didn't like Rocky. He was ... what had she said ... a wally? Even his own mates didn't like him.

These thoughts were circling in his mind like cattle in a closed-up pen when he arrived back at his own door. There was no release. He thought again about what Flagon had said — that he should go and talk to her. He knew Flagon was right, but he could muster no enthusiasm for the idea. He had tried once already and look what had happened. What if his fears were justified? He'd look a right fool walking up to her door and standing there with his mouth open while she explained that she was sorry and all that stuff, and her mother sniggered out of sight at the door of the sitting room. No, he told himself in a rush of self-pity. He could do without that, thank you. He slipped the key into the lock and went in to face his sister.

He found Maeve in the kitchen, preparing bottles for Stephen. She gave him one of her funny looks when he came in.

'OK,' he said. 'Don't start.'

She looked at him, wide-eyed and innocent. 'I'm saying nothing,' she said.

'I got stuck with her. She came down to Mooney's with Swamp and Orla, and then when we went to Casey's she had three G and T's. And, of course, muggins here got stuck to leave her home.'

Her eyes were amused when she looked at him. 'What made her take all that drink?'

He shrugged his shoulders. 'I dunno. Celebrating, I suppose. She was at the game today as well.'

'I see,' she said. 'You sound as if you can't stand the sight of her.' There was a faint hint of irony in her voice.

'No, she's nice enough — most of the time. It's just that I seem to be getting the job of taking her home ...' His voice trailed off as he caught her eye. He frowned. He guessed what she was thinking. 'No,' he protested. 'It's not like that. I don't really want to be leaving her home.'

Maeve put the bottles into the fridge and closed the door. 'Well, little brother,' she explained gently, 'you shouldn't be doing it if you don't want to.'

9

Next morning, as he strode in through the gates of the school, Donny was pleasantly aware of the admiring looks and calls coming his way from the younger boys in the school yard. At assembly, there was a sustained round of applause and a chorus of piercing whistles, when Brother O'Sullivan, beaming broadly, told the student body how proud he was of the team, and how they had made history.

At the eleven o' clock break in the senior area, the talk centred first on the semi-final, but soon drifted to the final.

'I see the papers are all tippin' St. Edmund's to win today,' remarked Donoghue.

'Yeh, who cares?' scoffed Flanagan. 'We'll take them, no bother.'

'They'll all be big bony ponces,' Miler announced. 'I know a bloke that's goin' to St. Edmund's, an' he has a neck like a bleedin' tree-trunk.'

'Yeh,' scoffed Flanagan. 'He'd be great in the middle of a ruck, but no ruckin' good when Donny here is nutmeggin' him on the eighteen yard line!'

'I wouldn't be too cocky,' Curtis warned. 'They'll be useful enough if they beat St. Jerome's. They'll have plenty of height, an' they'll be strong.'

'Yeh, but who says they *will* beat them?' asked Murray.

'Tell you what!' suggested Kavanagh. 'If they do win, we'll

beat them at football, an' then we'll challenge them to a game of rugby!'

This remark was greeted by a general clamour for places on the rugby team. 'I'm scrum half,' announced Butler. 'An' Kavo here can play prop. He's thick enough anyway.'

During the resultant maul between Kavanagh and Butler, the talk drifted on to the supporters' club disco in the school hall on Sunday night. 'Yeh, o' course we can go,' Donoghue stated. 'It's only the night before matches that Clint is paranoid about.'

Swamp, who had just arrived, sidled in beside Donny.

'I suppose you'll be goin', Don?' he remarked.

'Dunno, Swamp. I've work Sunday night.'

'Ah, you might be able to get the night off. It'll be great crack. An' it *is* for the supporters. Sure all the team'll have to be there.'

'Yeh. Maybe so, Swamp. I'll have a word with Murty tomorrow night,' said Donny thoughtfully. 'I could do with a break.'

'How did you get on last night?' Swamp asked casually.

Donny frowned. 'What do you mean?'

'With her nibs,' said Swamp cryptically.

Donny pretended ignorance. 'Which one?'

Swamp grinned at him knowingly. 'Oh, there's more than one, is it? Well, tell us about the one you left home last night, for starters.'

'You mean Fiona?'

'Don't tell me you left someone *else* home as well ...'

'Gerroff, Swamp!' retorted Donny indignantly. 'There's nothin' goin' on there. I just left her home because her *so-called* friends sort of abandoned her, after bringin' her to the pub in the first place.'

Swamp smirked, 'Oh, yeh. Well that's not the way *I'm* hearin' it.'

'You're listenin' to the wrong people, son.' Donny was becoming a little irritated with Swamp's disbelief.

There was something in Donny's tone that sobered his friend up. He motioned Donny away from the group. 'Seriously, though, Don. Am I barkin' up the wrong tree?'

Donny looked his friend square in the eyes and nodded.

'Wrong forest, Swamp,' he said.

Swamp exhaled his breath with a loud noise. 'Then I think we got a small problem here,' he said.

'What's the story, Swamp?'

'You mean, you haven't noticed anything?' Donny shrugged his shoulders. 'I mean,' went on Swamp, 'didn't it ever occur to you why Fiona was there in Orla's place every Tuesday an' Thursday when you called?'

Donny's irritation surfaced again. 'What the hell's wrong with that? She's a friend of Orla's, isn't she? There's no law ...'

'Yeh, Don. But *every* Tuesday an' Thursday!'

Donny saw red. 'Whaddya mean, every Tuesday an' Thursday. For all I know, she could be *livin'* in Orla's gaff!'

'OK. OK. Keep your shirt on, Don. Whether you noticed it or not, the fact is that Fiona has a mega-crush on you.'

Donny's eyes widened in disbelief. 'Crush! Well, you coulda fooled me. As far as I can see, every time I go near her, she acts as if she thinks I'm goin' to hop on her.'

'Ah yeh, Don. But ya see, that's only the way it comes *across*.' Swamp glanced around and lowered his voice. 'Orla was tellin' me that somethin' happened in the last place Fiona lived in. I'm not sure of the details, but some bloke she was keen on turned out to be a real bastard. An' she was awful cut-up about it. Orla said that Fiona often said that she'd never go out with any bloke ever again.'

Donny's anger subsided. 'Well, good for her,' he said, 'But what's that got to do with me?'

'That's how she felt before she met you,' said Swamp. 'An' now she thinks you're the greatest thing since Rudolph Valentino.'

'Who the hell was he?'

'Never mind. But just be careful. I think things are not great at home. There's this bloke that moved in with her mother, an' she hates the sight of him. Even Orla's not sure, but she thinks he's been tryin' to mess with her. Fiona won't talk about it.'

Donny stared at his friend. 'No kiddin', Swampy?'

The other nodded, his eyed bulging through the thick lenses

of his glasses. 'The only thing is, I wasn't supposed to say a word to you about this. Fiona'd *die* if she found out, an' I'd be dead if Orla heard I told you. *Right?*'

'Yeh. OK, Swampy. But did someone not tell her about Jacky?'

'*I* did, Don. At least I said I *thought* you were goin' with a girl from up Terenure way. But I don't think it sank in.'

'Yeh. Thanks anyway, Swampy. I'll keep it in mind.' Donny was beginning to feel a bit uncomfortable now, and he wanted to change the subject. Then deep in the building the hated bell jangled. 'I'll see you later, Swampy. OK?' And he headed for class.

It was lunch hour before Donny was alone with his own thoughts again. When class was out he headed homewards for a bit to eat. He felt pretty good now. The various subject teachers had all commented on the previous day's game, and Donny had been very aware of the eyes of the junior boys on him, as he moved through the crowded corridors between classes.

At home, he fixed himself a monstrous cheese sandwich with lashings of sauce to tart it up and made a pot of tea. He wanted to keep the good feeling for as long as possible, but as he poured the tea, the memory of Fiona sitting there at the table came back to him. He frowned. This was getting a bit too complicated, he thought. OK, so she might have a crush on him. That sort of thing happened to everyone. Most guys in his position would just play along with the situation to see where it took them — that is, provided they didn't hate the sight of the girl. And maybe at another time, the idea would have even been attractive. Fiona was not a bad looker and she had curves in all the right places. But Jacky was on his mind. Ever since the disco, he just couldn't get her out of his system. And then, as if things hadn't been bad enough, she had turned up with those two blokes yesterday. No, he decided, jumping up from the table, he wouldn't start thinking about that again. He turned on FM104 — loud! A good blast of music would clear the head. He'd think about the whole thing later.

On his way back to school, the thoughts came back. But this

time he was defensive. Why should he be the one to go running off after her. After all, it was she who decided to come to the game with Rocky and Bruce. *She* was the one, he told himself, who should be doing the explanations. And as if to convince himself of the rightness of the idea, he said it aloud. 'Yeh, it's up to her!' But how was she going to contact him? He had no phone. Would he expect her to come down and stand outside the gates of St. Colman's, as he had done outside her school? No way! he told himself. He wouldn't have her humiliating herself like that. What about a letter? Yes, that was probably what she would use. She'd done it already. But that would take ages. His impatience pulled and dragged at him like a lively dog on a leash. That might be next week, *if* she decided to do it.

'Damn!' he said, as he turned in through the school gates.

After school, Donny went straight home. Flagon and Swamp had to head off immediately after class on various errands, so he had only spoken briefly to them. He dumped his schoolbag in the hallway, went into the sitting room and collapsed onto the couch. He lay back with eyes closed, trying not to think. If only he could sleep. He focused his mind on the game yesterday, re-living the good things he had done, playing them over in his mind and savouring them. An image of the railing crowded with people floated in, and he pushed it away. He moved back outfield and stroked a long pass out to Kavanagh, but the railing swam into sight again, and this time there were faces there.

Donny sat up and put his feet on the floor. He looked at his watch. Twenty past four. He stood up, felt in his pocket for change, and headed for the door. When he reached the kiosk round the block he went straight in, pushed in the money and dialled. It occurred to him that Jacky might not yet be home from school. He had a sneaking fear that he wanted her to be still out. The ringing tone started. If her mother answered, would he speak or put the phone down? He tensed. The ringing went on. It became harder and harder to listen to it. Then suddenly, he dropped the phone back on the hook. He was aware of a certain relief as he left the kiosk. Well, at least he'd tried, he consoled himself.

Back at the house, he pottered around with dishes until it was time to pick up Stephen. It was with a certain pleasant air of suspense that he left the house and set out for McIntyre's. He wondered would Fiona be there and, remembering Swamp's warning, he began to order his thoughts so that he wouldn't give any hint that he was aware of how she felt.

Mrs McIntyre answered the door, with her big generous laugh. 'Just in time,' she boomed. 'The little gurrier was beginnin' to fret. He knows when to expect you.'

Donny took a deep breath before he entered the room. When he stepped round the doorjamb, however, the room was empty, except for Stephen in his outdoor suit, already strapped into the buggy. Donny listened for sounds from other rooms in the house, but there were none. Then, as if in answer to his unspoken question, Mrs McIntyre said, 'The girls went to the shops for me. They should'a been back by now. You might meet them on the way.'

Five minutes later he did meet them. They came out of the Post Office just as he was passing the door.

'Well!' exclaimed Orla, looking straight at Stephen. 'Look who's here.' Fiona looked at Stephen too, but she seemed unable to keep her eyes there. After a moment, her cheeks reddened and she lifted her eyes to Donny's face. He tried to be cool.

'Hi, girls,' he said casually. Then to Orla, 'Your mammy thinks you're lost.'

'She's waitin' for these,' replied Orla, holding up a plastic bag with some groceries in it. 'So I'd better go. See ya later, Fee.' Donny thought there was a plea in the look which Fiona shot in her friend's direction, but if she noticed it, Orla showed no sign. She just gave the others a big cheesy smile, turned on her heel and walked away. This is a set-up, thought Donny. Not again!

'Donny,' Fiona began, her fingers playing with the button of her jacket. 'Thanks ... for looking after me last night. It was really stupid ...'

'It's OK,' he said. Her discomfort was making him uncomfortable. 'Don't worry about it.' He rocked the buggy backwards and forwards to keep Stephen happy.

Fiona glanced along the street. 'I'm goin' this way ...'

He pushed on and she walked beside him. He searched for something neutral to say. 'Are you goin' to the disco Sunday night?' Even as he asked it, he had a sense that this was the wrong question.

'Yeh, probably. If me mam lets me. Are you going?' The shortness of the question betrayed her interest in the answer. He tried to be casual. 'Have to work weekends. But I'm going to see if I can get off for a few hours.' He felt the need to leave things vague. He didn't need any commitments.

Fiona gave a nervous laugh. 'I'm sure your girlfriend won't be too happy about that.'

A loaded statement, thought Donny. Careful now. 'Ah, I didn't ask her yet. 'Cos I don't know whether I'll be able to go.'

'Oh,' she said.

They came to the junction and Donny stopped. The route to Fiona's house lay to the left. He noticed the colour in her cheeks again and suddenly, he felt sorry for her. On an impulse he said, 'You'd never know. I might see you there, yet.'

She brightened. 'Yeh, that'd be great.'

He pushed the buggy out onto the road. 'Seeya,' he said. He didn't look back.

Later, when Maeve had put Stephen to bed, Donny thought again about ringing Jacky. But his first impulse was against the idea. He let it sit in his mind for a few moments. Then he went into the sitting room and turned on the TV. It would suit better another time.

10

Donny was hurrying to his first class along the school corridor next morning when Swamp caught up with him.

'Hey, Don. There was a phone call for you in my gaff last night.'

Donny stopped, frowning. 'Who was it, Swampy?'

'Well, it was a person of the female persuasion an' you're to ring her.'

'Who, Jacky?'

'Yeh, probably. The thing is, I wasn't in myself, an' Helen took the call, an' as usual, she didn't write the bleedin' message down. We're always on at her to write down the ...'

'But did she get the name?' Donny interrupted.

'Well, no, not exactly,' replied Swamp defensively. 'But sure it's either Jacky or Fiona, an' didn't you see Fiona yesterday evenin'. So *she'd* hardly be ringin' *me* wantin' to talk to *you*, now would she?'

Donny ignored the question. 'I suppose Helen didn't get a number either?' His tone was mildly sarcastic.

Swamp shook his head sheepishly. 'Well, that's bleedin' great, Swampy. There's a call from somebody, but we don't know her name, an' I'm to ring her, but we don't know her number. It's OK. Whenever I have a few hours free, I'll start ringin' all the women I know. It'll be bound to be *one* of them.'

The bell for class sounded through the corridor.

Swamp's face took on a pained expression. 'Lookit, Don. *I* didn't take the bleedin' call. In fact, I'm beginnin' to be sorry I ever mentioned ...'

Donny reached over and punched Swamp lightly in the ribs. He grinned. 'No sweat, son,' he said. 'It's probably Jacky's mother trying to contact me, to tell me that she still loves me.' Swamp's wry smile left him free to turn towards the classroom.

'Poor, misguided woman!' shouted Swamp after him.

Moments later, as he sat in the French class taking out his books, Donny smiled. He had just had the bizarre vision of Mrs Anderson talking to Swamp over the phone. 'Tell him to call immediately. Jacky hasn't eaten or slept since the night of the disco. Ask him please to come. Oh, will he ever forgive us?'

'Yeh, that'll be the day,' said Donny to himself.

'Did you say something, Donny?' asked Miss O'Callaghan, the French teacher, sweetly.

'No, Miss,' replied Donny. 'Just practisin' my French verbs.'

It wasn't until he started home for lunch that Donny had time to think more about the mysterious phone call. While his head argued that the caller could have been any one of a number of people, his heart told him it must be Jacky. It *had* to be her. She probably wanted to explain about Wednesday, to say that she realised now what a mistake she'd made going with Bruce and Rocky. She had finally realised what a shaper Bruce really was, and she had told him that she could never go out with him again. She was ringing to tell Donny how sorry she was, and to ask his forgiveness. As he strode along the footpath, Donny nodded to himself. Sure, he thought. It made sense. And now he would have to decide what to do. Keep her waiting? Let her stew for a while? Make her think he was very offended?

In the house, over lunch, Donny wished Flagon or Swamp were there with him, so that he could test out his ideas on them. They would help him to sort it all out. He ate quickly, threw the dishes in the sink, and headed back for school. Swamp might be back early. (Flagon was always sloping in the gate of the school when the last bell was sounding.) But the five-minute bell had already gone when Swamp arrived, and he was deep in discussion with Flanagan, so Donny let him go with only the customary salutation. 'Yo, my man!'

After school that day, Clint assembled the squad for a short meeting in his classroom before they went to the gym. He wanted to talk to them about the St. Edmund's team, who had beaten St. Jerome's three-one in the second semi-final. 'I won't keep you long,' he said. 'But there are a few things that you ought to know. I saw St. Edmund's playing. They can play football, make no mistake about that. They're very strong in a couple of positions; weak in a few. They're going to be as good as any team we've met so far. Maybe better. The one good thing is that the papers have made them favourites.' He looked around at them. They were studying him with serious and unflinching interest. He pulled a notebook from his pocket and turned to the blackboard. 'This is what we have to look out for.'

For the next twenty minutes he spoke about the opposition, about their pattern of play, their strengths and weaknesses, and about individual members of the team. Borghi, the Italian lad in midfield, was the playmaker. Everything went through him. So the first task was to close him down. McNeill, the blondy centre-half (Donny recognised Bruce's surname), was good in the air but didn't like the ball at his feet. Cantwell, on the right side of midfield, was lanky, but very fast. Matthews, the centre-forward, had a powerful shot, but he was slow in the wind-up. Copeland, the keeper, liked the low balls, but had suspect hands. Clarke, the winger, was fast. The rest were OK. They could put themselves about, and some of them could play a bit.

Donny's curiosity got the better of him. 'What about Stewart? I think he plays right fullback.'

Clint thought for a moment, his eyes staring at Donny but not really seeing him. 'A stopper,' he said then. 'A mullicker. But he takes no prisoners.' He waited for their attention again. 'One thing to remember,' he said, 'is that we need to be aware of their strengths. But we're not going to be afraid of them. They can be beaten, and we're the ones to do it!' There was an assenting grumble from the group as they rose and headed for the gym.

'Right, boys,' said Clint, as the squad assembled on the pitch a short time later. 'This is the second last session. We'll have a light one on Tuesday, when we'll go over all the set pieces and take a few pennos. But today's the last hard one, so let's get started. Lead them out, Anto. Four laps.'

The squad worked hard. There was little small talk, only a quiet determination to push the bodies to the limit of their endurance in the early, physical part of the session. Once that was over, they did the ball work, honed their skills, worked at perfecting that understanding between themselves and that familiarity with one another's style of play that had already been transforming them into a cohesive unit. They worked on passing and then more passing — keeping control under pressure, keeping their shape even when Clint told them to imagine they had just gone three-nil down. 'Work for one another!' was his constant shout. 'No narking. Leave that for me. I'm good at it!'

When the session was over, forty minutes later, Clint called them together at the touchline. 'That was good, fellas,' he said. 'Very satisfactory. There's just a few things before we go. I presume everyone'll be here on Tuesday.' They all nodded. 'Right. We'll go through all the set pieces again on Tuesday. And do the pennos. Now, you guys, no burning the midnight oil, or the candle at both ends, over the weekend and early next week. You'll have plenty of time for partying after Wednesday. OK?' Quiet and serious, they all nodded again. 'Right, that's it. Have the shower.' And they headed for the gym.

After he had showered and changed, Donny hung around the dressing-room while Flagon applied his spray-on Brut to various parts of his lean torso, dressed himself and tied up his long blond pony tail. Flagon, of all his friends, was the one who knew Jacky best. He had been with Donny in England the previous summer. He had shared the ups and downs with Donny. Donny knew that Flagon liked Jacky and got on well with her. Flagon was the man to talk to.

'I'll go some of the way with you,' said Donny, as his friend slung his kit-bag onto his shoulder.

'Tough oul' session?' said Flagon, when they were out on the street.

'Yeh. Tough enough,' replied Donny shortly. He was thinking about how to raise a certain subject with Flagon.

'Did you find out who that phone call was from yet?' Flagon's question took him by surprise.

'How did *you* know about that?'

'Never mind that. Did you figure it out?'

'No. Well, I'm not sure ...'

Flagon turned to look at him now. 'Don,' he said patiently. 'wouldn't any eejit know who it was from. Why don't you bleedin' ring her? I mean, the worst that can happen is that she'll tell you to sod off. Or her mother might tell you to sod off, which wouldn't be as bad. But neither of them things is goin' to happen, I'll lay a hundred to one.'

Donny thought about that. His strong sense was that Flagon didn't really understand the situation fully, that he was still working out of his memories of last summer.

'Did it ever strike you,' Flagon went on, 'that Jacky might have gone to the game on her own, met those two blokes that she knew before, and hung around with them for a while?'

'Yeh, but why didn't she wait after the game?'

Flagon shrugged his shoulders. 'I dunno. Maybe she had to go. An' now she's ringin' to tell you why.'

'Yeh. Maybe.'

Flagon halted. 'Lookit, Don. Will you do me a favour? Just pick up a phone this evening, an' ring Jacky. You're getting yourself into a black knot over this. The next thing you'll be going off your food.'

Donny knew he was right. 'Yeh. I'll do it, Flag.'

'You really are in love with her, aren't you?'

'Naw, Flag. It's not like that. I *like* her. There's something about her ... I mean, from the first time I met her, there was something there. It's like you kinda know what someone's thinking.' He tried to find a better way of saying it. 'She's someone I can talk to. It's like ... we're compatible ...'

'Yeh,' said Flagon softly. 'I know what it's like. You're in love. That's what you are. An' there's no use in denyin' it.'

When Donny left Flagon at the street junction, he was fully

resolved that he was going to ring Jacky. The time was five-thirty. She should be well home from school by now, he thought. No. On second thoughts, just in case, he'd wait till just after tea. She'd certainly be there then. But when he and Maeve had washed the dishes, he lay down on the floor and began to play with Stephen. I'll make the call from work, he promised himself. He stayed on the floor for a while, with Stephen pummelling his face with his fists. But as he lay there, Donny began to feel annoyed with himself. Suddenly he sat up. 'C'mon,' said to himself. 'You can't keep chickening out of this.' He got up and carried the baby into the kitchen, where Maeve was working. 'Can you hang on to him? I'm just going out for a few minutes.'

'Where to?'

'Just a phone call. One of the lads,' he lied. He grabbed his jacket and was outside the door before she could say more.

The kiosk was empty. He put in the coins and dialled. He tried not to think about anything when it started to ring at the other end. Someone lifted the receiver.

'Hello. Andersons,' said Mr Anderson's voice.

'Hi, Mr Anderson, This is Donny.' He felt he should have added 'O'Sullivan'.

'Ah, Donny. How are you?' The tone sounded warm and friendly.

'I'm OK. Fine, in fact. Eh, I was wonderin' if I could have a word with Jacky.'

'Well, Donny, you're just five minutes too late. Her mother's just taken her across to Miriam's. That's her friend. She's staying the night with her, I believe. Can I give her a message?'

'I don't believe this,' thought Donny. Then aloud he said, 'Ah, not really. Sure I'll give her a bell tomorrow some time. OK?' For some reason he was anxious to get off the phone.

'That's fine. I'll tell her that. And by the way, congrats on winning the semi-final. Jacky showed me the report in the paper. I believe you're meeting St. Edmund's in the final.'

'Yeh.' A pause. 'Well, OK, Mr Anderson. I'll see you. Bye.'

'Goodbye, Donny. And good luck in the final. I hope you win.'

Donny put the phone down. 'Yeh. Like hell!' he said when he was sure it was well down. The man sounded as if he actually meant what he said. Donny's estimation of Mr Anderson took a dive. He could just have said, 'Good luck', and left it at that. He didn't have to go and say things he didn't mean. Glumly Donny pushed open the door and stepped out into dull evening. The sun had disappeared behind a bank of clouds in the west and it was getting cold. As he plodded home, he thought grimly of his next meeting with Flagon and he began to prepare the speech. He loaded on the sarcasm.

'Yeh, brilliant idea, Flag. Just ring her up an' everything'll be OK, huh? Now her Dad is doin' it — givin' me the bum's rush. An' he even has the cheek to tell me he hopes we win the final, an' him up to his tonsils in that rugby club that most of those St. Edmund's guys are hangin' around. You're right, Flag. Now I know for sure, all right!'

'Well?' said Maeve, when he came into the house.

'Well, what?' he retorted.

'Well, did you get through to your friend?'

'Yeh,' he snapped, taking the baby from the pram. 'C'mon, buster. Let's have a fight.'

'Don't get him laughing,' she warned. 'You know it gives him the hiccups.'

Donny arrived at the pub a little before eight o'clock. He went around collecting glasses straight away, and put them in the washer. Then he began to serve the scattering of customers that appeared at the bar. Shay, the other barman, kept himself busy by wiping the surface of the counter with a cloth.

'You're all go today,' he remarked drily, as Donny went past him with a drink-laden tray.

'Somebody has to do it, you know,' Donny slagged back.

Murty, the bar manager, was in the little back office, doing some paper work. Donny waited for a slack moment, and then he knocked at the office door and went in. Murty looked up from his work. The furrows on his forehead became fat and ridged when he lifted his eyes.

'Yeh. How'ya, Donny?' he said in that gravelly voice of his.

'Eh, I was just wonderin' if I could have a few hours off Sunday night,' Donny said.

'What for?' Murty didn't beat about the bush.

'You see, there's this disco, for the supporters, in the school. An' all the team are trying to go.'

Murty thought for a moment. 'I'd like to let you go, Don. But what am I goin' to do for a barman?'

'Maybe one of the lads that's off might do it.'

'Yeh, OK. I'll try Paddy. If he can do it, it'll be OK.'

'Thanks, Murty.' Donny went back to the bar and began serving again. Paddy was usually OK for filling in at short notice. A widower with a grown-up family, he seemed to like being in the pub.

Several minutes later, Donny heard his name being called. It was Murty, shouting from the doorway that led to the office and basement. 'Phone call, Donny. She's checkin' up on you.'

Donny put down the tray he was carrying and went towards the phone. What could Maeve want with him now? He picked up the receiver.

'Hello? Donny here.'

'Donny?' It was Jacky's voice. 'This is Jacky. I hope you don't mind me ringing you at your job ...'

'Jacky!' A swarm of butterflies suddenly took off in Donny's stomach. 'Howya,' he said lamely.

'I'm great. Did you get my message?'

'Yeh. Sort of. Helen couldn't remember who you were. She just said some girl called. So I wasn't sure ...'

'But did it not even cross your mind that it might be me?'

'Yeh. I *rang* you. This evening. But your father said you were out.' He was aware of the edge in his voice.

'Yes. I'm over at Miriam's. She's my friend. I'm staying the night.' Her voice sounded so relaxed. How could she be so relaxed? Donny thought. He moved closer to the wall to let Murty's stocky figure pass him by in the narrow passageway. He glanced out at the bar. It was filling.

'Yeh, well ...' He couldn't think of anything to say. He was getting anxious. He knew he should ask her about Wednesday. But how?

'Oh, well done in the game!' Her exclamation cut across his thoughts. 'You played very well. You all played very well.'

'Yeh. I saw you there.' He grasped at the opening. 'I was just wondering ...' He moved out of Murty's way again as he came back from the cellar. He thought he heard Murty mutter something about 'all bleedin' night' as he passed.

'But that's why I'm ringing you, Donny. I knew you were probably wondering. I didn't want you to get the wrong impression.'

Donny gave in to a nasty impulse. 'Yeh. You didn't want me to think that you came to the game because of me, is that it?'

There was slight pause. 'What do you mean, Donny? That's not funny, if you think it is.' In his mind he saw her eyes flashing.

'It's not meant to be funny.' Out at the bar, the line of waiting customers was getting longer. Then he heard Murty calling his name. 'Listen, Jacky. I'm here in the middle of work. I can't stay ...' He was beginning to regret his smart-assed remark already.

'Donny, can we meet, and talk? What about Sunday evening? Are you doing anything?'

'Yeh, I'm working, an' then I'll probably be going to a disco in the school. It's just for the supporters' club. So all the team are trying to go,' he explained.

'I'll come over,' she said with sudden enthusiasm. 'What time is it at?'

The suggestion took him aback. 'It's at nine o'clock. But I wouldn't be able to get you till near ten, 'cos I won't be knockin' off till ...'

'But there's no need, Donny. I'll take a taxi. It's simple. To St. Colman's, Walkinstown, isn't it?'

'Yeh,' he said. He felt that he needed more time to think about it. It couldn't be as simple as that. 'But, what about your folks? What're they going to say?'

'But that's the thing, Donny. They're going out to a show. They think I'm staying in to watch telly.' He felt the old excitement in her voice again. 'They won't *know*. The only thing is,

I'll have to be home before half-eleven. But we'll have plenty of time.'

'Yeh,' he said, aware that his tone didn't match hers for enthusiasm. 'Yeh. OK. But I have to go now. Seeya Sunday.'

'That's great, Donny. See you then.'

Something was nagging at the back of his mind, as he put down the phone, and he couldn't remember what it was. He hurried out and started to take orders. He'd think about it later.

The evening passed quickly. Closing time took Donny by surprise. He was in good form, chatting and cracking jokes with the regulars, when Murty switched off and on the lights, and the last orders were being served. Donny was whistling as he cleaned up. It was funny, he thought. The very sound of her voice seemed to banish all the doubts and questions. Donny had a feeling now that everything was going to be all right.

Then, before he left, Murty came back to him to say that Paddy could come in at nine on Sunday evening, so Donny could take time off then, as long as he started at seven instead of eight. That was no bother to Donny. He could do with the money.

11

On Sunday evening, Donny dressed in his best clobber and lashed on the after-shave before he left the house. He felt more settled in his mind and was confident that Jacky would explain what had happened on Wednesday. There was only one little cloud on his horizon. Fiona was expecting to meet him at the disco and he had a hunch that Jacky's presence there might be a problem. At least, he thought, Swamp and Orla would be there as well. So he wouldn't be stuck again.

The clock over the bar showed twenty-five minutes past eight when, to Donny's surprise, he saw Swamp coming in through the bar door. Behind him were the now familiar figures of Orla and Fiona. Donny felt a twinge of irritation. What was the story?

Swamp gave Donny a peculiar look as he weaved his way between the tables, a sort of say-nothing-I'll-tell-you-later look. 'Ah, how's it goin', Don?'

'Great, Swamp. Howya girls?' returned Donny, trying to sound welcoming. 'What brings you here?'

Swamp and Orla glanced at Fiona, who was standing behind them. Her face was slightly flushed. 'Ah, we just decided to call an' see if you're goin' to the disco,' she said, making an effort to smile.

Donny tried to sound vague. 'Yeh, probably. But not till after nine.'

'Ah, sure, we'll wait so,' said Fiona. Donny thought her voice was slightly louder that usual. 'Can you give us a drink, Donny? Just the one, while we're waiting.' Her eyes were bright as she spoke. He noticed the make-up on her cheeks and lips.

Donny glanced at Swamp and Orla again and then along the bar. 'Yeh, well, soft drinks — no bother. You know yourself. But the boss doesn't want us serving anyone underage.'

'Ah, c'mon, Donny. Just the one. Be a sport.' Fiona's cheerfulness was a little forced, Donny thought.

'Well, all right. Just the one,' he replied. He didn't want to be the spoilsport. 'You lot sit over there and I'll bring them over to you.'

Several minutes later, he took two Cokes and a gin and tonic over to his friends' table. Swamp was still giving him the funny look, but they had no chance to talk, so Donny said nothing.

Fiona took the gin and tonic.

'Right,' said Donny. 'I'll be less than half an hour.' He thought of telling Swamp that Jacky was coming to the disco, but it didn't seem to be the right time.

Several minutes later, Swamp appeared at the bar counter. He beckoned Donny with his head. 'She wants another G and T,' he said ominously.

Donny felt annoyed. 'Another one, Swampy. Jeez, this is crazy! Why does she have to be doing this in the first place?'

Swamp held up his hands, proclaiming his innocence. 'This was not my idea, Don. In fact I was totally against it, an' Orla too. But Fiona decided she wanted to come here an' we couldn't get the idea out of her head. So we came with her.'

'Yeh, but what if she gets sozzled again?' Donny argued.

'Don, she was comin' here anyway, even if Orla and me didn't come. An' she says she's only havin' one more, an' if I don't get it for her, she says she'll get it for herself.'

Donny glanced at the clock. The time was a quarter to nine. Then he happened to glance over Swamp's right shoulder. A slim girl in a light-grey jacket had just walked into the lounge.

'Jacky!' he exclaimed. Swamp swung round, and his eyes bulged out when he saw Jacky. He turned back to Donny. 'Holy cow! What's *she* doin' here?'

Jacky had seen Donny and was coming in his direction, so Donny had no chance to reply. His nervousness came back to him with a bang.

'Donny! Paul! Hi!' Jacky called. She waved. Her pleasure at seeing them was unmistakable.

'Hi, Jacky,' they both said in unison. 'Didn't expect to see you here,' Swamp went on.

'I just thought I'd come over early and watch Donny working,' she joked.

'Workin'!' exclaimed Swamp. 'All he ever does is talk to the customers. He's a waster.'

Donny ignored the jibe. 'Yeh, anyway. Great to see you, Jacky,' he said. 'I'm out of here in ten minutes. Will you have a drink, while you're waiting?' He thought she looked terrific. The pink sweatshirt under the grey jacket seemed to catch the colour of her skin. Her hair was swept back in a ponytail.

'Yes, a Coke, please,' she said brightly. 'And now I'll have someone to talk to while I'm waiting. Brill!'

Swamp cast a brief but ominous look in Donny's direction. 'Sure. Come on over and meet Orla ... and Fiona,' he said.

'Go ahead,' said Donny. 'I'll bring the drinks.'

Donny was uneasy as he prepared the drinks. He was concerned about Fiona and he couldn't shake off the feeling that something bad was going to happen. He felt a strong need to be where his friends were, to know what was happening. Hurriedly, he put three Cokes on the tray. Then he glanced at the clock again. It was almost five to nine. Just the one more could hardly do Fiona much harm, he decided. He put a smaller measure of gin than usual into a glass, opened a bottle of tonic, and poured a small amount into the gin. As he made his way through the scattered tables, he tried to read the faces. Jacky was talking, her face animated just as he had seen it often before when she was excited. The others seemed to be listening, but Fiona was looking down and her face was in shadow.

'Right,' he said cheerfully. 'Here they are. Last drinks. I'll be ready in a few minutes.'

As he put the gin and tonic in front of Fiona, he was conscious of her looking up into his face. He didn't meet her gaze, however, but started to pour the tonic, intending to fill the glass. She reached out, caught the bottle and lifted the neck to stop him pouring.

'Don't drown it completely,' she said.

'Damn!' he said to himself as he went back behind the bar. This was not what he wanted. The thought flashed into his mind that he shouldn't go to the disco at all, but just slip away somewhere with Jacky and have a long talk. No, he decided. That would be too awkward to organise now. It would be easier to go along.

Paddy, the other barman, arrived at five to nine. 'G'wan with yeh,' he said to Donny. 'An' go aisy on the girls.'

'Yeh,' said Donny. 'Thanks, Paddy.'

When he reached his friends' table, Fiona moved in to make room for him at one end of the U-shaped bench. After an awkward moment, however, he took a stool from another table, put it next to Jacky and sat down.

'Aren't you going to have one yourself, Donny?' asked Fiona, her hand going to the pocket of her jacket. 'I'll get it.'

'Naw, it's OK,' he said. 'Sure we'll be heading in a few minutes.' He didn't want to leave any excuse for Fiona to have another drink. She persisted, however, and stood up.

'Naw, Fiona,' Donny protested. 'I don't feel like one now.'

In the end, it was Orla's and Swamp's intervention that persuaded her not to go to the bar. She wasn't too pleased. Donny looked around the table. Everyone had finished their drinks except Fiona. He was impatient to go. He knew he wouldn't be able to relax until they were out of the pub. 'OK,' he said. 'Are we right?' The others began to gather themselves for departure. Fiona put the glass to her mouth and drained the rest of her drink. 'We're right,' she said.

The school was less than ten minutes from Carey's, so the group set off walking. Donny wanted to explain about Fiona to Jacky, but it was not possible because Fiona didn't seem to want to walk with Orla and Swamp, who were ahead, but hung back close to him. He wished they were at the school. He wished he felt more relaxed and could think of something to say. He wished Fiona wasn't sticking to him like a leech. He wished he was alone with Jacky so that he could talk to her. He glanced at her and she smiled at him, but he saw questioning in her eyes.

'Should be a good crowd there tonight,' he observed. 'The supporters deserve a good night. They're great.'

'They were great at the last match,' agreed Jacky. 'They really cheered you on.'

Donny tried to draw Fiona into the conversation. 'Yeh. Fiona and Orla were there. They were brilliant too.' He looked down at her, wanting her to smile, to say something that would make things all right again. But she kept looking at the ground ahead of her.

'Will you be at the final, Fiona?' Jacky asked, her tone amiable and relaxed. After a long pause, during which Donny felt himself becoming more tense, Fiona spoke, so quietly that he could hardly hear her. 'Maybe,' she said.

'Will *you* be there?' Donny asked Jacky.

'Of course I will,' Jacky retorted. 'Wouldn't miss it for anything.'

He thought of asking her who she would be supporting, but he resisted the urge. It would sound too sarky.

The dark mass of the school building loomed ahead of them. Already they could hear the distant throb of the music and, as they neared the gates, they saw other groups of young people drifting in.

Inside the gym, the sound was ear-splitting. Beams of light from the stage stabbed and whirled. A mass of dancers on the floor pulsed to the beat. Donny smiled as Orla hauled a reluctant Swamp out to join the throng. Disco dancing wasn't Swamp's favourite pastime. When Donny looked for Fiona, he saw that she was right beside him, so near that their shoulders almost touched. His eyes searched the dark crowd for Flagon's distinctive pigtail. If old Flag were around, he'd be able to chat with Fiona for a while, and take the pressure off Donny. But there was little chance of finding him in that melee.

Jacky was shouting something in his ear. He bent his head.

'Do you want to dance?' she shouted. He nodded. 'Yeh. OK.'

When he was out on the floor, Donny looked for Fiona again. She was still standing where he had left her. Her face was white and peaked against the darkness behind her. She seemed to be looking at him. Then Donny was sorry that Swamp had told him anything about her. If he knew nothing about how she felt, it would be easier for him.

Jacky was talking to him again. He bent again to her smiling face. 'I hope you haven't arranged for someone to come and push me in the back tonight,' she said.

He grinned down at her. 'Nah,' he said. 'That only happens in the posh clubs. Not here.' She waggled a warning finger under his nose, but her smile gave him reassurance. Somehow the ice was broken. Now it would be easier to talk, he thought. He looked around the gym for some place that would be quiet. Maybe the dressingrooms. No, they'd surely be locked. Then it would have to be outside. After this round of dances, he told himself, he would take Jacky outside and talk. Get it sorted out. Then they could enjoy the rest of the night.

'Who's Fiona with?' Jacky asked.

The question took Donny by surprise. 'She's just a friend of Orla's,' he said, his cheeks flushing.

Her look was long and searching. Then she nodded, but her eyes looked away.

'C'mon and we'll have a chat,' he said, when the music subsided and the DJ's voice started its suave chatter.

She nodded. 'OK.' He turned to lead the way and ran smack into Flagon. 'Whooo!' yelled Flagon, when he saw Jacky. His eyes lit up. He grabbed her and swung her off her feet. 'How's it goin', Jacky, me oul' flower? Long time no see!' He aimed a huge wink at Donny. 'Surprise visit, eh, Don?'

'Yeh, you could say that, Flag,' retorted Donny. He smiled as Jacky planted a kiss on Flagon's cheek, while *he* pretended to swoon. 'Wow!' he shouted. 'Bet you don't kiss *him* like that!'

Jacky laughed and poked him in the ribs. 'I've been saving that one for you, Flag,' she joked. Then the chat began. Jacky wanted to know all about Leandra, Flagon's girlfriend. His response was to make a sorrowful face and to throw his head dramatically onto her shoulder.

'She's still over there,' he wailed. 'An' I'm over here.'

'Ah, poor Flag,' she consoled.

Watching them, Donny began to relax. This was the Jacky and Flagon that he had known in London the previous year. As they chatted, it was plain to see that they were both pleased to have met again. Maybe, thought Donny, things *can* be as they were before.

'Hey. Do you remember that day we went to Battersea Park?' Flagon shouted. The music had started again. 'An' the go we had on the roller-coaster?'

'I remember,' she said. 'That was the time you two were bragging about how much fun it was going to be, and you both came off it as sick as parrots.'

Flagon laughed. 'No. That's not what happened at all, was it, Don?'

'Naw, Flag,' said Donny ruefully. 'We were even *sicker*!' And all three of them laughed at the memory.

They had been talking for some time and the subject had swung round to football, when Swamp's rounded figure appeared beside Donny. His face looked serious. 'Hey, Don. Can I have a word?' he said into Donny's ear, while at the same time pulling him away from the others.

'What's up, Swampy?'

'It's Fiona. She's lost the head altogether. She's in there in the Ladies an' won't come out.'

Donny glanced across towards the door of the ladies' toilets. 'What do you mean, Swamp?'

'She's after lockin' herself into one of the cubicles an' Orla can't get her to come out. She thinks she's cryin'.'

'Oh shit!' exclaimed Donny. The bad thing that he had feared had arrived.

'Orla thinks she's a bit jarred. An' she says she wants to talk to *you*.'

'What? In the *Ladies*!' Donny retorted.

Swamp's face mirrored Donny's disbelief. 'Yeh, Don. That's

what Orla says.'

'You're not serious. Where's Orla?'

'Gone back in to her, I think. Will you come over, Don?'

Donny hesitated. 'But there's nothing *I* can do, Swampy. You don't think I'm going to go into the Ladies! Can't Orla talk to her?'

'She is, Don. But it's no use. She's talkin' crazy.' He paused and swallowed. 'Orla said that she said she was goin' to commit suicide.'

'You're joking!' exclaimed Donny. 'But why, Swampy? Why would she ...?' Swamp had a strange expression on his face. 'Ah, no! You don't think she's ...!'

Swamp's eyes were huge. 'I dunno, Don. It's just the way Jacky suddenly turned up. Even if you'd *told* us she was comin', we could have warned her.'

'Yeh, but ... I didn't know myself till last night,' Donny protested. 'And anyway I never thought ...'

'Lookit.' Swamp's tone was urgent now. 'C'mon over an' we'll talk to Orla.'

Reluctantly Donny agreed. 'Hang on a minute.' He turned back to Jacky and Flagon, still chatting enthusiastically. 'Hey. Something's come up. Can you hang round for a couple of minutes, Flag? I'll be back soon.' He left them staring after him in mild surprise.

It was several minutes before Orla came out of the ladies' toilets. Her face was white and frightened. 'She still won't open it, Paul,' she said to Swamp. Donny saw tears hovering in her eyes. 'She wants to talk to you, Donny. Will you? I'm afraid she's goin' to do something crazy.'

'OK,' Donny said. 'Just get her to come out. I'll talk to her.'

Orla looked doubtful. 'I'll try,' she said. She turned and went into the Ladies again.

The scared feeling that had started in Donny's stomach was growing. 'What do you think, Swamp?' he asked.

Swamp pushed up the glasses along his nose. He stared up at Donny. He was frightened too. 'Maybe we should get one of the teachers,' he said. 'Miss O'Callaghan's somewhere around.'

Donny thought about that. A teacher would probably know what to do. But there'd be a big fuss, and in no time at all the story would be all over the place. And Donny didn't want his name mixed up in the business if he could help it, either.

'Just hold on a sec,' he said. 'And see what Orla says.'

He had hardly finished speaking, when the door of the Ladies opened and Orla rushed out. 'Oh, Paul! Donny! Someone'll have to go into her. She's in a terrible state.' She put her hands to her mouth. 'I'm afraid.' By this time a small knot of girls had gathered at the doorway. One, who had just come out, was trying to tell something to the others, over the noise of the music.

Donny made a decision. 'OK, Swampy, just don't let anyone in for a few minutes. I'm going in to talk to her. C'mon, Orla.' He pushed the door open and went in.

There were only three cubicles in the small toilet area. The door of the one at the end was closed. Donny went to the closed door and listened. A quiet sobbing came from the other side.

'Fiona,' he called softly. No response. 'Fiona.' This time he heard a low moan. He crouched down and looked in under the door. He could see Fiona's boots. She seemed to have her back to the right hand wall of the cubicle. Then a dark blot on the floor caught his attention. As he watched, another blot landed beside the stain. Donny's hair stood on end. Blood! He jumped up, went into the next cubicle, stepped up on the bowl and looked in over the separating partition. Fiona was leaning against the wall and she was holding her left hand away from her body at a curious angle. Then Donny saw the blood on her wrist. 'No, Fiona!' he exclaimed. Beside him Orla let out a scream. 'What, Donny?' she asked.

Donny grabbed the top of the wall, hauled himself over and eased himself down into the cubicle beside Fiona. She didn't move, but looked at him with a bleak and empty gaze that frightened him even more. He caught her left wrist. She tried to resist but he was stronger and he closed his hand over the bloody part. From her right hand something metallic dropped to the floor. With his other hand, he started to release the catch on the inside of the door. Fiona stared at him, her eyes like pools of blackness in her white face. 'Oh, Donny,' she whispered. She came towards him and he didn't move away. She put her forehead against his chest. 'Oh, Donny!' He didn't let go his hold of her wrist even though he could feel the blood moist on his palm, but he put his other arm around her shoulders. 'It's OK, Fiona,' he said, although he felt funny inside. Orla's voice on the other side of the door was urgent and frightened. 'It's OK,' he said again. Fiona shook her head slowly against him. 'I'm sorry, Donny,' she whispered. 'But it's the only way.' Her body shook with the violence of her sobbing.

'She's OK,' Donny called out again, in reply to Orla's agitated queries. 'She's all right.' He waited for a few moments until Fiona's sobbing eased. He felt he should say something but he couldn't think what. 'C'mon,' he said then. 'Let's get out of here.' He pulled the brass bolt fully back and opened the door. Orla's frightened face stared at him. Donny put his fingers to his lips as a warning to her. When her eyes fell on the pool of blood on the floor, her mouth opened in a soundless scream. 'Oh, my God!' she whispered. Then louder, 'I'm going to get Miss O'Callaghan.'

'No! No teachers!' Fiona said, her words slurred. 'Just get me out of here, an' I'll be all right.'

Suddenly she felt very heavy on his left arm and he grabbed her before she fell. Her head lolled loosely against him. 'Give me a hand here,' he told Orla. 'She's getting weak.' Together, they put Fiona sitting on the floor with her back against the wall. She was trying to speak, but Donny couldn't catch the words. Donny looked at the door again. He didn't want anyone coming into the toilet area until Fiona had time to recover. For her sake, and for his own, too, he didn't want the story spread all over the place. They had enough problems as it was. He took some loo paper, damped it under the tap, and began to wipe away the blood from the damaged wrist. 'Just get that cleaned up, if you can,' he told Orla urgently, indicating the pool of blood on the floor. 'There's no need for the rest of them to know about this.' Orla grabbed some tissue and went into the cubicle. 'Oh, God!' she moaned. 'Oh, God, Donny! We'll have to get Miss O'Callaghan.'

Fiona lifted her head. 'No! No teachers!' she muttered again.

'Just leave it for the moment,' Donny said.

There were several cuts on Fiona's wrist, but when Donny examined them closely, he realised that they were not deep.

'She's going to be OK,' he told the crouching Orla. He wrapped some clean paper around the wrist and pulled the sleeve of her sweater down over it. Fiona was shaking her head slowly from side to side and moaning softly.

'Fiona,' Donny said urgently, 'Can you stand up?' She moaned again. 'Look. We're going to get you out of here, OK? Do you think you can walk?' She nodded again. 'I think so,' she whispered.

'Right. Orla, when we get to the door, just switch off the light and we'll get her out of the gym into the fresh air.'

Orla was in an agony of indecision. 'Are you sure, Donny?'

'Lookit!' he retorted. 'Do you want the whole place to know about this?!'

She shook her head. 'No,' she whispered.

'Well, then. Help me to get her out, and to a hospital. And remember, she only fainted!'

Orla switched off the toilet lights, and opened the door. A wave of sound hit them. Swamp was there, his expression asking wordless questions. He came to Fiona's side when he saw that Donny was supporting her.

'Just takin' her out for a bit of fresh air, Swamp,' Donny shouted. He pushed his way through a knot of curious spectators and headed across the floor for the door on the other side. 'She just fainted,' he told them as he passed through.

When they neared the door, he looked around for Jackie and Flagon, but he couldn't see them. He pushed open the door into the foyer, past Brackley and McGuinness who were sitting chatting at the ticket table, and out into the night air. He turned left into the darkness, away from the street lights, away from any prying eyes. 'You'll be OK now,' he soothed. 'We're going to get you some help.'

Donny halted in the darkness by the side wall of the gym. 'Just let her lean against it,' he said to Swamp. He took his arm from around Fiona's shoulders.

Orla, who had followed them out, came to Fiona and put her arms around her. She was crying. 'Oh, Fee!' she sobbed.

'What's the story, Don?' Swamp whispered.

Donny leaned away from the girls. 'Her wrist is cut, Swampy,' he said quietly.

'Oh, shit! No!'

Behind them Orla was talking to Fiona. 'It's OK now, Fee. We're here. Don't worry. We're here.'

'She'll have to go to hospital,' Donny told Swamp. 'We'll have to get a taxi.'

'I'll go an' ring,' Swamp said.

'An' Swampy,' Donny added. 'When you go in there, see if you can find Jacky an' Flag. Have a word. Just say I'm delayed.'

Fiona was sobbing again. 'No! No hospital!' he heard her say to Orla. 'I don't want to go to any hospital. Just let me go home.' He felt he should move away and let them talk, but he was concerned that Fiona might collapse again. In the faint light, he saw Orla's pale face turned up towards his, questioning.

'She should go,' he whispered. 'She needs ... She needs help.'

Suddenly, Fiona broke away from Orla and began to stumble off into the darkness. Orla screamed. 'Catch her, Donny! Catch her!' Donny ran and caught Fiona's arm, but she tried to pull away. He put his arms around her. At first she resisted, but after a moment, he felt her body go slack. She rested against him. Orla came and put her arms around Fiona from behind. 'Oh, Fee!' she sobbed. 'You have to go. They'll help you.'

Fiona's body was shaking again and Donny knew she was crying. He held her tighter. 'Don't worry,' he whispered.

They stood together for a long time, it seemed to Donny. Yet, although he was standing motionless, his body was shaking and his mind was in turmoil. Why had Fiona done such a terrible thing? What did it have to do with him? Surely it hadn't been his fault? he asked, with a sick feeling in the pit of his stomach. He wondered again should they call Miss O'Callaghan. But she might just get all upset like Orla. Where the hell was Swamp? Had he called a taxi? Had he spoken to Jacky and Flagon? Why wasn't somebody coming out to help him? What was happening? In the end, he could stand the waiting no longer.

'Orla,' he whispered. 'Would you go and see what's keeping Swamp?' Silently she nodded and disappeared in the direction of the gym entrance.

Alone with Fiona, Donny became more aware of her breathing. It was calmer now, but every now and again, she gave an involuntary sob.

'How is it?' he whispered.

'Better now,' she said. 'But I don't want to go to the hospital. I'll have to go home. I don't want them to know ...'

Donny thought about that. 'But you *need* to. You need to get your arm ... looked at. They'll help you. Anyway, they won't keep you in. If we go now, you can be home at the normal time.' He was feeling more and more that he was in the middle of something that was too big for him to handle. They'd know what to do at the hospital.

A dark shape came round the corner of the gym. It was Swamp, followed by Orla. 'There's a taxi coming,' he said. 'We should wait out on the street, so's he won't miss us.'

'But I don't want to go to a hospital,' Fiona said again. 'I want to go home.'

The others looked at Donny. Silently, he nodded his head. 'We'll stay with you, Fee,' Orla said then. 'We'll stay with you at the hospital, an' take you home afterwards.'

Reluctantly, Fiona allowed Orla to lead her towards the entrance to the school grounds. Donny edged away towards Swamp.

'Did you see them, Swampy?' he whispered.

Swamp shook his head. 'Scoured the place, Don. Couldn't find hide nor hair of them. I dunno where they've gone.'

'Are you sure?' Donny queried, frowning. 'They must be there.' But his friend shook his head. 'Right,' Donny went on, 'you hang on there a sec, and I'll have a look. Get the taxi to wait.' He sprinted towards the door of the gym. Once inside, he stood up on a chair by the wall and scanned the crowd of dancers, lit only by the sporadic flashes of light from the stage. Then he did a tour of the gym, keeping close to the wall where the chairs were, but nowhere could he see Flagon or Jacky. 'Shit!' he said. He couldn't believe this. He couldn't believe everything that was happening to him. It was like a jinx. 'A bleedin' jinx!' he exclaimed, as he pushed towards the door again.

When he arrived back at the gates of the school, however, Flagon had arrived, but Jacky was not with him. 'Hey, Flag. What's the story? Where's Jacky?'

'Jeez, Don. She's just gone.'

'What do you mean, gone?'

Flagon's eyes widened for effect. 'Home, Don. She took a taxi. I wanted to get her to came back. I *told* her you weren't gone far ...!'

'But how? Where did she get ...?'

'Lookit, Don. Keep your shirt on. What happened was: we saw you goin' out, an' after a while she decided she wanted to go after you, in case you needed a hand. But we went out into the street. We didn't know you were round the side of the gym. We went all the way down to Bulfin Road, thinkin' that you were gone home with Fiona, but there was no sign. An' then she decided to get a taxi. An' I tried to persuade her to ...' Flagon broke off when he caught Swamp's anxious glance towards Fiona, now leaning against the gate pillar supported by Orla. He lowered his voice to a whisper. 'She just wouldn't come, Don. She said she had to be home, before her folks got back. She said you could get in touch with her, if you wanted.'

Donny had heard enough. He looked up at the clear starry sky above him, wound himself up, and exploded. 'Christ!' he said. Then louder, 'That's all I bleedin' need!' He walked away from them then. 'Why don't you all leave me alone!' he shouted back at them. He wanted to hit something, *somebody*, to vent his pent-up frustrations on something that would hurt. He walked past the high front door of the school and round by the laurel hedge at the side. Viciously he kicked out at the high bushes, hearing them splinter and snap under the force. 'Can you not leave me *alone*?' he shouted.

Suddenly he felt strong arms around him. 'Come on, Don! Cool it!' It was Flagon's voice. Donny tried to wrestle himself free, but Swamp was there too, and the grip around him tightened.

'Come on, Don,' said Swamp. 'You'll have the boss over from the monastery, or Jaws, if you keep roarin' like this. Lookit, there's even lights on over there already.' It was true. High up near the third floor of the looming monastery to their right, they could see two lighted windows. 'They're just after comin' on,' warned Flagon.

'Lemme go, guys!' yelled Donny. 'Lemme go, or I'll wake the whole god-damn town!' They released him then. He sat against a low window-sill, breathing heavily, and ran his hands through his hair. 'Such a cock-up I never saw in me whole life!' he said then. They waited. They knew there was no point in saying anything until he had gotten it out of his system. 'I tried nearly everything, an' I *still* can't get it right. I thought it'd be OK tonight, an' then Fiona goes an' does this to herself. Why would she do a thing like this? Why did she have to ...?' He shook his head, but the guilt and anger and confusion inside him wouldn't ease up. His friends were silent, and he looked up at them then. 'Why did she do it, Swampy?' he asked quietly. 'Was it because of me ... and Jacky?'

Swamp started to say something, but shut up again. He shook his head, looking towards Flagon for help.

'Go on, Swampy,' Donny went on, his voice rising again. 'You can say what you're thinking. You can say...'

Flagon grabbed him by the shoulders. 'Donny! Shut up! He's not thinkin' nothin'! Stop blamin' yourself. It wasn't you ...!'

Flagon broke off at the sound of hurrying feet coming from the direction of the street. It was Orla. 'The taxi's here,' she said. 'Are yiz comin'?' She was looking at Donny as she spoke.

Donny looked at her and then at Swamp. Swamp just stared at him.

'C'mon,' said Donny. 'We'll *all* go.' Then he got up and started towards the street.

12

It was nearly two o'clock before Donny got home that night. He was exhausted. The crowded taxi had taken them to James's Hospital and they were left waiting for half an hour before a nurse and doctor saw Fiona. Orla went with her, while Donny, Flagon and Swamp sat in the dingy waiting room, talking occasionally in subdued tones.

'I'd say it's your man in the house with her mum that's the problem,' Swamp said after a while. 'Orla thinks he might be messin' with her.'

'You mean with Fiona?' Flagon asked in surprise.

'Fiona didn't say anythin' much. But Orla thinks there's something there.'

'Something should be done about blokes like that,' growled Flagon. 'There's a number you can ring, isn't there?'

Donny abruptly stood up. 'I'm going to stretch the legs,' he said. They were silent as he headed for the door.

Outside, in the lamplit streets, Donny thought about what they'd said. He knew they were trying to make it easy for him, so that he wouldn't blame himself for what had happened. But he felt it had something to do with him, and it frightened him. He began to think back over the past weeks, about all the times he had met Fiona in Orla's house. *Had* he given her the wrong idea? Sure, he'd chatted and had the crack with the girls. Sure, he had to admit that he liked Fiona, in a kind of a way, just as he liked Orla's wit, and Flagon and Swamp. But he'd never said or done anything to make Fiona think that she was more to him than just that, a friend. All right, he'd been caught a couple of times to take her home, but that was what any guy would have done with one of his friends who was a girl, at that time of the evening in Dublin. It just wouldn't have been safe for her on her own.

When Donny got back to the waiting room, Orla was there. She looked worried. 'They want to keep her in ... for observation,' she said. 'But she doesn't want to. They want us to get her mother, but Fiona goes crazy when she hears that. An' she won't give them her address or telephone number, an' she doesn't want me to do it either. What'll we do?'

'Why doesn't she want her mum to know?' Donny asked.

The others looked at one another, each waiting for someone to speak. 'Well, none of us would,' Orla said. 'You know.'

'Yeh, I suppose so,' replied Donny. 'So, what do you think?'

The three boys looked at Orla. This was a girl's business. If anyone knew, it would be Orla.

'If she doesn't go home tonight, her mother'll *have* to be told somethin' or else she'll go to the guards.'

'Suppose,' said Swamp, 'that we were to get a message to her mum that she was stayin' the night in your gaff? Say it was because the disco was so late, or sumthin'.'

Orla thought about that. 'Yeh, but *how*?'

'Jus' ring her up,' said Swamp, as if it was the most obvious thing in the world.

'Yeh, but *who*?' she asked. The three boys gave her the answer. They just stared at her. 'I dunno,' she said uncertainly. 'What if she wants to talk to Fiona?'

Flagon spoke. 'Just tell her that she's in the toilet ... No, that she's dancing, an' that she asked *you* to ring an' ask.' He looked at the others for approval. They were nodding hopefully. 'It'll work. No sweat,' he assured her.

'We have to do it, Orla,' argued Swamp. 'We can't take the chance of lettin' her out. In here there'll be someone to look after her. An' she might go for it if her mother thinks she's in your gaff.'

'OK,' Orla decided. 'I'll try it.'

They found a coinbox, and the boys stood tensely around Orla while she inserted the money and dialled. Donny looked at his watch. The time was twenty to twelve.

'Maybe we should do the sounds of a disco while she's talkin',' observed Swamp drily. 'Make it more realistic.'

'Hello,' said Orla. 'Is that Mrs Grady?' A pause. 'Well, this is Orla. An' I was just wonderin' if Fee — if Fiona can stay the night in my house — after the disco.' The knuckles of her right hand were white where she gripped the phone. 'Yes. She's in at the disco.' Orla's eyes were huge as she looked up at Swamp. 'She's dancin' an' she asked me to ask.' Another long pause. Orla's white face gave no clues. 'Oh, thanks, thanks, Mrs Grady.' She put the phone down, her face registering her relief. There were sounds of approval from the others. Swamp gave her a playful punch on the arm. 'Her mother said she'll see her after work tomorrow,' Orla explained. 'Ya boy, ya!' he said.

Then Orla went away to inform Fiona of the plan, and to try to get her to agree to it. When she returned, several minutes later, her face again broadcast her success. 'She's stayin',' she announced.

'How is she?' Donny asked then.

'She's ... She's OK,' said Orla enigmatically. Donny wanted to know more, but he felt that this wasn't the right time to ask questions.

'The nurse said that Paul and I can stay with her for a while, till she goes to sleep,' Orla went on apologetically. 'I asked about you, but she said two was the most...'

Donny nodded. 'That's OK,' he said. He didn't really feel like talking to Fiona anyway. He wouldn't have known what to say. He glanced at Flagon. 'Me'n Flag'll just slope off home. I'll give you a bell in the morning, Swampy,' he said.

'Fair enough,' said Swamp. 'See ya.'

'I'll go with you a bit, Don,' said Flagon, as they emerged into the night air. They turned towards home.

'What do you think, Flag?' asked Donny.

'Jays, I dunno, Don,' replied his friend. 'Nothin' like this ever happened before.' They walked on, Flagon taking huge strides with his long legs. 'She was hardly serious about it, was she?' he went on.

'She was serious,' Donny stated. 'You should've seen her wrists, an' the blood on the floor of the jacks.'

'Yeah, but ... People sometimes do that just to make a point. Just to get someone's attention. It's like a cry for help, you know.'

'Flag, I did nothing. I never said anything or did anything to make her think ...' A lump in his throat seized up Donny's vocal cords. He tried to swallow it down. Flagon said nothing so he went on. 'OK, I took her home a few times. But that was because someone had to do it. You couldn't let a girl walk home ...'

'That's OK, Don,' Flagon interrupted. 'Nobody's sayin' anything. There's no point in you blamin' yourself. Didn't Orla herself say that that bloke in her house was probably messin' with her? That sort of thing really messes up a girl.'

Donny swallowed hard. He knew that Flagon was trying his best to make him feel better. 'Well, it's just that it *looks* like I had something to do with it. Maybe it was because Jacky came. But I never thought ... I mean, I didn't think there'd be any problem with Jacky coming.'

Flagon looked at him then. 'Jacky thinks you set the whole thing up, Don. To get her back for that time in the rugby club. I tried to tell her, but she wouldn't listen.'

'Ah, shit!' said Donny.

'Well, you have to admit that it did look a bit hairy. You were hardly in the gym door before you did a legger ... into the ladies toilets!' Flagon started to grin, but wiped it off. 'An' a few minutes later you come out with your arm around this other girl. I wouldn't mind if we hadn't *seen* you. But me an' Jacky were standin' there *lookin'* at you headin' out into the dark with Fiona. An' *then*, when we went out to look for you, you were gone, disappeared! I mean, what did you expect her to think, Don?' Flagon's tone was gentle, but insistent.

'Flag,' said Donny hoarsely. 'I wouldn't do a thing like that. Not to Jacky. Not to anyone.'

'I know that, Don. We all know that.' Flagon's tone was intense and serious. 'We know you're not like that. But that's what *she* thought. *She* doesn't know you as well as *we* do.'

Donny felt the traitor tears welling up and he struggled to swallow them down. It wasn't fair, he told himself. It wasn't right!

'Don,' said Flagon quietly. 'It's not your fault, what happened to Fiona. It's somethin' else that's happenin' to her. An' she's getting help now. An someone'll have to see that that bloke gets sorted out. But you're goin' to have to go an' talk to Jacky. It's the only way.'

'Yeh, Flag,' said Donny, when he was able to speak. 'I think I'll do that.'

They walked on towards home in silence. When they came to Flagon's turn-off, Donny gripped his arm. 'Thanks, Flag,' he said.

Flagon patted him on the shoulder. 'No sweat, Don,' he said.

Later, as he lay in bed in the darkness of his room, Donny tried to get his mind to settle. He wanted to forget everything and sleep. But sleep would not come. He tried to blank out all the insistent images, but no sooner had he shaken one away, than another popped onto the screen of his mind. He wondered should he wake Maeve and tell her what had happened, but then he thought that she might be upset. She might start blaming him. He decided against it.

He turned his attention to the following day. He tried to remember what classes he had on Monday mornings, just before lunch. When he couldn't visualise his timetable, he rolled out of bed, switched on the light and hunted for his journal in the canvas rucksack that held his books.

The last two classes before lunch were Irish and French. Old Morris and young Miss O'Callaghan would hardly notice if he wasn't in their classes. They never checked attendance anyway. First after lunch was English. That'd be OK. Bill Moloney could be squared. At least he wouldn't question a note. The last two classes of the day, however, were Technical Drawing. And that meant Jaws. He'd have to be back to school in time for these. He did a calculation in his mind. If he left at eleven-forty, he'd easily be at Jacky's school by one o'clock. All he'd need would be fifteen minutes with her. That'd be enough time to sort things out, if they were *going* to be sorted. That'd give him over an hour and a quarter to get back. It'd be plenty, he calculated. There was, of course, the question of the note for Bill Moloney explaining his absence from class. That'd do on Tuesday. He'd worry about that later.

Donny's mind was more at ease when he crawled back into bed. At least he had made some kind of a decision. In a short time he was asleep.

13

Monday morning was hazy and cool, but it held a promise of spring. When he got to school, Donny made his way round the side of the building to the wide paved area by the laurel hedge where the seniors usually gathered. Flagon was with the gang, but Swamp was not to be seen. The subject of conversation was football, with particular attention being paid to the weekend results in Britain, and there was the usual slagging of boys whose favourite teams had been beaten. Donny joined the group, standing silently after he had returned the customary greetings. He was on the lookout for Swamp, and he didn't feel like joining in the chat. After a while, Flagon came over.

'How's it, Don? Any sign of Swampy yet?'

'No,' replied Donny. 'He's probably still in the scratcher.'

Butler shouted across the group. 'Hey, Don. Do you know a bloke called Stewart — Rocky Stewart?' His voice, as always, was loud and braying. Donny turned to look at him, frowning.

'Yeh,' he said. 'Why?'

'Is he a *friend* of yours?' Butler demanded, his eyes narrowing.

'Nah,' said Donny. 'What about him?'

'I met him, over the weekend. He plays for St. Edmund's, you know.' Donny nodded. 'He was with a bloke that lives near me that goes to St. Edmund's, an' he was slaggin' you off somethin' awful.' Butler's leer irritated Donny. 'I was just wonderin' was he serious or only messin'.'

Donny glanced at Flagon, but he was staring at Butler. 'Well now you know, don't you,' Donny said shortly. 'He's not!' He was going to turn away — Butler could be a pain in the ass at times — but curiosity made him stay. 'What was he saying anyway?'

Butler seemed reluctant to continue. 'Ah, nothin' much. Just stupid things. No, the reason I asked was I thought he might a' been a mate ...'

Donny wouldn't let it go. 'I *do* know him. What was he saying?'

Butler half smiled. 'Well, he said that we'd — that you'd better have the John's Ambulance at the game on Wednesday. Stuff like that, you know. He was only messing, really.'

'Oh, yeh? Is he expecting to break a leg, or somethin'?'

Butler laughed now. 'That's what *I* said to him. But he didn't think it was funny. He's a bit off the head, if y'ask me.' Butler paused and looked at Donny intently. He lifted his butt off the window-sill where he'd been sitting and strolled round the outside of the group till he stood beside Donny and Flagon. When he spoke again, his tone was quiet and confidential. 'He was goin' on about how he was goin' to take Jacky up to the Pine Forest after the victory celebrations on Wednesday. He's a headcase, Don, I'm telling you ...'

'Did he say that?' Donny's tone was hard.

'Yeh. But he's just a headcase, anyway, Don.' Butler was trying to pull back. He had said too much.

'Did he say that, though, really?' Donny insisted.

Butler nodded. 'Yeh, Don.' His face was apologetic. 'Maybe I shouldn't have said anythin'. But I thought he was a friend of yours.'

'It's OK, Kev. You didn't know. Don't worry about it.'

The bell for class jangled inside the building, and the group began to drift towards the corner that led to the side door.

'He wasn't really *with* us, Don, anyway,' Butler called, as Donny moved away from him. 'We just met him more or less by accident.'

'It's OK, Kev. No sweat,' repeated Donny. 'It'll all be sorted out on Wednesday.' He quickened his pace now, needing to get away from Butler before everyone in the place heard him. 'Once and for all,' he added to himself.

Swamp was five minutes late arriving for class, so Donny didn't get to talk with him till after the double period had ended.

'She was much better when we left her last night,' his plump friend told him, as they pushed through the crowded corridor at twenty past ten. 'Orla an' her mam are goin' in to see her this mornin', an' Mrs McIntyre's goin' to talk to a social worker. If that bloke's really been messin' with her, he could get the jail.'

Donny was relieved. He needed to hear that someone else, someone grown-up, had taken responsibility for Fiona. As he headed for his Maths class, taking the damp stairs two steps at a time, he promised himself that he would call to see her — soon.

The next two periods passed quickly, and when the bell for the end of the fourth sounded, Donny slipped out along the narrow path that led to the side gate and from there onto the street. Soon he was on a bus, heading east for Ranelagh, where he changed to a south-bound one.

As he neared Mount St. Oliver's, he thought about the coming meeting, that's if the nuns let him see Jacky at all. She'd probably be angry with him, but he knew he could explain about last night. And she still must feel something for him, otherwise she wouldn't have come to the school disco. But what about his own feelings? Was he really in love, as Flagon had said, or was it just a teenage thing, a 'crush', as Maeve would say?

The word 'crush' brought the events of the previous night swirling back into his mind, and the bad feeling started again. It had been there, lurking like a black cloud, all morning, and now its depressing weight sank down on him again.

'No,' he told himself. 'It wasn't your fault. Stop blaming yourself!'

He turned his thoughts to Jacky again. When he'd sorted out about last night, he'd talk to her about the disco in the rugby club, and about her being at the game with Bruce and Rocky. He wasn't looking forward to that bit, because it reminded him of the difference between his world and Jacky's. And then the traitor doubts came back again.

'Cop on to yourself,' he said aloud. An old lady, sitting on a seat opposite, looked at him sharply. No, he told himself, there was no turning back now. The one thing he knew was that he didn't want to lose her, and with that thought, his resolve hardened. He wasn't going to give her up without a fight. Grimly, he watched the lines of traffic flow past the bus, his chin firmly set, waiting for the journey to end.

It was five to one when he reached the gates of Mount St. Oliver's. He stepped off the bus and paused for a moment, surveying the pile of buildings that lay bright and forbidding in the pale noon sunlight. He pushed his hair back with his hand and checked his clothes. The jeans looked shabbier than ever, and there were scuff marks on the once-white runners which he had never noticed before. His tummy felt tight and empty. He started to walk towards the tallest of the buildings, which had imposing double doors halfway along the ground floor, and a medieval-looking tower on the right-hand corner.

A sign on one of the doors said 'Reception', so Donny pushed it open and stepped inside. As the door creaked shut, he gazed at the polished wooden floor that stretched away from him to a wide stone stairway. His eye followed the stairs upwards. The wide granite steps were tinted blue and red by the gloomy stained glass windows which stood narrow and pointed above them. Higher still, the vaulted roof echoed to the squeaks of his runners on the varnished floor. There was a strong smell of polish.

To his right was a door with 'Office' written on it. He knocked on it and a female voice called, 'Come in.' He pushed it open and entered. Behind a high counter, at a desk upon which stood a computer terminal and visual display unit, sat a sharp-nosed woman who looked up when he came in.

'Yes?' she said, her arched eyebrows accentuating the thinness of her face.

'Excuse me,' said Donny politely. 'I'm looking for Jacky Anderson.' He found it hard to smile.

'Jacky Anderson,' she repeated slowly, glancing at the clock on the wall to her right. The time was one minute to one. 'Is she expecting you?' Her voice was polite, but firm.

'Eh, no,' said Donny. 'But I'm a friend of hers.'

The woman studied his face for a moment. 'A friend,' she said, with a slight frown. He was glad that the counter concealed his jeans and runners. 'I'm afraid we don't allow our girls to have ... visitors during school hours. But if you want to give me a message for her ...' The woman was interrupted in mid-sentence by the chime of a distant bell. The red numbers on the control box on the wall beside her told Donny it was one o'clock.

'I have a message for her, an important message.' He made his voice sound polite and sincere. 'It'll only take a few seconds, an' it's kinda private.'

Through the window beyond the woman's left shoulder, Donny saw a group of girls moving into a space between two buildings. Some of them were coming towards him; others just crossed the space and disappeared behind the building to the right. The woman read his eyes and turned to look. Her eyes searched his face again. He could see her wavering.

'Does she have her lunch at the school?' she asked.

Donny nodded. 'Yeh.'

'OK,' she said then. 'She'll probably be going into the refectory with the other girls.' She pointed her thumb over her left shoulder. 'You might spot her there. But don't tell anyone you were talking to me.'

'Great! Thanks!' said Donny, turning towards the door. 'See you.' Gratefully, he hurried out through the main door again, and began to jog along the tarmac, more aware than ever that the gear he was wearing was in rag order. Now he heard the chatter of girls' voices. A quick glance told him that Jacky was not among the first group that he met. He passed them, his gaze fixed on the groups that were crossing his path ahead, and steeled himself for the eyes that he knew would soon be upon him. Then, as he drew nearer, the hurrying line petered out. The last few girls glanced at him curiously and then disappeared from view behind the building. Donny quickened his pace. Whatever about spotting Jacky in this moving stream of her school-mates, he definitely didn't want to have to follow them into the building on his right to enquire for her there. He decided he would intercept the tail-enders and ask about Jacky. As he rounded the corner in hot pursuit, however, another wave of turquoise uniforms appeared on his left hand. He found himself directly in their path. He braced himself, fixed his eye on a tall girl who was on the outside, and waited for her to draw level with him.

'Excuse me,' he said. 'I'm looking for Jacky Anderson. She's in Leaving Cert.' He moved off the path as the girl and two of her companions stopped. The tall girl leaned her head closer to him as if to hear better.

'Pardon?' she said.

Aware of the amusement in her eyes, he repeated himself. Now there were three girls giving him their attention.

'I'm looking for Jacky Anderson,' he said again.

'Jacky?' said the tall one, turning to scan the stream of girls that flowed out from a distant doorway. 'She should be along soon.'

'She was in French with Matilda,' a short girl with pigtails offered. She too, began to scan the crowd.

'There she is now!' announced a third, dark-haired girl. 'Hey, Jacky!'

Donny saw Jacky before she saw him. She was engrossed in conversation with a slim pale-faced girl. She looked different in the uniform, years younger to Donny's eyes.

'Hey, Jacky,' the tall girl sang out again. This time she heard her name being called and looked. She stopped abruptly in her tracks when she saw Donny, her face flashing her surprise to him. 'Donny!' The girl beside her looked too, but he kept his eyes on Jacky's face, as he advanced towards her. 'Donny! What are you doing here?' she asked, stepping onto the lawn.

'I just came over ... to see you,' he said quietly, uncomfortable with the closeness of the others.

'Is something wrong?' she asked, her eyes searching his face.

'No. Nothing. I mean nothing serious.' He looked around him. 'Is there anywhere we can talk?'

Jacky glanced quickly towards the doorway from which she

had come. 'Yes. Over here,' she said, pointing towards the left-hand corner of the two-storied building into which the girls were going. 'We can go down by the hockey pitch. Come on. Hurry.' From behind her came a catcall. 'Oooh, Jac-ky!' She ignored it.

'Come on, quickly, before Consilia comes.'

'Lookit,' Donny said, as they hurried towards the corner, 'I don't want to mess up your lunch hour, but I just wanted to come over an' talk ... about a few things.'

'Yes,' she said, as if she had been expecting him to say that.

When they turned the corner, Donny saw a path winding away and downwards through tall evergreen trees. Between the gaps in their trunks, he saw a level grassy field in the distance.

'About last night,' he said. 'I'm sorry about what happened. Flag was tellin' me that you thought ... well, that I did a bunk out of the place deliberately.'

She looked at him, then looked away. Then she nodded. 'Yes. I did say something like that.'

'Well,' he went on, 'I don't blame you. But it wasn't like that. It's just that when you an' Flag came out looking for us, we were round the other side of the gym ...'

Her eyebrows lifted in surprise. 'And what was going on round the other side of the gym?'

'Yeh, well, it's kinda complicated, Jacky. There's this girl, right? An' she's havin' a hard time at home. She's a friend of Orla's — you know, Swamp's girl friend. An' she got a bit upset at the disco an' locked herself in the girls' jacks an' wouldn't come out, right?'

'Right.' Jacky's expression was serious, listening. 'In the jacks,' she repeated.

Donny was feeling strange. He took a deep breath. 'Well, the truth is she started to cut her wrists with a bit of glass.' He paused because she had halted and was looking at him in surprise and horror. 'So Orla — that's her friend — came out for me ... an' Swamp. An' we had to go in an' get her out, an' take her to the hospital ...'

Jacky's eyes were searching his face. 'Are you serious, Donny?' she said. 'Are you telling me the truth?'

'Yeh,' he replied. 'But we got her before ...'

'But *why*, Donny? Why would she do something like that?'

Donny sighed. The bad feeling he'd had last night was coming again. 'Listen, can we sit down somewhere?' he asked.

'Yes. There's a place along the hockey pitch.'

They followed the path until it brought them down onto a benched hockey pitch. Along the right side was a high grassy embankment, on which grew an assortment of trees and shrubs. Jacky led until she found a sheltered nook, surrounded on three sides by bushes. The fourth side opened out onto the green sward below. 'We can sit here,' she said, sitting down on the faded grass of last year.

'This girl, Fiona,' Donny went on, when he was seated, 'has some problems. Swamp said that she's having a hard time at home. An' he thinks that that had something to do with what happened last night.'

She looked at him for a long moment, as if trying to read his inner thoughts. 'Donny, I know what you're saying is a terrible thing, if it's true. And I understand that she would have to be taken to hospital. But what I don't understand is why you had to go with her.'

Donny took another deep breath. 'Look, Jacky. Swamp said that ... well, that Fiona had a crush on me. And when it happened, she said she wanted to talk to me. That's all.'

Her face told him that she was struggling to believe him.

'A crush?' she said, frowning.

'Yeh,' he replied defensively. 'Lookit, Jacky. I don't know whether it's true or not. I just hope that it's not, because I don't feel good about the idea that maybe *I* had something to do with her doin' what she did. But what I want to say is, I didn't do anything or say anything to her to make her think, or feel, like that, in case that's what you're thinking.' He looked her in the eyes now. 'I'm telling you the truth, Jacky.'

He hated to see the conflict in her face, the indecision in her eyes. 'OK,' he went on in a rush, 'I know it looks a bit funny — me goin' off like that last night. But it's just that I got such a fright when I saw the blood ...' He had to stop because his throat seized up again as the memory came back to him. He looked down at the ground so that she wouldn't see his face. She made an involuntary move towards him, but stopped herself. 'All I wanted was to get her out before the rest of them copped on to what was happening. You know how a story like that would get round. And I sent Swamp in to find you and Flagon, but you were gone.'

Jacky looked away at the houses which showed through the scattered trees on the far side of the pitch. 'Donny,' she said, after a long moment. 'Before you came today, I thought I knew what happened. I mean, there was this girl, Fiona, in the pub and she didn't have a boyfriend. And she completely ignored me when I arrived. Then she came along to the disco with us ... with you.'

'Yeh, I know what it *looks* like,' he agreed. 'But that's not how it *was*! It's just that she has this *thing* about me.'

She looked down at her hands now. He noticed again her long slender fingers. 'Donny, I went to a great deal of trouble to get over to Walkinstown last night. Mum and Dad were out and they didn't even *know* I was going ...'

On the defensive, he turned to attack. 'Oh, yeh? You didn't want them to know that you're meeting me. How do you think that makes *me* feel?'

'No, Donny,' she protested. 'That's not the point. I came over because you invited me. And when I arrived ...'

'You invited yourself, Jacky,' he corrected cruelly. 'You said on the phone ...'

Suddenly, Jacky got to her feet and he knew she was hurt. 'Donny, if you didn't want me to come, you should have said so. I wouldn't have ... I just thought you wanted me to. I'm sorry. And I'm sorry about your ... your friend, Fiona. But ...' She stood there, swallowing hard. Then she turned away. 'I'm going back to the school now ...'

Donny sprang to his feet. 'No, Jacky. Don't! Please don't!' She started to walk down the sloped bank, but he caught her by the arm. Remorse welled up in him. 'I'm sorry. I shouldn't have said that ...'

'You shouldn't have. But you *did*, Donny,' she whispered,

her face turned from him.

'No, Jacky,' he pleaded, coming round to stand before her. 'It was stupid. I didn't mean it. I swear I didn't mean it. It was just that I felt bad about ... about you being at the game last week.'

She looked up in surprise. 'At the game? What do you mean? I came to the game to see *you*!' Her voice trembled with emotion. She brushed a wandering tear away from her cheek.

'Yeh, right,' he said. 'But what about those two blokes that you were with? I mean, I couldn't believe it, after everything that happened that night at the disco. You came to the game with that guy Rocky!'

She was shaking her head. 'No, Donny. You're *wrong*! I didn't go with them! I went on the bus! I left here at lunch hour, and took the bus. On my *own*!' The tears were welling up again. 'Bruce and that Rocky fellow saw me at the game and came over. They stood with me at the railings. I couldn't just tell them to get lost. Bruce is a friend of mine ...! Oh, I *knew* you would get the wrong idea, Donny. That's why I wanted you to ring me, or call. So that I could explain. Why didn't you ring me? Now everything is a mess.'

The sorrow in her face was like a knife inside him. He reached for her but she stepped back. 'No, Donny,' she said, her hands up defensively. 'It's ...' She struggled to find the words. 'It's just a mess.'

He dropped his outstretched hands. 'I did ring,' he said quietly. 'Lots of times.' He ignored the disbelief on her face. 'And each time, your mother said you weren't in.'

Her face showed her disbelief again. She shook her head. 'Oh, Donny. Why are you saying that? You *didn't* phone me. You *know* you didn't!'

His anger was gone. 'Look,' he said gently, 'let's just sit down.' They sat once again in the shelter of the shrubbery. A foot of matted grass lay between them, but to Donny, it seemed like miles. 'It's true,' he said. 'I *did* ring, several times. Did she not tell you?'

She looked at him for a long moment. Then she shook her head. 'No, Donny. She never said anything about you calling.

When did you ring?' He could tell she wanted to believe.

He listed off the times. 'Thursday after the disco. Friday after the disco. Following Tuesday. Day after the semi-final. Sometimes there was no reply, but I got your mother several times, and she said you were out each time.'

She thought about it, her brow creased with the effort. 'The Thursday after the disco,' she mused. 'I was *in* that evening. I was in every evening that week, because I thought you might ring, or call. How could she have forgotten to tell me? She *always* tells me when somebody rings ...' She stopped when she caught Donny's eye. Her hand went to her mouth in a gesture of dismay. 'Oh, no!' she gasped. 'She wouldn't do that! She *couldn't* have done that!'

But Donny was nodding slowly. 'She could. And she did. She must hate the livin' sight of me. That's for sure.'

'You mean, she answered the phone, was talking to you, and said that I wasn't in! I don't believe this!' Jacky exclaimed. 'How could she *do* such a thing!' She looked in puzzlement at the ground in front of her.

''S funny. I had a feeling she was doing it,' Donny said. 'Her voice sounded sorta quiet, as if she didn't want anyone to hear her.'

Jacky's eyes stared at the distant roof tops, but they were seeing something else. 'And all the time I was thinking that you just weren't bothered,' she said at last. 'Oh, she's a bitch! She's a rotten, mean *bitch*!' She spat the last word out with passionate force.

'Yeh, well. You always said she was a snob, didn't you,' Donny remarked, grinning, trying to ease her out of her anger.

'I even came over here one day after school to see you.' Her eyes widened with surprise. 'But what I didn't realise was that the cars all go out another gate. There I was like a nerd, waitin' at the front gates for your mother's car to come back out, so I could at least let you *see* me here. An' then, when I realised none of them were coming out, I did a legger over that fancy hedge along the avenue to try an' catch you. Nearly bleedin' killed myself.' Her eyes were huge as he spoke, but her face grew softer. 'An' then, to cap it all, I was there cursin' like a madman after you drove off, when this little nun pops up from behind a bush an' gives me this filthy look.'

She was laughing now. 'I don't believe it, Donny! That was probably Pius. She's always sunning herself on the seat by the avenue, saying her prayers.'

'Yeh,' he said, more serious now. 'Someone must have been prayin' for me all right.'

They looked at each other now, and the moment was filled with emotion. He wanted to reach over and catch her hand and draw her towards him, but he didn't know how she would take it.

'Does this mean we're friends again?' he said.

She hesitated, her eyes scanning his face. 'Donny, you *are* telling me the truth?' she asked. 'About last night?'

'Lookit, do you think I'd be here right now, if I wasn't?'

She thought for a moment. Then she smiled, and his heart sang. 'No, I don't think so. I believe you, Donny.'

'That's cool,' he said. He lay back on the sloping bank, his hands under his head. 'I'm sorry about last night. I mean I really messed up your night.'

She smiled. 'It's OK. You didn't have a great night yourself. And *I'm* sorry about what happened at the game. I couldn't get rid of that Rocky fellow.'

'No sweat.' Above him, the clouds were breaking into scattered white fleeces in a sea of blue.

'What are you smiling about?' she demanded, flicking his face with a long stem of grass.

'You should have seen me last night when Flag told me you were gone home. I was like an anti-Christ, roarin' and shoutin' around the school. I think I woke up ol' Jaws with the racket.'

She leaned forward, her elbows resting on the grass beside him, her face close to his. 'Well, I wasn't in the best of humour myself,' she said. She swatted his face again with the dry stem.

'Gerroff!' he retorted, and made a grab for her. She struggled to escape, but he pulled her down towards him. Impulsively, he kissed her on the cheek, then on the mouth. For a moment he felt her respond, but then she pulled back.

'Donny, do you realise that if Consilia or any of the other nuns catch us here, I'll be expelled.'

'Yeh,' he joked. 'Sure you can always come down to St. Colman's. It's time we got a few girls there.'

'No, seriously, Donny.' He released her then.

'What time do you have to be back?' he asked.

'Two o' clock.'

He looked at his watch. The time was twenty to two. 'Ah, just take the rest of the day off,' he suggested, half jokingly.

Her eyes shone with the old spirit. 'Why don't we?'

'What? An' head off somewhere?'

'Yes,' she said, and he knew she was serious. The thought of Jaws' drawing class flashed into his mind, but he pushed it away.

'Right. Do you have to get anything ? A jacket?'

'I will,' she replied, getting to her feet. 'I'll only be a minute. And don't go away.'

'I won't.' In a rush of footsteps, she was gone.

Donny lay back on the grassy slope and stretched out his legs. He tightened up his stomach and shoulder muscles and then released them, feeling the tension draining out of his body. He felt contented, but excited too. He was glad he had come.

It wasn't long before he heard the thump of footsteps on the nearby turf again. When he got to his feet, Jacky was there, wearing a blue jacket, her face bright and flushed and her breathing quicker from the exertion.

'Great!' he said. 'Where'll we head for?'

'How about Battersea Park, London?' she suggested, smiling.

'Yeh,' he exclaimed enthusiastically. 'That'd be cool. What a place!' She started walking along the side of the hockey field that was sheltered by the shrubbery, and he fell into step beside her. 'But do you remember the whatchacallit — the roller coaster? It was mad!'

'Yes,' she joked. 'That was the one that you and Flag couldn't wait to get off, if I remember correctly.'

He grinned sheepishly. 'Yeh. I remember. You'd want to be a madman to go up in one of those, I'm telling you. Anyway, where'll we go? Seriously.'

'Let's go to Dun Laoghaire, or Killiney. It's a lovely day for the sea.'

'You're on.'

A short distance from the school, they caught a bus to Blackrock, and sat upstairs on the front seat of an almost deserted deck.

'Anyway,' said Jacky. 'I never got to tell you about the semi-final. That fellow Rocky Stewart is despicable. He *knew* I was there to see you, but he kept saying these awful things about your team.'

'Yeh, I know. He was trying to get at *me*, too.'

She was silent for a moment. 'Yes,' she said then. 'He did say some very nasty things about you. He's so *stupid*! I was delighted when you kicked the ball at him.'

'Where were you when I did that?'

'I couldn't stand him any more, so I had moved away. *And* I had to leave early and catch a bus back here, so that I'd be here when Mum arrived. That's why I wasn't there at the end, in case you were wondering.'

He allowed himself an ironic smile. 'Yeh. I was wondering — a bit. Fact is, I looked all over the gaff for you when the game was over. So I reckoned you were gone off for a spin in Bruce's big car.'

She stabbed him in the ribs with her elbow. 'I *could've* got a lift ... He *offered* me a lift right up to the school, I'll have you know. But Rocky was with him, so I declined the offer. Now look at the things I do for you, Donny O'Sullivan!'

'Yeh,' he said seriously. 'I can see them.'

'Now, tell me about this girl, Fiona.'

He shot her a quick glance. 'Do you still not believe me?' he demanded amiably.

'I *do*. But you've told me so little about everything. I want to know ... what's been happening in your life.'

'Right,' he said, with an exaggerated sigh. 'I'll start from the beginning.' And he did.

'Something should be done, Donny,' Jacky said, when he had told about Fiona in the hospital. She turned in her seat to look at him. 'I mean, if that man is really abusing her, she can't go home. Surely they wouldn't let her go back to that house.'

Donny shook his head. 'Naw. The social workers should be able to sort it out. They can get the cops onto it if something's really wrong. Flag says that your man could get jail.'

'Let me know what happens, won't you?'

'Yeh,' he promised. 'I'll give Swamp a shout later on.'

At Blackrock they boarded the Dart for Killiney. The sea to their left was shimmering and calm. The tracks hugged the sea shore all the way to Dalkey. When the train shot out from the Dalkey tunnel, they saw the long curving Killiney beach below them, stretching away towards the bulk of Bray Head, a solid mass between sea and sky.

'Oh, isn't it beautiful!' Jacky exclaimed.

From Killiney station, there was a flight of steps down onto the almost deserted beach. The waves lapped on the wet sand, with hardly a sound. They stepped down onto the pebbled shore, holding hands, while the gulls wheeled and called above them. By the water's edge, they strolled barefoot, their toes sinking into the cool oozy sand. Donny felt great. The uncertainty and questioning of the past few days had been lifted from him, and his heart was full for the graceful girl who walked so unselfconsciously beside him. Her hand was firm and warm in his. He would not doubt her again, he told himself.

At the north end of the beach, where the cliffs rose in benches to the railway high above, they found a small cove, bounded on three sides by granite walls, and overhung with gorse and last year's brambles. On the dry sand, honeyed by the afternoon sun, they sat, leaning back against the granite wall, content to be together, shut off from the world outside.

'Imagine if we were on that ship, Donny,' whispered Jacky. Far out, near the horizon, a long ship plodded slowly northwards.

'Yeh,' he joked. 'We'd probably be covered from head to toe with coal dust!'

'OK, smarty-pants. That plane, then.' She squinted upwards to where a silver plane, tiny with distance, was laying twin white tracks southwards across the blue. 'I wonder where it's going to.'

'London, probably.'

'If we were on it, we'd make it go wherever we wanted. We'd hi-jack it. And we'd tell the pilot to go to ...'

'I think London first,' he said. 'London was cool. We could

go back and see all the places where we were last summer.'

She laughed, and leaned against him. 'That'd be nice.'

He slid his arm around her waist, aware that the uniform made her seem much younger, but feeling also the warmth of her breast against his side.

''Course we'd have to call to see your Gran in Leatherhead,' he went on, enthused by the dream. 'She's cool.'

'You're saying that just because she likes you.'

'Well, that's more than I can say for your mother.' At the mention of the last word, reality came back to him with a bang. 'Speakin' of which, aren't you supposed to be at the school at four o'clock, for when she comes to collect you?'

'Yes.' He waited for her to say more. 'She can wait, for all I care.'

Donny looked at his watch. The time was twenty to four. Jaws would be just telling the rest of the lads to tidy up. He would no doubt be wondering where Donny was.

Jacky heaved a long sigh. 'All right, I'll go and phone her.'

She started to get to her feet, but he held her waist. With his other hand he touched her cheek and gently turned her face to him. He kissed her on the lips. 'Just before you go,' he said. 'I want to say that I'm glad I came over today.'

Her lips were soft on his mouth again. 'Me too,' she whispered. He turned her till she sat across his thighs, and cradled her shoulders in his left arm. Her closeness was like a drug. Her caress woke feelings in him that were strange and new and exciting. She clung to him, her breathing deep and vital. He buried his face in her hair, aware of the smoothness of her neck and shoulders.

'Maybe,' he said after a while, 'maybe we should go and make that call.'

Her hand on his neck clung tight for a second and then relaxed. She smiled and kissed him again.

'Maybe you're right,' she whispered.

Near the station they found a kiosk. Donny held the door and Jacky went in. 'Come in,' she said. He stood behind her, his arms protectively around her waist, as she plunked in the money and dialled. 'She could already be gone,' she said, as the distant ringing began. Donny half hoped that she would. Suddenly the ringing stopped and Donny, his ear close to Jacky's, heard her mother's voice saying the number.

'Mum,' said Jacky. 'It's me. Don't bother coming to collect me. I'll be home later.' Her tone was cool and distant.

'Oh, is there something on in the school?' Donny heard the mother say and tightened his arms around Jacky's waist.

'No. There's nothing. I'm not at the school. I'm in Killiney.'

Donny steeled himself. 'Killiney? What are you doing in Killiney?'

'I'm with Donny.' Silence at the other end. Jacky let the statement sink in. 'He told me about the telephone calls — when you said I was out.'

'Jacky ...'

'Mother, how could you *do* such a thing?!'

'Jacky ...'

'Just don't say anything!' Jacky's voice quivered with indignation. 'I'll see you later. Goodbye!' Slam! The phone came crashing down on the holder.

She turned to face him, her eyes bright with anger. 'If she's lucky,' she added with passion.

'You did great,' he said, kissing her on the forehead. 'What do you think she'll do now?'

'I don't care. She can call the police for all I care.'

'Right,' said Donny. 'Before we go, do you mind if I phone Orla, just to find out how Fiona's doing?'

'No. That'd be good. Please do.'

He phoned McIntyres' then, and got Orla. 'Hi, Orla. How's it going?'

'Donny? I'm grand. Where ...? Why are you calling?' she asked bluntly.

'I was just wonderin' how Fiona is, so I thought I'd give you a shout.'

'Fiona's ... OK. They're keeping her in for another day. She wants to go to the game tomorrow, but they won't let her.'

'But what about her mother?'

The social worker's goin' to talk to her this evenin'. Me Ma was talking to her this mornin'.'

'OK, that's good. I'll try to drop in later ...'

'No, Donny. The doctor said not to.'

'What do you mean? Nobody's to call to see her?'

Another pause. 'No, Donny. Just you ...'

Anger flared in him. 'Me!? What do you mean, me!? Is she trying to ...? Are *you* trying to blame this whole thing ...?'

'No, Donny! No! We're not! It's just that the doctor told me to ask you not to visit her for a while. She's going to get in touch with you. I think she wants to talk to you.'

'Who? Fiona?'

'No, the psychiatrist.'

'What about?'

'I dunno, Donny. About Fiona, I suppose. Donny, nobody's blamin' you about what happened. It's just that Fiona likes you, an' the doctor thinks that maybe you can help her.'

'Lookit, Orla. You know that other things happened to her.'

'Yes, I know, Donny. That's what's really bothering her. But the social worker's goin' to do something about that. She's goin' to try an' find someplace else for her to stay.'

'Yeh. Well, I'll see you later, then. OK?'

'OK, Donny. And Donny, good luck with the game tomorrow. I'll hardly be there if Fee can't come.'

'OK,' he said grudgingly. 'An' thanks.'

When he put the phone down, Donny was annoyed and upset.

'What?' asked Jacky. 'What did she say?'

'She said that I'm not to go to see Fiona. The *psychiatrist* said it, an' that she wants to talk to me.'

'But it wasn't your fault, Donny. She has no right to ...'

'I know that. But you can see what people would think. And you know how they talk. They'll be sayin' that I was messin' with her.' The bad feeling started to come back, and Donny leaned back against the glass wall of the kiosk. He sighed. 'I just wish it never happened.'

Jacky's eyes were huge as she looked at him. 'Donny? What you told me about Fiona, is it the truth?

He stared back, pained by her doubt. 'I swear to God, Jacky ...!'

She stopped him with her fingers on his mouth. 'I believe you, Donny,' she whispered. 'I'm sorry. I just had to ask. I believe you.' She leaned against him and put her arms around his waist. Her blond hairs brushed against his chin as she rested her head on his chest. 'Don't worry about it, Donny. It'll turn out OK. You'll see.'

He encircled her with his arms, but the cloud on his mind stayed. 'Maybe,' he said. They stayed there, holding on, for a long moment.

'What's going to happen when *you* get home?' he said then.

'To *me*?' she asked in surprise. 'Nothing. She knows she was wrong, that's all there is to it.'

'Yeh, but staying out like this? Won't there be a kick-up?'

'Not when Dad finds out about it. He'll be on my side. He likes you, you know.' When he didn't respond, she looked up at him, her arms tightening around him. 'Don't you know that?'

He remembered his last conversation with her dad. He had been friendly. 'Yeh, maybe,' he reluctantly agreed.

'What about you, Donny? Will you be in trouble?'

He shook his head. 'At home, no. But at school ...' He was remembering Jaws' class that he had just missed. She squeezed his waist again, and her eyes were full of cheerful optimism. 'Naw,' he said. 'School'll be OK. I'll just get a note from Maeve. No sweat.'

She smiled up at him, the old smile that he remembered so well. He bent his head and kissed her on the lips. A warm feeling flowed through him. He felt her response, more urgent now, her breathing faster.

An insistent knocking against the glass wall of the kiosk brought Donny back to reality. Outside stood a red-faced man, his grey hair all awry on his balding pate. 'Are youse goin' to stay snoggin' in there all day?' he demanded. 'There's a whole bleedin' beach an' a whole bleedin' hill beside ye. Why can't ye go an'...'

'OK,' Donny called through the glass. 'Keep your shirt on.' He pushed backwards out of the kiosk, holding Jacky's hand.

The red-faced man caught the door.

'Thank you!' he said sarcastically.

'No bother,' replied Donny, trying not to laugh. 'Right,' he said to Jacky, in a voice loud enough for the man to hear, 'is it the bleedin' beach or the bleedin' hill?'

Her smile was half amused, half embarrassed. 'Let's climb the bleedin' hill,' she suggested.

The climb to the top of the hill took them first along narrow, tree-lined roads that sloped steeply upwards. Then they reached a gateway in a low granite wall, through which they saw a narrow path rising amid ferns and bracken. As they climbed, the figures on the beach below them became smaller and smaller.

'Wow!' exclaimed Jacky, when they reached the summit. The view was panoramic. Northwards, Dublin Bay swept in a great curve from Dalkey Island to the distant hazy mass of Howth Head. The slim chimneys of the Pigeon House power station stood like sentinels at the entrance to Dublin Port. Westwards lay the city itself, shimmering in the late afternoon haze.

'Dublin's fair city!' Donny exclaimed. 'It doesn't look so great from here.'

'It's better this way,' Jacky said, turning to look southwards towards Bray Head and the Sugarloaf there, and beyond them, the ranges of the Wicklow Mountains.

'Yeh,' said Donny. 'Just looking at them would kind of put a longing on you ...'

'For what, Donny?'

'Oh, just to get away. To travel. See strange places that you've never seen before.'

She sighed and leaned closer to him. 'Do you not like Dublin, Donny?'

'It's OK. But there's so much to see out there.' The sweep of his arm took in the sea and the distant mountains.

They sat together on the grass facing the sea. Below them the thin white curves of breaking foam on the beach made the sound of distant whispering.

'Donny,' said Jacky, after a while, 'what are you going to do next year?'

He looked down at her, puzzled by the question. 'Well, I'm going to head for Timbuktoo, and when I'm finished there I'll buy a camel and ...'

'No, seriously, Donny.'

He was silent for a moment. 'On second thoughts, I might stay around for a year or two till Stephen grows a bit bigger, or until Maeve meets some bloke that'll be good to her and look after her. She deserves it, anyway.'

'Yes, but what are you going to *do*?'

'Well, I'm going to play loads of football, probably go to a few concerts at the Point ...'

'No, you silly. I mean work, or college.'

'I dunno. It depends on a lot of things.'

'You know you can get grants for going to college?'

'D'you know who you're beginning to sound like?' he retorted. 'Your mother!'

'Yes, I know,' she conceded. 'But I'm not thinking of mother's stupid reasons. I think you *should* go to college. You might be sorry later, if you don't give it a try.'

'Yeh. I chatted with Maeve about it last week. She wants me to go, even though she hasn't got a spare tosser to her name. So I went an' had a chat with old Corcoran — he's our Careers teacher — an' he's going to get the forms for me.'

'It would be nice if we were both in college. Then we could meet as often as we liked.'

'Instead of once every six months, like it is at the moment,' he remarked wryly.

'We'll meet more often from now on, Donny. I promise.'

'Yeh,' he said, wanting to believe it was true. 'But it's not going to be easy.'

'Don't say that, Donny. It'll be OK. Don't mind Mum. She'll have to get over her stupid ideas.'

He took the long strands of her hair in his hand and let them spill back against her shoulder. 'Yeh, I know. But it makes things that bit harder — you know — for me calling up, and for us going places.'

'But we *can* go places,' she insisted. 'There's lots of places ..!'

'Yeh, like that disco?' He hadn't intended the remark to sound so bitter.

'No, Donny.' She turned to face him now. 'Forget about that! That was just stupid. Even Dad said so. He said you were right to get up and leave that night. I was just a bit upset that it wasn't working out better.'

'Yeh,' he said. 'But let's face it. We're different. I'm different ... from you. We come from different places, from different worlds.'

'But, Donny, I *know* you're different. You're not like those others at the club. You're kind and ... and brave, and you're not always pretending to be what you're not, like them. Even Bruce — he's a terrible snob, although when I'm with him, he's mostly OK, 'cause he knows that I'm not impressed with all that rubbish.' She paused, searching his eyes for a response. 'You *are* different, Donny, but that's why ... that's why I want to know you.' She caught his fingers and squeezed them hard, her wide eyes forcing him to look into them. 'That's what you want too, isn't it, Donny?' The question was serious and searching.

He nodded. 'Yeh. 'Course it is.' He held her gaze, looking deep into the translucent depths of her eyes.

'You're sure?'

He had never been surer of anything in his life. He drew her nearer to him. Her face was below his, her eyes still searching. He bent to kiss her. 'I'm sure,' he said huskily. He kissed her lips, her closed eyes, her hair, her cheek.

'I'm sure,' he repeated.

15

'Donny, do you know what I think we should do?' It was over an hour later and the westering sun was tipping the horizon, scattering a brilliant orange-and-red glow across the sky. The friends were sauntering downwards toward the station again.

'No, what?'

'I think we should go home — to my house, that is, and talk to them.'

He looked at her, startled. 'Are you serious?'

'We have to do it sometime, Donny. So we might as well do it now. As well as that, I don't want Dad to be worried about me. It's not his problem.'

'But what are we going to *say*?'

'Just say what we think — what we want.'

He thought about that. 'An' what do we want? I mean, what exactly?'

'Well, we can't have *everything* that we want, but at least we want to be able to meet whenever we'd like to. And you should be able to talk to me on the phone whenever you ring.'

'Yeh,' he agreed, but his heart was quailing at the thought of the proposed meeting.

She looked at him, sensing his hesitancy. 'That is, if you want to, Donny.'

'I *want* to, but the idea scares the shit out of me.'

She caught his hand and squeezed it. 'It won't be too bad,

Donny. Remember, Dad is on our side.'

He knew then that he had to do it. It was the test and he had to go through with it. 'Right,' he decided. 'Let's go and get it over with.'

The last traces of day were lingering in the sky when Donny and Jacky at last dismounted from the Number 18 bus and began to walk the half mile of pavement that separated them from Jacky's house. Although it was tainted a little by the thought of the ordeal to come, Donny had already stored this day into the inner sanctuary of his mind, where it would remain a treasured memory. His only regret was that he hadn't taken his courage in his hands and come on a lunch-hour visit to Jacky before this.

'So, what's the plan?' he asked.

'I think, if they're both at home, that we should talk to them together. OK?'

'That's cool,' he replied, although he felt far from cool himself. He started to think about what he might say, but the thoughts filled him with so much anxiety, that he pushed them out of his mind. He would play it by ear, he decided. It had always worked before.

There was a light in the hallway of the house when they reached it, and the Volvo and Toyota were parked in the drive. Donny tried to manufacture some saliva in his mouth as Jacky inserted her key in the door and pushed it open. Impetuously, she reached up and kissed him on the cheek. 'Remember, I love you,' she whispered.

There was a sound from somewhere inside. Then a door opened towards the back of the hallway, and Mr Anderson came out.

'Jacky!' he said. Donny thought he sensed relief in the voice. 'Donny! You're welcome. Come in.' The big man shook Donny's hand vigorously. Then he opened the sitting-room door, switched on the light and stood back to let them enter.

'Hi, Dad,' Jacky said softly. 'I suppose you heard?' Her father nodded, his face serious, but not grim. 'Where's Mum?'

He tilted his head towards the kitchen. 'In there,' he said. 'She's been worrying about you.'

At that moment, Jacky's mother appeared from the lighted doorway behind her husband. She seemed even more elegant than Donny remembered her. 'Jacky!' she cried. 'Oh, thank God you're back safely! We've been so worried about you!'

Jacky stared at her mother unmoved. 'You knew where we were,' she said coldly. 'There was no need for you to be worried. I was with Donny the whole time.'

Mrs Anderson's face coloured a little. 'Yes, but ...' She couldn't ignore Donny's presence any longer. 'Donny! Thank you for taking her home safely,' she said, her eyes strangely uncomfortable. 'She's never done anything like this before.'

'No sweat,' said Donny. 'It wasn't too difficult.' The sarcasm slipped out, despite his good intentions. He really felt like saying, ''Cos we ran out of drugs an' condoms.' But he restrained himself.

'Well,' Jacky fired back. '*You've* never done anything like this before, *either*! I just can't believe that you could *do* such a thing! How could you tell Donny that I was out when I was in the house all the time!'

'Listen,' interrupted Mr Anderson, trying to calm the waters. 'Why don't we sit down and chat about it, eh?' He indicated the soft padded chairs in the sitting room.

Donny went in and seated himself at the end of the plush couch that dominated the back of the room.

'No, Jacky dear,' said Mrs Anderson, sitting on the edge of a higher chair by the fire place. 'It's not what you think at all. Of course I wouldn't do that. It's just that you were studying at the time, and I didn't want to disturb you. I meant to tell you, and it just went out of ...'

'Mum! Donny rang at least *three* times, and each time you said I wasn't in. All you had to do was *tell* me.'

The woman tried hard to keep her composure. 'Jacky, dear. I'm sorry. I ... I was only thinking of your welfare ... I mean, of your studies.' She looked at her husband for support, but he just stared impassively at Jacky. Again, she was forced to look at Donny. 'Donny, I'm sorry,' she said simply. 'It was silly of me. I hope you'll forgive me.'

Donny could see how difficult it was for her. Her embarrassment made him uncomfortable, but he wasn't going to let her off too easily. He waited. 'It's OK. No sweat,' he said then.

He looked at Jacky. She flashed him a glimmer of a smile, a glint of triumph.

Mr Anderson spoke. 'I vote we all have a cup of tea, and a muffin.'

'Yes,' agreed his wife expansively. 'What a nice idea. I'll go and put the kettle on.' She rose from her seat and fled into the kitchen.

Half an hour later, when Donny was ready to go home, Jacky saw him to the door. He stepped out into the cool night air and she followed him. 'Well,' he said. 'What'cha think?'

'I think you can phone me any time you want to now,' she said, smiling.

'Yeh. I think so,' he replied. 'You did good.'

She stepped close to him. 'Good luck on Wednesday.' She reached up and kissed him. 'I'll see you there.'

'After the game?'

'*At* the game. You'll have a job getting rid of me on Wednesday,' she said with spirit. 'Win, lose or draw.'

When he got home, Donny found Maeve waiting for him in the living room. 'Well,' she said with exaggerated emphasis. 'Where have you been? Or should I say, what have you been up to?'

'Ah, me an' Jacky decided we're going to get a flat an' live together,' he said carelessly, as he hung his jacket on a chair.

'You *what*?'

He grinned. 'It's OK. Don't get your knickers in a twist. I was only kidding. Listen, is there any grub? I'm starving.'

Over the meal, he gave her a brief account of the day's exploits, concluding with his visit to Jacky's house.

When he finished, he found Maeve regarding him with mock severity. 'You're a right chancer. But it's no harm that that woman was put in her place. She's a bit too stuck up for my liking.'

'Anyway, I'll need a note for tomorrow,' he said then.

She lifted her eyebrows. '*Another* concoction? What am I supposed to say this time? That you were sick?'

'Naw, I was in school this morning. They mightn't go for it. Just say I was at the dentist again. It always works.'

She shook her head in disapproval. 'One of these days, you're going to be caught out badly. And I won't be a bit sorry for you. Go on, then. Get me the writing pad.'

16

It was after the second class next morning, that a Second Year boy told Donny that Bill Moloney wanted to see him. During the mid-morning break, therefore, he went down towards the staff room in search of his form tutor.

Bill had that familiar semi-apologetic expression on his face when he came out into the foyer in answer to Donny's query.

'It's about that note, Donny. The one about the dentist. I'm afraid the year head isn't too happy about it. He seems to think that you used the same excuse recently and that you didn't go to the dentist at all.'

'I thought all I had to do is bring in a note from Maeve. She's my guardian, an' if it's OK with her, then ...'

The teacher nodded. 'Yes, Donny. That's the theory. The practice, I'm afraid, is that Brother Sharkey wants the name of the dentist you went to.'

'Why's that?'

'He just wants to check out your story.' The teacher paused when he saw the expression on Donny's face. 'Is there a problem with that, Donny?'

'Yeh, Mr Moloney. There is! Why can't that man just leave me alone? He's always on my case. He makes a hobby out of picking on me!'

The teacher nodded. 'I know, Donny. But you know the man in question. The easiest thing for you to do, is to give him the name of the dentist.'

Donny decided to tell Bill Moloney the truth. 'There was no dentist, sir. I went out to Mount St. Oliver's to see Jacky.'

'Ah, I see. A romantic rendezvous.' The other pursed his lips thoughtfully. He knew about Donny's long-standing relationship with Jacky. He had met her and he liked her. 'That puts a different complexion on it. I don't know what you're going to do, so.'

'Listen, Mr Moloney. Just tell him that I'll get that information for him tomorrow. I'd prefer not to deal with it today on account of the practice this evening and the game tomorrow. After that, I don't really care.'

Bill Moloney's expression was doubtful. 'I'll do my best, Donny. But you know him, when he gets an idea into his head. The best thing for you to do is to keep out of his way for the rest of the day. Right? Now don't be late for class.'

Donny took Bill Moloney's advice. On his way to French class, he did a detour to avoid passing Brother Sharkey's room. When French was over, he appointed Flagon as vanguard and Swamp as rearguard while he made his way cautiously to the Physics Lab. Then, just three minutes before the lunch bell, when Donny had already packed away his Science books and was mentally reviewing the contents of the rickety fridge in his kitchen at home, there was a peremptory knock on the Lab door, and the forbidding features of the Jaws appeared. He nodded towards Mr Conway, the Science teacher. 'Is O'Sullivan here?' he snapped, his black eyes traversing the class.

Donny, at the back, muttered, 'The name's Donny,' but not so loud as to be heard. He glanced at Flagon, sitting on his right. He heard Conway say, 'Yes, he's here,' and then the call, 'Donny?'

'Keep the cool, Don,' urged Flagon in a whisper. 'Don't let him get to you. He's bleedin' dangerous.'

'Yeh,' Donny answered aloud. 'Here.'

Jaws looked at him and said, 'Out here,' his head jerking in the direction of the corridor. The class went silent as Donny picked up his bag and walked out through the open door. He closed it after him, and turned to face the black eyes of the Brother.

'That note you gave to Mr Moloney this morning ... about the dentist — who wrote it?' said Jaws, his tone hard and grating.

Donny returned his gaze steadily. 'My sister, Brother,' he said coolly.

'I don't believe she wrote it.'

'She did, Brother. You can ring her if you don't believe me. Her number is two, eight ...'

'Never mind about that,' Jaws snapped. 'Where's the dentist?'

Donny remembered visiting a dentist years before somewhere in Kimmage. 'Kimmage,' he said.

A glimmer of triumph flashed in the Brother's eyes. 'You told me last week the dentist was in Ranelagh!'

'Yeh. Well, I went to a different one yesterday,' said Donny.

'What's the address?'

'I don't know. I just know where it is and I go there.'

'Well, what's the name of the dentist, then?'

Donny could see the vein on the Brother's neck beginning to bulge and the colour of his face deepen. He gazed out through the window of the corridor, as if trying to remember, and just then the rhythmic chime of the lunch bell started to ring. 'Can't remember,' he said. The corridor was suddenly full of noise as the doors burst open and the bodies swept out. Donny put on a frown of concentration and said, 'I think it started with M. Or was it P?' He looked blankly at the Brother again, spread his hands wide and said, 'It just won't come to me.' Over Jaws' left shoulder he saw the stationary figures of Flagon and Swamp looking in his direction. But he knew the man was angry and he tried to keep his eyes focused on his face.

'OK, you smart aleck,' said Jaws. 'While you're at home for your lunch, you look up the directory and get me the name of that dentist and bring it to me before two o'clock. Do you understand me, O'Sullivan?'

Donny tried hard to keep the anger from showing in his voice. 'Yes, *Brother*,' he said. Then he turned and walked away.

'What're you goin' to do?' Swamp asked, when Donny had

angrily related the incident to his friends.

The question irritated Donny. 'I dunno what I'm going to do,' he said shortly, picking up his bag and heading for the door.

The others were silent as they followed him out through the gates of the school into the warm noon light.

'Yeh, well, you'll have to tell him *something*,' Flagon said then. 'You know him. The next thing is he'll have you in detention after school.'

'He will an' his arse!' vowed Donny.

'Why don't you tell him the truth?' suggested Swamp.

'Are you crazy, Swampy?' Flagon demanded. 'An' him already after sayin' that he was at the dentist? He'd have him up for lying to a teacher. You'd be playin' right into his hands. You couldn't say that.'

'Well, then, the only thing to do is to find a dentist in Kimmage, ring up the receptionist, tell her the story with a lot of sob thrown in, an' get her to say you *were* there yesterday.' Swamp spread his hands wide. 'Simple,' he said.

Donny stared at him for a moment. 'Yeah, Swampy,' he said then. 'That's not a bad idea at all.'

They went straight to the telephone kiosk. In the tattered Golden Pages they found three dentists in the Kimmage area. Donny dialled the first number, while the others looked on through the open doorway of the kiosk.

'Hello,' said Donny, when a woman's voice answered the phone. 'I have this problem, you see.'

'Do you want an appointment?' she asked curtly.

'Well, yes. In a way. But ... '

'We're booked up till next Thursday ... '

'No, hang on. I need an appointment for yesterday. The thing is ... '

'Yesterday? Is this some kind of a joke?' The voice was cold now, suspicious.

'No. You see, I was *supposed* to go to the dentist yesterday, but I didn't make it. I mean I didn't get an appointment. But there's this teacher in school that *thinks* I was there yesterday, but I wasn't, you see. I was somewhere else.'

'Really?' said the cold voice at the other end.

Donny pushed on. 'An' he's going to ring you up to check whether I was there or not. So I was just wonderin' if you might *say* I was there yesterday ... even though I wasn't.'

There was silence at the other end. Then the voice said, 'Am I to understand that you want me to say you were here for an appointment yesterday, even though you weren't here, and even though you didn't have an appointment ...?'

'Yeh. You see, I'll get into trouble ... '

'I'm sorry, sir,' the frozen voice cut in. 'We treat dental conditions here. We do not provide an alibi service for boys who are mitching from school. Good afternoon.' Click! The phone went dead.

'You lousy, rotten, miserable, uncooperative bitch!' Donny shouted into the mouthpiece. 'It wouldn't have bleedin' killed you!' And he slammed down the phone in disgust.

'OK,' said Swamp. 'Let's try the next one.'

'No. I'm not doing any more!' Donny stated. 'It's poxy!'

'OK. Let me try,' said Swamp, taking up the phone.

'No,' Donny protested.

'Just one try,' pleaded Swamp. 'It can't do any harm. OK?'

Swamp put in the coin and dialled. Flagon and Donny watched sceptically. 'Hello,' said Swamp after a moment. 'My name is Paul Marsh, and I have this very good friend that's in a spot of bother.' There was something weird about Swamp's accent. A pause.

'No, he hasn't a toothache. It's just that he had to leave school yesterday on a very private and personal matter, and — well, he has to explain his absence to this very unsympathetic teacher, and he was ... well, I was wondering if you could possibly be so kind as to help him out.' Another pause, longer this time. 'Well, no. If he could say that he had an appointment with the dentist yesterday ... ' Donny and Flagon heard a garble of words spoken in a raised tone, then Swamp's polite reply. 'Excuse me! I've never heard such rude language in my life ...' The others heard the phone clicking at the other end. Then Swamp shouted, 'Ya frosty-faced oul' biddy!' as he brandished the phone in front of his face. He shook his head in disbelief. 'I dunno. Women! They usen't be able to curse at all. Now they're worse than us.'

'What did she say to you, Swampy?' Flagon enquired.

'She told me to eff off,' said his friend drily. 'An' she was only a young wan.'

The other two looked at Donny now. 'It's a waste of time,' he said. 'We'll just have to ... Hold on. I just remembered something. Maeve works in Kimmage.'

They stared at him blankly. 'So?' they both said in unison.

'Listen! All we need is a telephone number in Kimmage and someone at the other end that will say, "Yeh, this is a dentist's surgery" and "Yeh, Donny O'Sullivan was here yesterday".' They stared at him, still not understanding. He laughed at them. 'Maeve'll do it!' he announced. 'Simple! She works in an estate agent's. She's by a phone all day, and she's the only secretary there, so she *has* to answer the phone.'

He waited for their reaction. It was guarded. 'Yeh, but what if he cops it?' Swamp demanded. 'He mightn't be that stupid, just to take your word for it that the name and number you give him are right.'

'Yeh,' added Flagon. 'An' will Maeve go along with it?'

'Course she will,' Donny argued. 'She *has* to. 'Cos she wrote the note in the first place, and if she doesn't I'm rightly up shit creek! I can't go an' tell him I was lying. He'd *really* sow it into me then. The way *he* is, it'd be a suspension, an' he'd probably insist on me doing it during the game tomorrow.'

'Nah, he couldn't do that,' scoffed Swamp.

'He could, too!' retorted Flagon. 'Remember Henno, a couple of years ago. He was suspended, an' they didn't let him play on the cup team. It'd be just like the bastard to pull a trick like that.'

'Listen, guys,' said Donny. 'I don't care what he does, as long as it's after the game tomorrow. All I have to do is keep him off my back till the game is over, and then he can do what he likes.'

'Supposin' it's a draw tomorrow, an' there's a replay?' said Flagon, the devil's advocate.

Donny grimaced. 'Shit! I never thought of that.' Then he shook his head. 'No way, Flag! We're going to win tomorrow.

Nothing surer.'

'Lookit, Don,' said Swamp. 'Is it not possible to keep out of his way till after the game tomorrow?'

'Yeh,' Donny retorted. 'Go on the hop! That's the only way. 'Cos knowing him, he'll be waiting for me inside the school door.'

'Yeh,' smirked Flagon. 'You could always get a note from Maeve sayin' you were at the dentist!'

Donny fished a twenty-pence piece from his pocket. 'I'm going to ring Maeve,' he announced. 'It's the only way.'

But when he rang Cooney's Estate Agency, a man's voice told him politely that Ms. O'Sullivan was on her lunch break, and she wouldn't be back till two o'clock. 'Shit!' said Donny.

'Where does she go for her lunch?' asked Swamp.

'Haven't a clue. I'll only have to leave it till a few minutes before two, and hope she's back early. C'mon, lads. Let's go an' have some lunch.'

It was five to two when the three friends met again at the kiosk. Donny dialled Cooney's number. 'No, she's not back yet,' he was told.

'You go ahead, guys,' he said. 'I'll hang on. She's bound to be back any second.'

Reluctantly, they turned towards the school. But Swamp gave some parting advice. 'Whatever you do, Don, don't antagonise him. Keep the cool. An' don't forget, plenty of "Yes, Brother Sharkey" and "No, Brother Sharkey" ...'

'An' "Kiss me arse, Brother Sharkey",' added Flagon sourly.

'Just be careful, Don. I'm telling you, he's bleedin' dangerous.'

'Right, guys, see you in a few minutes,' said Donny, and he popped another coin into the box.

Donny's watch showed twenty seconds before two o'clock, when the phone beside him suddenly jangled to life. He had left the number with the man in Cooney's office with instructions to tell Maeve that she must phone her brother urgently.

'Listen,' he said, in answer to her puzzled greeting. 'Can you to do me a favour?' He explained his difficulty and his plan. At first, she positively refused to cooperate, but when he reminded her about the game on the following day, and what had happened to the unfortunate Henno, she reluctantly agreed. 'This is the *last* time I'm *ever* going to lie for you, Donny!' she vowed.

'You're a pal!' he said. 'I'll babysit every night next week. But I have to go now. I'm late as it is.'

The long corridors of the school were deserted when Donny loped in by the side door, several minutes later. There was no sign of Jaws. He thought about going to the staffroom and asking for him, but decided instead to take the easier course. He bounded up the terracotta stairs, taking three steps at a time. He needn't have worried. When he turned onto the corridor where his class was, there was the black figure waiting outside the door.

'Well,' he growled, 'did you find the name?' His tongue made a sucking sound against his teeth.

Donny oozed sincerity. 'Yes, Brother,' he said. 'The dentist's name is Cooney and the number is nine, two, one, eight, six, six. Here, I've written it down.' He handed the Brother a scrap of paper torn from his English copy. 'An' I'm sorry about not having it earlier. It just went out of my head.'

The black eyes stared at him and Donny felt the tension grip him inside, but he forced himself to hold his ground and stare back into them. Then, when he felt sure that he would have to look away, the Brother looked down at the piece of paper.

'Cooney?' he repeated slowly. 'Cooney? Never heard of a dentist in Kimmage called Cooney. Must be new. Well, we'll see.' The cold eyes once again glared at Donny. 'Go on to class.'

Donny was relieved to get inside the classroom and close the door. He made his excuse to Old Conway and went to his desk. He knew Flagon and Swamp were staring at him, and when the coast was clear he gave them the thumbs up. 'It's cool,' he whispered. Their relief was obvious.

When the class ended, Flagon and Swamp crowded round him, expectation in their faces. He told them what had happened.

'Is he going to ring?' asked Flagon.

'He didn't say. But as soon as school is over I'm going to call Maeve an' find out.'

'We'll be with you, Don,' Swamp promised.

But Donny never had a chance to make that phone call. The four o'clock bell had just gone, and Donny was heading for the public phone outside the staff room, when he heard his name being called behind him in the crowded corridor. He recognised the harsh tone immediately, and his heart sank. 'Hang on a sec,' he said to Swamp, who was trailing him to the phone. He turned to see Jaws' burly figure approaching him. There was something ominous about the cast of his face. Under his left arm, he carried what appeared to be a telephone directory. As he got nearer, Donny became aware of the gleam in the Brother's eye.

'You thought you'd get away with it, didn't you?' snapped Jaws.

Donny affected surprise. 'What do you mean, Brother?' He saw the flash of anger in the other's face.

Jaws brandished the directory in front of Donny's face. 'Dentist!' he sneered. 'That's the first time I ever heard of an estate agent pulling teeth.'

Donny knew the game was up. He started to change tack, allowing the hint of a sheepish grin to creep into his face.

'This is no laughing matter!' roared Jaws. He made a sudden lunge towards Donny, but pulled up before contact was made. Donny was aware of the curious glances of the few stragglers in the corridor.

'I'm not laughing, Brother,' he said evenly. 'And I'm sorry I didn't tell you the truth. But my sister knew where I was yesterday, and it was OK by her ...'

'If your sister knew, O'Sullivan, she wouldn't have told a pack of lies, would she?' The ruddy face was close to his now, and Donny could smell the rancid breath.

Donny reddened. 'It was my fault, Brother. I asked her to write what she wrote.'

'You're a liar, O'Sullivan,' sneered the other. 'And I'm going to show you how we deal with liars here. Get down to the detention room.'

The corridor was empty now. Donny chose his words carefully.

'Brother, I know I shouldn't have lied, and I am prepared to do a detention on Thursday or Friday, but we have the last training session now, and Mr Eastwood wants us all to be there.'

A cold smile was spreading at the corner of the Brother's lips, and his head began to nod slowly. 'You should have thought about that before you lied, shouldn't you. They'll just have to get on without you this evening. And it won't be too hard, because you are useless! You were never any good, and you never *will* be any good. Now get down to the detention room!'

Donny felt the hurt and the anger welling inside him. 'That's not true,' he said, standing his ground. 'And it's not fair. If I don't go to the practice, Mr Eastwood will drop me from the squad.'

'Listen!' demanded Jaws, his voice rising to a shout. 'Are you going to go down ...?'

Now Donny was shouting too. 'This is what you've always wanted, isn't it? You were always picking on me! For the last three years, every chance you got ...'

The boiling anger in the Brother's face made him step back, but he kept shouting. 'I want to see the principal! I want to see Brother O'Connor! I have a right to ...!'

Suddenly, out of nowhere, Jaws' fist came swinging. It caught Donny high along the left cheek bone and flung him back against the wall. Then, to his surprise, he was lying on the ground, the tiles cold on his cheek. Dazed, he lifted his head, shaking it to clear the fuzziness, but keeping his arm across his head in case of another attack. Somewhere along the corridor, he thought he heard Swamp's voice. He looked for the Brother's feet and they were there, a yard from his head. He heard Swamp's voice again. 'Don't, Brother!' it said. 'Don't hit him again. It's not fair!'

The Brother's feet turned away from Donny. 'Get out, Marsh!' he roared. 'Get out of this building at once!'

'No, Brother,' said Swamp quietly. Donny, now struggling to his feet, saw Swamp advancing towards Jaws, his eyes huge behind the thick lenses of his glasses. 'I saw what happened,' Swamp went on. Then his voice lifted a tone. 'I saw you punching Donny, Brother.'

The Brother took a step in Swamp's direction. 'Are you going to get out, Marsh?' he shouted again.

Swamp halted, but stood his ground. Then he said slowly and clearly and with menace, 'I was a witness, Brother.'

Jaws stood like a wounded buffalo, glaring at Swamp. Then he made a lunge in his direction. But just when Donny thought that Swamp was going to be battered to the ground, the Brother rushed past him along the corridor. 'You two will be sorry!' he shouted back over his shoulder. 'You'll be sorry.'

When the hurrying steps had merged with the distant sounds of the building, Swamp spoke. 'How is it, Don? He gave you a right one there.'

Donny felt his cheek. It was puffing out already. 'I'm not bad, Swampy. But I'll have to get something onto this or the eye will shut up altogether.'

'C'mon,' said Swamp. 'There's an ice pack in the fridge in the Lab. I'll get the keys from the cleaners.'

Several minutes later, the friends were sitting on a bench outside the Lab. Donny held the stinging ice pack to his face.

'Ah, shit!' he said. 'I can't believe this.'

'Wha', that he took a swing at you, the bastard?'

'Nah, that I didn't see it coming and duck.'

'Maybe it's as well that you didn't,' replied Swamp thoughtfully. 'This could be the biggest mistake the man ever made.'

'Lookit, Swampy. I'll have to go to the practice. Clint'll have a seizure if I don't, an' as well as that, he'll probably drop me from the team.'

'Hang on, Don. You're in no condition to go anywhere. Except to old Boc's office.'

'Yeh. What use would that be?'

'He's the principal, isn't he? Lookit, Don. You've just been assaulted by one of his teachers. That's illegal! It's against the law! It's a case for the courts. You *have* to go an' tell him. You'll never get the chance again to get that bastard back for all the grief he's laid on you. You just *have* to go, Don. You can go out to the practice after that. Clint'll understand.'

'Yeh, but what if Jaws is down there already, covering his ass?'

'So what? That'd be the best reason *I* can think of for you being there, before he spins a pack of lies.'

Donny pressed the ice to his cheek thoughtfully. 'Right,' he decided. 'We'll go.'

There was a light showing under the door of Brother O'Connor's office when they arrived there. Donny knocked tentatively, taking the ice pack down from his face. They heard a muffled, 'Come in' from within, and Donny turned the handle and pushed open the door. The principal, alone in his cluttered office, looked up from his desk.

'Excuse me, Brother,' said Donny. 'Can I ... can we talk to you?'

'Donny? Paul? Come in,' said the Brother, pushing his papers back from him. He looked more closely at Donny's face. 'What happened *you*?'

'I just got punched in the face, Brother.'

The skin on the principal's forehead suddenly became corrugated. 'Punched,' he repeated, making a clicking sound with his tongue. 'What uncouth youth would do such a thing? Sit down, boys.' His hand indicated the chairs standing against the right-hand wall. 'And tell me about it.'

Donny backed towards a chair. 'It wasn't a student, Brother. It was Brother Sharkey.'

The principal's eyes looked at him now as if they were seeing him for the first time. 'Brother Sharkey,' he repeated, his glance now switching to Swamp. Swamp nodded his head.

'Yes, Brother,' said Donny.

Swamp felt the need to explain his presence. 'I was there. I saw it happen.'

Brother O'Connor, took a deep breath and leaned back in his chair. 'Do you want to tell me about it, Donny?'

Donny did, and he started from the beginning, with the note he had presented to Mr Moloney. He explained where he'd actually been the previous day, and why he felt it was necessary to say he had been at the dentist. He said he'd apologised to Brother Sharkey, and that he had made the reasonable request to have the detention deferred till Thursday or Friday because of the practice after school. When he was finished the Brother was silent, studying Donny's face with a thoughtful expression.

'There's no need for me to remind you what the consequences will be for you both, if I find out that what you've just told me is not true,' he said then, emphasising his words by holding the index finger of his right hand stiffly in front of his face. 'But if you're telling me the truth, and I think you are, I'm sure both of you are intelligent enough to know that this is a serious matter. You do understand, however, that I'll have to get the other side of the story from Brother Sharkey. It seems clear that you have had some injury to your face, Donny, and I'm sorry about that. I hope it won't interfere with your chances of playing in the final tomorrow. In the meantime, it would be well for you to go out to see Mr Eastwood as soon as possible, and explain that I detained you.' Now he leaned forward over the desk. 'I think you will understand if I ask you not to speak about this incident until I have had a chance to speak to the man in question.' The lines on his face softened a little as he waited for an answer.

Swamp spoke. 'There's just one thing I'd like to say, Brother. Brother Sharkey's been pickin' on Don here, for ages now. Every chance he gets he hops on him ...'

The principal held up a restraining hand. 'That may be so, Paul. And if it's true, it'll come out in the wash. I think it would be in order for me to say that the Brother in question is a fine teacher, but that he is suffering from a little stress at the moment. I'm not trying to excuse what has happened. I'm just asking you to keep it in mind, OK?'

'Fair enough,' said Donny, rising from his chair.

'I'll be in touch with you tomorrow.'

'Sufferin' from a little *stress*!' exclaimed Swamp, as he and Donny walked away from the office. 'The man's a bleedin' nut case!'

'Yeh,' agreed Donny. 'You could sing that if you had a tune to it.' He turned to face his friend. ' Here, Swampy, what does it look like?'

Swamp examined the side of Donny's face critically. 'It's all red an' battered lookin'. An' the eye is beginnin' to close. Keep the bleedin' ice on it, Don. It's your only chance.'

'Shit!' exclaimed Donny. 'That's all I needed. I'm going to get my gear and go to the practice.'

'I'll go as far as the gym with you,' offered Swamp.

Donny stripped quickly and got into his gear. He knew Clint was going to be annoyed. 'What time is it?' he asked Swamp when he was ready.

'Nearly a quarter to five,' his friend said glumly.

Ignoring the throbbing of his cheekbone, Donny hurried out onto the pitch, where the practice was in full swing. Clint stopped shouting at the players when he saw Donny coming. He came to meet him. 'Where the hell were you, Donny?' he demanded, obviously annoyed. Then he saw Donny's face. 'What happened your face? Christopher! You've got a real shiner there. What happened you?' He examined the damage with expert fingers.

'I had an accident, sir. I ran into a door. I'm sorry I'm late.'

'Did you get ice on this?' Clint demanded. 'That eye is going to close unless you work on it.'

'Yeh, I had ice for the last half hour. I'll be OK.'

Clint glanced at his watch. 'It was hardly worth your while togging out, you know. We're nearly finishing.' His face was serious. 'And you know the score about missing a practice, Donny. That's the way it's been all through the season ...'

'But, Sir, I couldn't help it!' Donny protested. 'Swamp'll tell you. There was nothing I could do ...'

But Clint was shaking his head. 'I'm sorry, Donny. When you didn't turn up I asked Doyler to do the set pieces in your place. It wouldn't be fair ...'

Donny spoke with a low passionate voice. 'Sir, I wasn't supposed to say this, but I have to now. I didn't run into a door. Brother Sharkey hit me, with his fist.'

Clint's eyes grew wide with surprise. 'You're not serious, Donny.'

'Ask Swamp. He saw it all, Sir.' Donny looked to Swamp for support.

'Yeh, I did,' asserted his friend, his eyes distant behind the thick glasses. 'He just belted him one. An' Donny wasn't givin' him any hassle. He was only askin' him ...'

Clint held up a restraining hand. 'OK, Paul. I haven't the time to go through this now. If it's true, I'll have to think about it.' He turned to Donny again. 'Either way, Donny, that eye's going to look a sight tomorrow, the way it's behaving now. And there's no way I'm going to play you unless you're fully fit. It wouldn't be fair to the team. You understand that, don't you?'

Donny nodded. 'Yes, sir. I'll keep the ice on it all night if I have to. It'll be OK tomorrow.'

'Right. We'll see,' growled Clint. He turned and walked back towards the goals where the squad was gathered. Donny followed him, a sinking feeling inside. Doyler was the twelfth man, a midfield player. He'd been waiting his chance to get into the team.

'I'll be fine in the morning, sir,' Donny called after Clint, but even as he said it, he was straining to see with his left eye, the swelling was closing in so much.

In the dressing room a little later, the rest of the team wanted to know what had happened. Remembering Brother O'Connor's final request, Donny tried to joke it away.

'Ah, there was a mosh in the corridor, an' I got pushed against the door. I'll be OK.' They were concerned, though.

'What'd Clint say?' Flanagan asked.

'Nothing much. Just said to keep the ice on it, an' it'll be OK in the morning,' Donny lied. But suddenly the disappointment hit him. He wouldn't be fit to play tomorrow, he told himself. Now all the work — the training, the games over the past few weeks — was to be for nothing. It was so unfair. The dim dressing room became clouded as tears welled up in his good eye. He quickly tossed his gear in his kit bag, and headed for the door. 'Hey, Don,' called Flagon, 'hang on a sec. I'll be with you.'

Outside, the evening had clouded over, and a light rain was drifting down. Donny pulled the collar of his jacket up around his neck, and waited for Flagon. Swamp had gone home earlier.

When Flagon came out, he eyed Donny sceptically. 'C'mon, Don. I don't believe that bullshit about a mosh. What really happened?'

Donny could lie no longer. 'He hit me. Jaws hit me!' he said, his voice overflowing with anger and sorrow.

Flagon stopped, disbelief registering in his face. 'You're kiddin'!' he said. 'How? Where?'

Haltingly, Donny told the story, fighting back the emotion as he went.

'The bastard!' exclaimed Flagon when he had finished. 'He can't get away with that, Don. That's assault. You can get jail for that!'

'Yeh, I know.'

'But what are you going to *do*?'

'Dunno yet, Flag. I don't want to think about it till after the game tomorrow. But there's one thing sure. This game tomorrow means a lot to me, and if I can't play tomorrow, it's going to be his fault. And he's going to have to pay for that, and pay dear!' His voice choked up and he said no more.

The first thing Donny did when he reached home was to raid the ice box of the fridge, upend the tray of frozen cubes into a plastic bag, smash them to pieces against a wall, wrap the lot in a kitchen towel and apply it to his eye. He did all this while recounting the events of the afternoon to a concerned and angry Maeve. When he was finished, she vowed that she would take the next morning off work and go to the school to talk to Brother Sharkey in person. Donny tried to dissuade her, but she was inflexible.

Later, lying on the couch, he thought of phoning Jacky, but he couldn't face the thought of having to tell her that he mightn't be playing in the final, so he just stayed on the couch. He went to bed early, clutching another ice pack, with the radio volume turned high, in an effort to keep his mind off the game. He drifted off to sleep with the memory of Maeve's passionate anger on his behalf vivid in his mind, and it gave him a good feeling. Up to now, it was he who had been looking out for Maeve, supporting her while her ill-fated marriage went on the rocks and disintegrated, leaving her with a baby and no means of support. But she had grown stronger through it all and now it was her turn to come to his help.

17

Donny had been lying in bed, vaguely aware of the distant morning sounds of Dublin streets, when he suddenly remembered his eye. He leapt out of bed and rushed to the bathroom mirror. The flesh around the eye and down the side of his face was a mixture of wonderful colours: blues, reds, browns, each merging and mingling with the next in a bizarre display. 'Oh, shit!' he exclaimed. The eye, however, was not completely shut. He closed the good eye and stared around the bathroom belligerently with the other one. Apart from an unaccustomed dark shape bulging up from below, he could see perfectly. 'Please, God!' he breathed, descending the stairs three steps at a time, heading for the fridge again. The kitchen clock said six forty-five. He took the ice back to bed, applied it for fifteen minutes, and then dozed off again.

He was shaken awake by Maeve at ten past eight. His first question was, 'How does it look?' He could see her trying to hide her dismay when she studied his face.

'It's very discoloured,' she said.

'But I can see OK,' he argued. 'It'll be all right in a couple of hours.'

There was sadness in the look she gave him. 'I hope so,' she said. 'C'mon, get up now. I'm going with you this morning.'

There was something about the set of her face that told him there was no point in arguing.

The sister and brother arrived at the school at ten to nine. In her navy suit and pink blouse, Maeve had a business-like air about her. Conscious of the casual glances in his direction from the students passing through the foyer outside the principal's office, Donny knocked on the door. He heard a muffled call from within so he turned the knob and pushed open the door. Brother O'Connor rose from his desk when he saw Maeve.

'Ah, come in, Missus ...' He obviously couldn't remember Maeve's married name.

'O'Sullivan,' she said. 'Maeve O'Sullivan.' She sat on the chair which he proferred, while Donny pulled another forward from the wall.

'Ah, I suppose you're here to discuss Donny's little incident with Brother Sharkey. An unfortunate mishap ...'

Maeve interrupted. 'Brother,' she said icily, 'I do not consider an incident in which my brother is assaulted by one of your staff to be a *little* one. And what's more, I think it was anything but a mishap.'

The old Brother spluttered and stammered in his haste to assure her that, of course, he had just been using a figure of speech, and that, *of course*, he fully realised the seriousness of the situation. 'But I hope that we can sort things out between us, to everybody's satisfaction,' he added, with a weak smile.

'I'd like to see Brother Sharkey,' Maeve said matter-of-factly.

'Em, I'm afraid that isn't possible at the moment,' he replied. Donny noticed the colour rising in the old man's cheeks and he felt sorry for him. 'The fact is, he's gone away for a few days, for a rest. He hasn't been himself lately, so we thought it best to give him a break.'

'And when do you expect him back?'

'Em, that's something now that I'm not able to tell you, Missus ... Miss O'Sullivan. But I can assure you that an incident like this will never happen again. You have my word on it.'

'I wish I could have Brother Sharkey's word on that too,' she retorted. 'You realise, Brother, that this could be a case for the courts.' Donny glanced sideways at Maeve, to see what expression she had on her face. He'd never heard her speak like this to anyone outside the family before. This wasn't like her at all.

The old man swallowed hard. 'I do, Miss O'Sullivan. I do indeed. I know that you have every right to ... to seek redress elsewhere. But if there was anything we could do, anything at all to make it up to you, please be assured that we will do it. I have spoken to Brother Sharkey. I have pointed out that we cannot have incidents like this in our school. And furthermore,' he gulped again in his anxiety to please, 'I have told him that Donny here has an exemplary record in our school. He is a fine boy who has never been in trouble here.' He paused for a moment, and his face became even more apologetic. 'It's just unfortunate that the incident arose over Donny's absence from school on Monday afternoon, and that there was some question over the note sent in to explain his absence.'

'Brother O'Connor,' said Maeve firmly, 'I am Donny's guardian until he's eighteen. And if I wish to let him stay away from school for a good reason, I expect the school to respect this fact, and not to give *him* a hard time ...'

The Brother held up his hand in appeasement. 'Exactly. Exactly,' he said. 'I'm with you all the way there ...'

As the old man waffled on, Donny's sympathy for him grew. It was clear that he was trying desperately to avoid a public airing of the incident in question. Yet, he wasn't trying to excuse what Brother Sharkey had done.

When the Brother finished with another heartfelt assurance that such an incident would never happen again, Maeve looked at Donny for the first time since entering the office. There was a question in her eyes.

Donny shrugged his shoulders. 'Well, maybe,' he said doubtfully. 'But what I'm worried about is that he just can't leave me alone. Every chance he gets he hops on me. An' he's been doing that for years.'

The old man leaned across the table towards him. 'Donny,' he said quietly, 'I think you can rest assured that you'll have no further trouble from the man in question.'

The corridor was deserted when Donny and Maeve stepped

out into it several minutes later. Donny was bursting to speak.

'Jeez, Maeve!' he exploded, 'you really did the business in there. The poor old guy was pissin' himself in case you took him to court. You were terrific!'

Her smile showed her pleasure. 'Well, thank you, little brother. Sure, somebody has to look after you, don't they? By the way, what time's this game at today?'

'Three o'clock. Are you coming?'

She inclined her head. 'I'll see what I can do,' she said cryptically.

When Donny walked into Miss O'Callaghan's French class several minutes later, the whole process ground to a halt. There was a collective gasp from the class, which the young teacher echoed with her own exclamation, 'Oh, my God!' and her hand went to her mouth. 'What *happened* to you, Donny?'

Donny acknowledged the reaction of his friends with a grim smile. 'Didn't duck quick enough,' he said wryly, as he headed for his seat. It took the young teacher five minutes to re-establish order. During that time Donny was the object of comment from almost every boy in the class. But the first comment, from Donoghue, told him that the story was out. Donoghue said, 'I hope you made fish meal out of him, Donny!' Miler shouted across the class, 'Sue the ar ... the pants off him, Don.' Donny shot a reproachful look at Flagon, but he put his innocent face on and denied being the blabbermouth.

'The whole bleedin' place knew about it this morning,' he said. 'An', by the way. Clint was lookin' for you.'

'Why? What'd he say?' asked Donny expectantly.

'Nothing. He just asked were you in. Anyway you'll see him at eleven.'

At the mid-morning break, as the squad converged on Clint's classroom for the mandatory team meeting on the morning of a match, the rumours were flying thick and fast. 'Jaws is not in today,' remarked Butler. 'You musta hit him an awful wallop, Don.'

'Sure, isn't he *gone*,' scoffed Murray. 'One of the First Years that does a milk round saw him gettin' a taxi at some unearthly hour this mornin'. I swear to God!'

'Gerroff!' scoffed Flanagan. 'Doesn't everyone know they came in the mad waggon last night, with a whatchacallit ... a strait jacket, an' carted him off kickin' an' screamin' to the looney bin.'

The slagging stopped when they entered Clint's room. The teacher was waiting at the door for Donny. 'Give us a look at that,' he said, zeroing in on the damaged eye immediately. 'Can you see out of it at all?' he asked then.

'Yeh, no bother,' replied Donny. 'It's just a *little* closed, but nothin' worth talking about. It looks a lot worse than it is.'

Clint stood for a full minute turning and twisting Donny's head, holding up his finger to one side and asking Donny could he see it. His face was grim when he spoke. 'I'm afraid it's bad news, Don,' he said. 'The way you are, I can't start you. But you're in the subs. Doyler's been working on your set pieces, so he'll start the game in the number seven jersey. We'll just have to wait and see then.' He gave Donny a friendly pat on the shoulder, and went over to the teacher's desk to give the pep talk. Donny could feel all eyes on him as he went to take his place, but he couldn't look at any of them. The disappointment was like a great ocean inside him, and he struggled to keep it from overflowing. When he sat down beside Flagon, the other said nothing. He just put his arm around Donny's shoulder and patted him several times. The sympathy nearly finished Donny altogether, but he swallowed hard and kept his head down.

Donny didn't hear much of what Clint said. It was the usual stuff about how it was up to them now, and how they had got this far through playing good football. Then Clint called out the team and, when he came to the right side of midfield, he paused. 'I know Donny is disappointed,' he started. 'And it's hard luck about his accident ...' Donny didn't wait for any more. He got up and headed for the door. 'It wasn't a bleedin' accident!' he said bitterly, as he left the room.

18

The squad left the school a little after twelve o'clock, with no hubbub or fanfare. The coach took them straight to Mooney's, where they were to have lunch. As Donny was entering the wide burnished doors of the pub, Clint called him to one side. Donny felt a sudden surge of hope, but when Clint spoke, it subsided just as quickly. In his hand was a green paper.

'This came to the school about an hour ago. It's for you.' He handed Donny the telegram. 'Thanks,' said Donny. Clint started to turn away, but changed his mind. 'How's the eye?' he said. He examined Donny's face for a moment. 'Umph,' he grunted then. 'It's improving. How does it feel?'

'A bit tender,' said Donny jauntily. 'But most of the time I don't even notice it.'

'Go ahead and have a bit of lunch then,' said the coach cryptically.

When the teacher left him, Donny opened the folded telegram with some curiosity. The message was short.

'Good luck, Donny. Score a goal for me. Love you, Jacky.'

He smiled sadly and stuffed the paper into his pocket. He felt unhappy that he hadn't phoned Jacky the previous night to tell her the bad news. He sighed. She'd find out soon enough, he told himself.

The meal was a subdued affair, with only the hum of quiet conversations being heard above the clink of cutlery. Donny, sitting between Flagon and Butler, found them reluctant to talk about the game, and he knew it was because of him. Flagon skirted around the subject several times, but when he had exhausted the conversational potential of the weather, and of how badly the city needed a proper football stadium, and of the capacity of Wembley Stadium, he fell silent for a moment.

'Jeez, Don,' he blurted then. 'I really feel bad about you an' this game. I mean, it's such shitty luck! The lads are the same. I mean, if that bastard had *planned* the whole thing, he couldn't have done a worse job.'

'Yeh,' said Donny ruefully. 'Looks like I won't be able to give your man Rocky a dig after all. I was kinda lookin' forward to that. Maybe you ...'

'A dig, is it?' retorted Flagon, brightening. 'Just say the word, son, an' I'll gut him.'

The coach reached Dalymount Park at a quarter to two. The street outside the stadium reeked of normality, with pedestrians and cars going about their everyday business. 'Leave the gear in the dressing rooms and get out onto the pitch,' Clint told the team as they dismounted from the coach. 'Have a good look.'

Donny walked out with Flagon onto the green sward. Apart from a worn patch like a spear head at each of the goalmouths, the pitch had a healthy covering of grass. The cool wind that ruffled Flagon's locks blew weakly from the north-east, and patches of blue showed between the fluffy white cumulus clouds.

The sun, when it broke through, made sharp shadows on the freshly-mown grass. Donny felt nervous, but now he knew it was for the lads. He feared for them even more, now that he would be unable to do anything to help them.

Doyle, the tall, gangling one that was taking Donny's place, appeared at his shoulder. 'I just want to say I hope there's no hard feelings, Don,' he said, apologetically. 'I know you'd be the same if you were me.'

Donny took Doyle's hand and shook it. 'No sweat, Doyler. Just break a leg, will ya?'

Doyler grinned down at him. 'Yeah,' he said, uncertainly.

'No, have a stormer, Doyler. Score a couple for me.' The

phrase he had just used reminded him of Jacky's telegram, and he felt the pang again. He hoped he'd see her before the game started.

In the dressing room the atmosphere was tense and expectant. The players dressed in silence, while Clint spoke quietly, sometimes to the group, sometimes to individuals, going back over the plays, reminding them about the tactics, of the situations that might arise. So, they might go a goal down, even two goals down. So, they might have some bad luck early on. None of these eventualities were going to change their game. There was going to be no panic. What if they went one up, even two goals up? 'This team is not going to play defensive if they go ahead!' he commanded, thumping the wall with his fist to emphasise every word. 'Remember the simple rule. No team can score if they don't have the ball. So we're going to *play* with the ball, right? And we're going to keep it *simple*, right?'

Immersed in his preparations, each player nodded, as if in silent conversation with himself. Clint went on in his low passionate tone. 'And this is a *team*, remember. What does a *real* team do? We all know what they do. They *help* one another. They give the man with the ball *options*, right? They move and support and run, and then move again, and run again. And if in doubt, they put the ball *out*, right?' Grimly, they listened, as if hearing the words for the first time, although they had heard them so often before. And as Clint went on, their nervousness lessened. They had done their homework, he told them. They had prepared well. Win, lose or draw, if they played to their potential, if they played their best, then they would have done all that was being asked of them. And if they still lost, then it would be to a very good team, and there was no disgrace in that. St. Edmund's couldn't be bad. They wouldn't have got to the final unless they could play. But St. Colman's had met good teams before this and had beaten them. So today they were to play without fear in their hearts. Fear was the enemy. 'And each one of you guys must look fear straight in the face, must look into your own heart and outstare fear.'

Clint was standing in the middle of the floor, and there was not a sound in the room. They had never heard anything like this in a football dressing room before, but they sensed that this was a special, unique moment, and they turned to look at him. Somebody began to clap, and the rest took it up, and then Clint was clapping too, standing there in the middle of the room, clapping his head off, with his face all red and fired-up. When the noise subsided, he said, 'This may be the biggest moment in your footballing career. There may never be a day like this one again. Make the most of it, boys. And good luck!'

In the cramped dressing room they stretched off as they had been trained to do, tautening the hamstrings and the Achilles tendons, stretching out the groin muscles, loosening out the torso and shoulders. Then the referee was there inspecting the studs, telling them he wanted a good clean game and wishing them luck. They stood, grimfaced and waiting as Curtis said the last words. 'Right, lads,' he said hoarsely. 'This is it. We've come a long way to get here, and we're all goin' out there to die for one another, right? An' I mean that. This one's for our school, an' for Clint, our trainer. An' for Donny O'Sullivan. So let's go an' do it!' He pulled open the door and led them out.

Going through the tunnel, Donny felt a bit choked up, after what Curtis had said. Yet, when he came out into the brightness and the cauldron of sound, he stopped to look for Jacky. The St. Colman's supporters were to his left, so he walked along the front of the stand, scanning the lively mass of bodies, now in full cry as their team came onto the pitch. Up in the high rear section he spotted Swamp, wrestling to keep aloft a flagpole with a monstrous flag on top. Then, on Swamp's left, he saw Jacky's familiar blond hair, with Maeve beside her. They had spotted him and were waving and calling. Immediately Jacky began to work her way along to the aisle that led downwards. He sprinted up the wide sloping steps, not wanting to meet her in full view of the whole school. As she came nearer, he saw concern in her face, which changed to shocked surprise when she saw his eye.

'Oh, Donny!' she exclaimed. 'Your *face*!'

He tried to be casual. 'Yeh,' he joked. 'The lads were sayin' that it's a big improvement. But it'll ...'

'But it's *terrible*!' she went on. 'How could he *do* such a thing to you? That's what I've been asking Swamp ever since he told me.'

'It was easy. He just closed his big fist and let fly.'

She caught his hand in a gesture of sympathy. 'Oh, Donny, you must be very disappointed, after all the games and everything.'

He nodded. Her gravity forced him to be serious. 'Yeh.'

'I wish there was something I could do to help.' She squeezed his fingers, willing her strength into him.

'You came, didn't you?' he said, forcing a smile. 'That's help enough.' He glanced out towards the pitch where the two teams and subs were warming up. 'Listen, I have to go. There'll be photographs an' stuff. I'll have to stay in the dugout ... that concrete thing below, during the game. So I'll see you after, OK?'

She nodded. 'I'll be here.' Her sympathy weakened him momentarily and he coughed to force down the emotion. 'You'd never know. I might get on for a while yet. See you later.'

On his way down again, Donny saw that the St. Edmund's squad were limbering up near the right-hand goal area. They seemed huge. Their jerseys were dark green, with narrow red stripes running horizontally across them. The shorts were of the same red colour. Donny picked out Bruce's blond head immediately. He had his back turned, and the black number four showed clearly as he stood talking to another player. Donny searched through the shorter stockier players for Rocky Stewart, but he could not immediately pick him out. And suddenly the disappointment gripped his stomach again with a great emptiness. As he walked out towards his team-mates, he felt wretched. He heard Flagon's shout, 'Here, Don!' He looked up to see a ball skidding across the turf towards him. He trapped it with his left, swung it over and hit it with his right towards the goals, thirty yards away. It skimmed the top of the crossbar. He went in search of another loose ball and smacked it with his left. It curled long and glided down into O'Reilly's big hands. 'Good shot, Don,' the keeper called. Donny hoped Clint was watching. He stood still and rotated his eyeballs, trying to see wide on both sides without moving his head. The hill under his left eye was shrinking in size, he told himself.

A battery of photographers lined up in front of the St. Edmund's squad and took pictures of them for nearly five minutes. As the St. Colman's squad was assembling, Donny caught a glimpse of Rocky Stewart trotting away from him. He noted the muscular thighs and the arrogant gait. While the photographs were being taken, the St. Edmunds supporters were chanting, 'Oggy! Oggy! Oggy! — Oy! Oy! Oy!', waving their scarves and flags with the exuberant energy of schoolboys.

The photographers dispersed, the subs and trainers trooped across to their respective dugouts, and the din in the stands rose to a metallic crescendo. The black-suited referee called Curtis and McLoughlin, the St. Edmund's captain, to the centre circle and tossed the coin. St. Edmund's would kick off. The whistle blasted and the Leinster Final was on.

To Donny, sitting in the confined, low-roofed dugout, with O'Connell and Doherty on one side of him and Clint, shouting like a madman, on the other, the first ten minutes had the quality of a dream. In the past few weeks, he had often visualised in his mind what playing in the final against St. Edmund's would be like, how big, how skilful they would be. Mostly he had dreamed of being on the pitch, playing against them, but sometimes he had tried to imagine what the game would be like for Jacky, watching it from the stands. And now it seemed to him that he was playing that dream over again in his mind. Except that now the central element was missing. Donny O'Sullivan was not on the pitch. Instead he was sitting in the dugout, a swarm of neurotic butterflies playing havoc with his stomach.

He found himself watching the St. Edmund's players. They seemed strong and physical. There was no mistaking the dark legs of Borghi, the Italian midfielder. He was stocky and not very tall and it was clear that he was the play-maker, as Clint had said. He had two good feet, and in the first five minutes he threaded two pin-point passes through the St. Colman's defence which sent shivers of apprehension across the massed supporters.

O'Reilly, alert in the St. Colman's goal, snuffed out the threat in each case, by bravely spreading himself across the path of the onrushing forward, and smothering the ball.

'That bleedin' Italian!' Donny heard Doherty mutter to himself.

In defence, too, St. Edmund's seemed formidable. The first ball that Kavanagh whipped across from the right wing was met solidly by the blond head of Bruce McNeill, who soared above Donoghue's hopeful leap, and cleared the ball to midfield.

After ten minutes, however, St. Colman's nearly scored. Rocky Stewart slid late into Kavanagh, after the ball was gone, and conceded a free kick about fifteen yards outside the penalty area on the left side of the pitch. Doyle, Donny's replacement, curled a high ball across the area. Flagon leaped high to meet it and knocked it onwards towards the back post. The St. Edmund's defence, sensing the danger, had just begun to shift across, when Donoghue raced in from wide on the right. His head met the ball with a solid thump. The keeper's hands flailed the air in desperation, but the ball smacked off the upright beside him and bounced back into play. In the frantic second that followed, Keogh, the St. Edmund's centre-back, snaked a long leg out and glanced the ball away towards touch. Donny, Clint and the other subs sat back down, the rising shouts stifled in their throats.

'Hard luck, Dunno!' shouted the trainer.

'Jeez!' exclaimed Doherty, slamming his fist against his thigh. Donny felt the tension easing. This was promising stuff. A bit of luck and they would have scored.

His relief was short-lived, however. Less than a minute later, Copeland, the St. Edmund's keeper, caught a back-header at the front edge of his area, threw the ball up in the air and thumped it high and long. Murray, the St. Colman's centre-back, came thundering out from his eighteen yard line to meet it, but McKenna, the centre-forward, was there too. They clashed. Off balance, Murray mistimed his jump. The ball came to earth behind them and bounced high again. Next moment, Donny was aware of the brown legs of Borghi streaking goalwards. The ball began to drop just inside the penalty area. O'Reilly, in goal, started to advance, but changed his mind, seeing Curtis arriving from Borghi's left. Curtis lunged with his left for the bounce, but Borghi's toe got to it before it hit the ground and nudged it forward. Next moment, Borghi fell headlong. The whistle blasted loud. Penalty! The St. Edmund's players threw their hands in the air, their supporters went mad, but the stand to Donny's left was numbed and silent.

Borghi stood expectantly outside the area. He looked at the referee, then at O'Reilly in the goals. The whistle blasted again. Borghi loped forward. O'Reilly guessed 'right', and dived, but the ball bounced lazily into the left corner of his net. St. Edmund's were ahead.

'Damn!' said Clint, and ran his fingers through his thinning hair.

During the next fifteen minutes, St. Edmund's nearly scored twice. Borghi controlled the midfield with casual ease, teasing and tormenting the St. Colman's midfield players, making neat triangles around them with the ball as he passed and then ran to take the return from a team-mate. Once he slipped past Doyle and took the ball forward. His two wingers went wide, taking Miler and Butler with them. Borghi came on, stuttering his feet to confuse Murray, who was poised in front of him, his eyes glued to the ball. Curtis, sensing danger and responsible for calling for the offside trap, stepped out beside Murray, then began to back off delicately on his toes, as Borghi swerved towards him. Curtis was steeling himself for the tackle, when Borghi hit the ball with the inside of his right foot. The ball lifted, seemed to be heading to the right of the posts, then swerved viciously downward. O'Reilly danced on the goal-line as his mind judged the flight of the ball. Then he flung himself towards the left-hand bottom corner of the goalmouth. The crowd sucked in its collective breath. O'Reilly's clawing fingers touched the ball, deflected it fractionally, and sent it whistling round the upright and behind. 'Corner!' roared the St. Edmund's fans.

'Jeez!' said Doherty in the dugout. In the stands the St. Edmund's crowd were chanting, 'We will, we will *rock* you!'

The second chance came five minutes later, after Kavanagh,

the St. Colman's winger, had shot wide with a hopeful effort from fully twenty-five yards, and Flanagan had tripped over the ball with the goal at his mercy and only the keeper to beat. This time it was O'Reilly's mistake. A long, high ball soared in from the right side of midfield. Donny heard O'Reilly's high-pitched yell above the other sounds. He saw the keeper advance, his gloved hands raised. A jumble of bodies gathered in front of him and he jumped into them, reaching high as the ball descended. But he couldn't hold it. It dropped tamely on the outfield side of the cluster of defenders and attackers. Matthews of St. Edmund's trapped it with his right foot, tapped it towards his right, and wound himself up for a strike through the mill of bodies. Miler, nearest to him, stuck a desperate foot out to block, but Matthews was quick. Instead of kicking it, he tapped the ball a yard further to the right, and then hit it. Miler, off balance, strained to block the shot he knew was coming. Somehow, he got the tip of his boot across. The ball nicked it, and the trajectory changed by a fraction. But it was enough to send it skidding the wrong side of the post. The St. Colman's crowd groaned with relief. Another escape!

In the dugout, Clint became more exasperated as the first half wore on. When he grew tired of roaring at a red-faced and flustered-looking Doyle that he was to stick to Borghi's ass, to no avail, he changed tactics. 'Dave,' he called to Flagon, who was taking a throw-in at the touchline nearby. 'Go on eight! Tell Doyler to drop onto your man!' Flagon, grim-faced and impassive, nodded in acknowledgement. Once, Clint glanced in Donny's direction and for a moment Donny's heart leaped. But the trainer looked quickly away again.

The score was one-nil at half time. 'Come on, you guys,' said Clint to the subs as he headed for the dressing room. Inside, when he had got them all seated, handed round the drinks and locked the door, he began to talk. Donny was impressed. Clint's voice was calm and his tone measured. They were doing OK. Not playing to their full potential, but playing OK. They had weathered the storm, and only conceded one goal. That was good. 'These guys are cocky now, and that's the way to have them,' he went on. 'Just relax. Keep the body warm. We're not out of this by a long shot.' This time there was no lecture, though. Now he let them talk. Yes, he agreed, they had to close down on Borghi. Flanagan would start on him in the second half. Right, they had to keep the ball to *feet*, and spread it wide. Correct, they had to look for the free kicks in front of goal. They hadn't used a set piece more than twice in the game yet. And they had practised them enough.

Clint went quietly amongst them, checking on a bruise here, an abrasion there, speaking with individuals, advising, encouraging, cajoling. Donny, sitting in a corner, waited tensely for any sign of a change in the team. But when the referee came again to advise them that they had three minutes, Clint had still said nothing.

'Right,' he called, just before they went out. 'We have forty minutes left. The team that wants this cup the most is going to win it. And I'll tell you one thing. None of you wants it more than I do.' He looked at them and he knew there was no need to say anymore. He opened the door, and let them out.

The second half was barely three minutes old when Flanagan got himself booked. It happened the first time Borghi got possession. The stocky Italian stopped the ball dead and scanned the field ahead of him, looking for a channel. Flanagan came at him from his right but, with his foot on top of the ball, Borghi rolled it back and Flanagan's right foot swiped at empty air. Borghi set off towards the left-hand touchline, waiting for a run from his winger, Matthews, but Flanagan gave chase. Guessing that he would be sold another dummy, Flanagan went in recklessly with both feet and whipped the feet from under his opponent. Borghi's shoulder thumped against the hard turf, he rolled over several times and lay prone, his face twisted in an agonised grimace.

The whistle blasted. 'Hey, you! Seven! Over here!' snapped the referee, whipping out his cards. In the dugout, Clint waited tensely. Donny pressed his intertwined fingers against the backs of his hands so hard that pools of white appeared under the fingernails. The card was yellow. The St. Edmund's crowd whistled and booed.

Borghi, on his feet quickly, took the free kick. It floated high towards the penalty spot. Once again, Murray called and steadied himself. Just inside the area, he climbed high, right arm over the centre-forward's shoulder, and headed the ball away towards the centre circle. Rocky Stewart, alone just inside his own half, controlled the bounce and dribbled forward. Curtis, sensing another deep kick, screamed, 'Get out!' and the last line of defence set the off-side trap and moved out. Stewart swung the ball in again. It swirled in over Curtis's head. But, suddenly, Borghi had darted in behind the defence, caught the ball on his chest and hit it with his left as it came down. It flew into the top left-hand corner of O'Reilly's net. The whistle blasted. The St. Edmund's crowd erupted, but the swell faltered and then died. The linesman on the far side had his flag raised. Offside! Goal disallowed!

In the dugout, Donny and Doherty exchanged a wordless look of relief. Clint was encouraging. 'That's OK, Anto,' he called. 'That's OK.'

St. Colman's now attacked with renewed determination. Flagon sent Donoghue away on the left, but his attempted cross was blocked into touch by Stewart's full-blooded tackle. From the throw, Murphy crossed low, but Bruce McNeill volleyed the ball away. Inexorably the pressure mounted. Miler and Butler, the wing backs, began to overlap wide at midfield, carrying the ball forward along the wings into the St. Edmund's corners. Twice, Miler crossed from the right, but the massed defence headed to safety. Then Butler crossed from the other side and Flagon got his head to the ball, but the keeper snatched it out of the air as it looped goalwards. The tension in the stands mounted. The din increased as the supporters had their own private battle to see which side could out-shout the other.

St. Colman's tightened the screw. For a five minute period the ball never left the St. Edmund's half of the pitch. It seemed inevitable that a score would come. Flanagan and Kavanagh tried a clever one-two right in the centre of the defence, but Flanagan failed to control the return. The ball bounced away from him and his toe shot was well wide. Within minutes, Flagon had the St.

Colman's crowd on their feet when he raced onto a low cross at the far post, but the ball skidded away from his straining lunge, and went behind for a goal-kick. And still the defence held out.

Now even Curtis and Murray, the St. Colman's central defenders had moved up to the halfway line, where they mopped up the ragged clearances and pushed the balls wide to the wings again to begin another attack.

And then disaster struck. Curtis had just chipped a pass across to Murray and had made a forward run into space. McKenna, the lone St. Edmund's forward, followed the ball hopefully. He made a fake rush at Murray, hoping to pressure him, but Murray casually turned the ball away and looked for Curtis. He hit the ball too hard, though. Curtis had to change direction but slipped as he did so. The ball rolled past him, and suddenly there was Borghi running on to it. He tapped it once to get past Curtis, now rushing in to retrieve the error, and raced towards the halfway line. Clarke, the speedy St. Edmund's right-winger, came streaking out along the right touchline, leaving Butler ten yards in his wake. Murray, retreating towards goal, found himself confronted by two St. Edmund's players. Borghi dribbled straight at him, twisting and turning with delicate control. Murray, nearing his own penalty area, and aware of Clarke threatening on his left, decided to make a stand, hoping to delay matters until the rest of his defence could race back to help. Borghi feinted to the left. Murray began to adjust and then Borghi slipped the ball to his right and in front of the speeding Clarke. Murray turned, but it was too far. He could see O'Reilly advancing from goal, narrowing the angle.

O'Reilly gathered himself, staying on his feet till the last split second. Clarke touched the ball onwards. O'Reilly's eyes locked onto it. His feet did a little dance. Then he spread himself and dived, his hands straining for the approaching ball. But Clarke was fast, and his legs were long. At the last second, he reached with his left and tapped the ball again. It touched the tips of O'Reilly's fingers, slowed momentarily and then spun off to the right. O'Reilly scrambled. Clarke checked his headlong pace and reached back with his right foot for the spinning ball. He hooked it to him. Murray raced to protect the goal as Clarke hit the ball low. Murray stuck out his right foot in a desperate attempt to block, but the ball skidded under it. Next moment the ball was in the net. Goal!

In the dugout, when the hubbub subsided, Clint grimly looked at his watch.

'How long, sir?' asked Doherty.

'Twenty minutes,' said Clint. Then he turned to Donny. 'How's the eye, Donny?'

'Perfect,' replied Donny.

'Get ready then. You're going on.'

Donny climbed out of the dugout and began to jog to his left along the touchline. There was a half-hearted cheer from the St. Colman's front lines when they saw him, but he could tell their confidence had been dented. He heard a call from farther up and saw Maeve and Jacky waving excitedly down at him. He nodded towards them and went on with his warm-up.

'Right,' said Clint a few minutes later, when Donny had finished stretching off. 'You're going in for Doyler. You're to pick up Borghi and man-mark him. Everywhere he goes you're to stick to him like glue. We have to close him down, Donny. We have twenty minutes. There's still time. And have a cut yourself if you get the chance.'

The ball went out of play and the linesman signalled to the referee that St. Colman's were ready to make a substitution.

The boys were glad to see Donny. 'Ya boy, ya, Don!' called Curtis from afar. 'Yo, Don!' said Flagon from nearby.

Borghi didn't even look at Donny when he arrived beside him. Instead he began to point and shout instructions to his team-mates in a thick Dublin accent as if he didn't even know Donny was there. He was shorter than Donny, but broader in the shoulders, and his thighs and calves bulged with muscle. Up close, his black hair accentuated the sallowness of his skin.

The St. Edmund's throw was taken. The ball went to McGregor, the ginger-haired mid-fielder. Borghi broke away from Donny and called for a pass. Donny went with him but had to check because Borghi suddenly cut back into the open space behind him. The pass never came, however, because Flanagan closed down on McGregor and he had to go towards the touchline and chip the ball forward towards Matthews. Miler was vigilant at full-back, though, and snuffed out the danger. He passed to Flagon, in space near mid-field. Donny jinked right, then darted left, calling for the ball. It came. He trapped it and turned. There was Borghi, shepherding him. Donny feinted to the left, then took the ball right, but his opponent read his mind. Borghi stuck out a foot and stole the ball. He started on a run forward, confidently, almost arrogantly looking for an opening. Donny sprinted. Borghi was teeing up the ball to hit it when Donny arrived, nicked it with his toe, and came away with it again.

Murphy was free wide on the left and Donny swung a long ball over to him just as Borghi's sliding tackle clipped his ankle. The referee raised his arms, allowing the advantage. Murphy took the ball on. He waited for Butler to overlap him along the left touchline, then drew the defender and laid the ball out to Butler's feet. Butler raced for the corner flag, shaped to cross, but checked suddenly. Rocky Stewart over-ran. Butler saw Donny racing through from midfield and stroked the ball into his path. Donny steadied himself and whacked the ball with his right foot. It screamed low through the crowded defenders, but it was rising all the time. Copeland, the keeper, launched himself to the right, but didn't jump. The ball was too high. It cleared the cross-bar by six inches and rebounded tamely off the protective netting behind.

'Shit!' said Donny. But now the St. Colman's fans sensed something and a new surge of sound rose from their ranks. The team felt it too. 'Come on, lads!' urged Curtis. 'Flanno! Kavo!' He clenched his fist and pumped it forwards and backwards. 'Come on!'

Several minutes later, Rocky Stewart was shown a yellow card for chopping the legs from under Flanagan after the ball was gone. The offence occurred about ten yards outside, and opposite, the left-hand corner of the penalty area. Donny took the ball and placed it. He looked towards Clint, who was now standing beside the dugout. Clint looked at the goals and then back at Donny.

'Yeh,' he called. 'Yeh!'

Donny stepped back. The St. Edmund's defensive wall was assembling itself. Copeland, his left hand on the left post was shouting and flapping his right hand directionally. Satisfied, the keeper drifted back to his right. Donny saw the empty corner of the net. He took a deep breath and exhaled. The whistle sounded. He looked intently at the ball. Then he ran and hit it with the inside of his right foot. The ball lifted over the heads in the wall, was heading wide of the posts. But as it began to drop, it curled. Copeland, reading its flight, began to adjust. He scrambled crab-wise to his left. He saw the ball angling down, drove his feet into the dusty turf, and leaped. But his desperate fingers couldn't reach. The ball whistled past them into the top corner of the net. Goal! The St. Colman's stand went crazy.

'Great goal, Donny!' shouted Clint.

On the pitch, the celebrations were exuberant, but short. The team knew that time was running out, and they were anxious to restart.

Slowly the pressure grew again. The confidence was returning. St. Colman's harried and crowded when St. Edmund's had possession. When they won the ball back they began to play football, helping one another, giving and going, passing and running, always moving into space to make a target for the return pass. Now they were hungry for the ball, each player on the team wanting it and purposeful when he got it. But the time was pushing on too and St. Edmund's were packing the area with defenders, flinging themselves recklessly in the path of shots, belting loose balls in any direction as long as they were away from goal. And in the stands the tension was torture for the young hearts.

There were nine minutes left on the clock when St. Colman's forced yet another corner. Donoghue, being left-footed, went over to take it. Curtis and Murray stalked into the St. Edmund's box. Defenders darted here and there to pick up the hovering attackers.

Donoghue hit a high curler. It went way out and then started to come back with the wind. All eyes strained to watch its flight. Tendons and muscles tensed ready for the jump. Copeland shouted shrilly and committed himself to the catch. Flanagan came on a run from far out. At the last second, Copeland spotted him and changed the catch to a punch. He caught the ball solidly with his fist and it flew outfield in a high arc. In the melee Copeland fell over Bruce McNeill and tumbled to the ground.

Flagon, just on the edge of the eighteen yard box, judged the flight of the ball. He touched it with his right, killing the pace on it. Then he looked up and struck it immediately with his left. The high lob went over the head of McKenna, racing out to challenge him. It floated over the heads of the massed defenders and attackers, who seemed to be rooted to the ground watching its flight. Copeland, on his way back to cover the empty goalmouth, glanced over his shoulder, and what he saw galvanised him into action. He sprinted awkwardly; his head turned back to see the flight of the ball. He flung himself towards the goals, right arm stretched to the limit. But he was too late. The ball landed just inside the line and bounced up into the roof of the net. Goal!

The rest of the team caught up with Flagon on his knees by the touchline, pumping the air with waist-high fists at the delirious fans. They enveloped him, squashed the air out of his lungs, ruffled his hair, and honoured him with rough, manly kisses. Clint was there on the touchline too, eyes beaming wide through his glasses, his face and neck flushed red with passion.

'How much time, sir?' Donny called, as the referee's whistle popped a warning.

'Seven minutes!' Clint called hoarsely. 'No mistakes now. A draw will do!'

But Curtis, the team captain, had other ideas. 'Come on, guys!' he commanded them. 'There's still time!' He went among the team, while St. Edmund's were gathering themselves for the restart, growling like a wild thing, glaring at them with fierce determination. 'Come on! You *have* to!'

The game restarted. Borghi, in the face of Donny's challenge, passed the ball right back to McNeill. The blond defender was forced to rush his kick by the arrival of Kavanagh, and the ball came to Murphy at midfield. Donny, on Murphy's left, drifted wider still. Murphy spotted him and threaded a pass along the touchline for Donny to run on to. As Danny raced after it, however, he became aware of a burly shape approaching at speed from slightly behind and to his right. Sensing a charge, at the last split-second Donny checked his run and leaned his shoulders back. Rocky Stewart, unable to adjust in time, hurtled across his path. He didn't stop until he came up short against the tubular metal rail, three yards off the pitch. He almost catapulted head-first over it, but the weight of his legs saved him. Donny, seeing that the ball had angled into touch, turned back. 'Don't go yet,' he said sarcastically. 'We're not finished.'

'Piss off!' retorted Rocky, in a low voice. Donny turned to face him, but he knew immediately that it was a mistake. Next moment, he was nose to nose with the stocky full-back. He glared into the hard grey eyes.

'I'll be stayin' around for a while yet,' said Donny. 'We have to finish a job here.'

'Yeh!' sneered the other, grinding his forehead against Donny's. 'You want the other side of your face painted too?'

Then the hands came and pulled them apart.

'Here, you two!' snapped the referee, his hand going significantly to his back pocket. 'Cut that out!'

'C'mon, Donny. Keep the concentration!' called Curtis.

The game restarted. Stewart flung a long throw back to Copeland. The keeper bounced it three times, waved his team back towards the St. Colman's goal, and bounced it again. He rolled it on the ground and tapped it ahead of him. He was in no rush. St. Edmund's were playing for a draw. He didn't kick it until the referee warned him with the whistle.

There were two minutes left when Copeland caught another back-header and went through another bouncing ritual. His kick was high and long. Curtis's shout, 'Anto's ball!' could be heard throughout the ground. He met the ball solidly with his head and drove it out. Flagon chested it down, lost it to McGregor, but won it back again with a bone-jarring tackle. 'Play on!' called the referee. Flagon stroked the ball to Donny, now free on the right. Borghi closed in, but Donny pushed the ball further to the right to Miler and made a run forward. Borghi switched across to challenge Miler, but he slid the ball through to Donny. Kavanagh, his right winger, was wide and calling, but when the left-side full-back drifted over to cover Kavanagh, Donny didn't pass to him. Instead he looked towards the middle. Ten yards ahead, McNeill and Keogh, the St. Edmund's central defenders, blocked his way.

Suddenly Flagon appeared in the gap between the two big men. Taking his cue, Donny drove hard towards Keogh, on Flagon's left. At the last moment, he passed the ball towards Flagon and sprinted around Keogh. Flagon touched the ball once, a glancing blow. The angle was perfect. It slid behind Keogh right into Donny's path. There was a rising surge of sound from the stands. Donny saw Copeland rushing out, arms low, body crouched. Donny controlled the ball with a touch. Behind the keeper, the goals loomed huge. Five yards from the advancing Copeland, Donny stabbed his toe sharply under the ball. The stands seemed to have gone suddenly silent. The ball chipped up. It sailed over the keeper's head. It floated for an age above the level of the crossbar beyond. Then it dipped. It bounced. Before it hit the net, Donny was racing away towards the St. Colman's supporters. He knew it was in. Flanagan grabbed his arm as the stands erupted, but Donny shook himself free. It was ecstasy; it was delirium.

The fans were going mad: jumping, yelling, hugging, dancing; flooding in a dangerous wave down the stepped seats, flinging their caps and scarves and banners into the air. When he got to the railing, Donny caught a glimpse of Maeve and Jacky's joyous faces before the team landed on him. He suffered the physical assault, the exultant yells, the crushing weight, and when he thought they were all through, Clint swallowed him in a wild embrace that squeezed the breath out of him again.

'Ya beauty, Donny!' was all he could say, and he repeated it over and over again.

The game restarted. St. Edmund's mounted a desperate attack, but there was no way through. The clock ran out. The final whistle blew and St. Colman's were Leinster Champions for the first time in the history of their school.

For Donny, the time immediately after the final whistle was a hectic jumble of emotions. He remembered Borghi and Bruce McNeill shaking his hand before the class got to him. Then he was man-handled onto bony shoulders and chaired around the field. He grabbed Flagon's hand — he too was riding high — and held it aloft in a victory salute. Boys of all sizes pushed and shoved to grab his hand or just slap him — they didn't care where. He remembered Maeve's happy face with the tears rolling down, and Jacky's hand wiping his own tears from his face when he eventually got to her and grabbed her. Then Swamp was there, his face all red and sweaty, as hoarse as a crow, unable to say a word. After the back-slapping was over, he whispered into Donny's ear. 'Listen. Orla and Fiona are over there.' He nodded towards the stand. 'They did a bunk out of the hospital to see the game, but they don't want to come over. Maybe you'd say hello.'

Donny looked down at Jacky. She nodded. 'Yeh, sure, Swampy,' he said. They worked their way towards the outskirts of the throng where the girls were standing. Fiona's face was pale and serious. Orla held out her arms and Donny hugged her.

'Yiz all played grea'!' she said.

Donny turned to Fiona. The struggle showed in her face, but he caught her and hugged her too. 'Thanks for coming,' he said, feeling the momentary pressure of her hands on his waist.

'You played terrific,' she said, and the tightness round her mouth softened.

Flagon arrived, whooping and crowing. 'Yo, girls! Are ye comin' to Mooney's for the piss-up?'

'No. We'd better be gettin' back,' said Orla, 'before they send the cops out lookin' for us. But we'll stay for the presentation.'

A balding man from the Building Society, the sponsor of the competition, was making an attempt to be heard over a crackling public address system. In a toneless speech he praised the game and his building society up to the skies. Then there was the

...tation, and Curtis's big boyish mug as he turned to the ...owd, brandishing the cup over his head as if he were on TV, and Rocky Stewart's disappointed face as he came down with a runners-up medal, but he wouldn't look at Donny. And there was cheering and shouting and yelling and dancing out on the pitch and up on the benched seats of the stand.

Donny would remember the claustrophobia of the boisterous dressing rooms, the hoarse bawling of Butler, the Coke and 7-Up squirting and fizzing and the parents and teachers and well-wishers crowding in to shake hands and mouth inaudible words of congratulation. And most of all he would remember Clint, standing in the middle of it all, gawking proudly around at them, unable to say a word, and mopping his wet face with a ragged piece of loo paper. It was glorious stuff.

When the meal and speeches were all finished in Mooney's, later that evening, and the dining area had been thrown open to the public, Donny and Jacky drifted out to the almost deserted early-evening lounge. Donny flopped down on a wine-red seat. He stretched out, feeling the aches now beginning to complain.

'You know, Clint was just sayin' that every now and again you get a bunch of guys — a bunch of people — and they all just happen to be there at this particular time in history, and you get a team like ours, and they win the cup, and it won't happen again in yonks.'

Jacky, sitting beside him, regarded him curiously. 'Uh-huh?'

'Well, he was saying that he feels very lucky he was around when we came along. He said he's very grateful. Well, I feel kinda like that too.'

'What do you mean, Donny?'

'Well, there's the lads on the team, an' Clint too. An' then there's Maeve, the best sister anyone could have. An' there's Flagon an' Swamp, my best friends ... And there's you.' He looked at her now, taking her hand in his. 'You guys all came along at the right time ... the right time for me. An' I'm glad I was here.'

She looked at him, and her eyes were misty.

'And I'm glad I was around too, Donny,' she said simply.

He stretched out again, feeling the scars of battle, but [...] his strength too. 'You know, I think things are not going to tu[...] out too bad, after all.'

'Better than you expected?' She was smiling now.

'Yeh. A lot better.'

She punched him in the ribs. 'Isn't that what I've been telling you all along!'